Creatures

An Urban Fantasy

Brionna Paige McClendon

Brionna Paige McClendon
Visit my website at www.facebook.com/brionnapaigebooks

Printed in the United States of America

First Printing: Jan 2020

ISBN- 9781544198484

*"Witches
and
Werewolves
and
Vampires,
oh my."*

Table of Contents

Chapter One

Unexpected Meeting

THE ROOM WAS THICK with a haze of smoke from a hundred lit cigars. It thickened into a cloud, filling my lungs as I breathed the tainted air. The mere smell of it caused my nose to wrinkle. Many eyes were upon me, waiting, watching. Taking a breath, my hand wrapped around the microphone, parting my lips, I began to sing.

My voice echoed through the room, silencing the bar side conversations. The men became entranced by me, by the way my voice whispered between their ears, the way my body moved with the song. The bar was under my spell, captivated by the songstress.

They say that there are creatures, lovely and menacing.

Creatures that spellbind you with their beauty.

Women whom sing to your soul,

Whose voices whisper between your ears.

They trick you and play you,

For witches have not a care.

They lure you in and steal your soul away.

Before you know it, you are nothing more,

For you have become a witch's plaything.

Once the last note of the song echoed its way through the room, claps erupted around me, cheers shouted. A grin tugged at the corners of my black coated lips. So easily, I could have put this whole bar under my spell, but I did not.

"Thank you." I spoke into the microphone before stepping down from the wooden stage.

"Amazing as always, darling." Cindy, a blonde-haired woman in her late forties worked at the bar, serving drinks.

"Thank you, Cindy!" Flashing a quick smile, I grabbed my satchel bag and headed outside.

The air was heavy with moisture, the summer heat still lingering from the day. Mosquitos buzzed through the air, wishing for a drink of my sweet, sweet blood. They reminded me much of vampires, the blood thieving ancients.

Wiping my hand across my brow, I ventured along the sidewalk. The roads were quiet, not a soul could be found lingering about. But a witch always kept her wits about her. Our one rule was to never let your guard down, *never.*

My velvet, black boots sounded softly upon the concrete sidewalk. The streetlights that hung above my head buzzed and flickered. The silver chains of my many necklaces danced against each other, bouncing on my breasts. The tail of my midnight dress traveled along the ground, the concrete snagging it. Bunching it up in my hand, I tossed the end of it over my arm, and carried it.

Then, the sound of heavy footsteps made its way into my ears. I stopped in my tracks, took in a breath, and prepared myself to face the man that seemed to not comprehend the word *no.*

His balding head shone in the light from the street lamps, sweat glistening on his skin, rolling down his brow. Sweat stains formed beneath his pits and on his chest. He was a heavy-set man. When he was close enough, my nose crinkled at the scent of his body odor. I had to suppress the gag that rose in my throat.

I shook my head, my dark purple hair swaying in the slight breeze. "How many times do I have to tell you I'm not interested?"

The man was still catching his breath. "Oh, come on, sweetie. All I ask for is one night."

I readjusted my bag on my shoulder and placed a hand on my hip. "The only form of entertainment I provide are the songs from my lips and nothing more."

The man took a step closer to me, reaching for me with his sweaty hand. "Your lips could provide other forms of entertainment, sweetie."

My brow furrowed, my voice sounding low with warning. "Do not touch me, you will regret it. Now, move along. Find someone else to bother."

As I began to turn away from him, the man lunged toward me. His large hands gripped my arms. "Every night, I ask nicely. Do you like men that aren't so gentle? I can give you that, *sweetie*." His breath reeked of beer; his face so close to mine that the smell of it caused my eyes to water.

A snarl curled my lips, disgust rising within me at the feel of his sweaty hands on me, his breath tracing along my face. "Let. Me. Go. *Now.*"

The man shook his head. "You aren't getting away from me tonight."

Lifting my knee, I rammed it into his groin. The man let out a yelp of pain, his chubby face turning bright red. But it only caused his hold on me to tighten. *"You bitch!"*

The man lifted one of his hands into the air, ready to slap it across my face. My eyes narrowed on his hand; time slowed around us. Raising my own hand into the air, I was preparing to use my magic. It thrummed deep inside me, bottled up.

As the cap began to untwist, the magic slowly spilling out, there was a flash of darkness, and the man was sent flying. It happened so fast that I barely had time to blink. The man lay on the concrete, staring doe-eyed at the man that loomed over him.

"Leave her alone." A voice that dripped with darkness and mystery escaped the dark clothed man.

"She's mine tonight, buddy! Get your own woman!" The man stood from the ground, panting.

"A woman belongs to only herself." The mystery man said.

The sweat drenched man made to swing at the man, but he caught his fist with such speed that I never saw his hand move. The chubby man stood there wide-eyed, blinking at the man. Fear drained his face of color and the smell of piss began to fill the air.

The man shook his head, disgusted, and released his hold on the other man. "Leave."

He needn't say more; the piss pants man took off down the sidewalk and disappeared into an alleyway.

The mystery man slowly turned to face me. His ghostly-blue eyes took me in with concern and fascination, they seemed to draw me in. And I began to see the long, long years he's lived within his gaze and the pain hidden away behind the green flecks in his blue irises.

His hand brushed through his brown hair, one side of it was shaved down short, while the other was kept combed to the side neatly. He was tall and lanky, his black coat stopping just below his knees. His face was perfect; too perfect. I knew right away, from the moment he appeared from the darkness, that he was not human.

"Are you alright?" He asked, that same darkness still coating his voice.

Straightening my dress, I said, "Yes, though I could have handled that myself." A sigh escaped my lips, "But, thank you."

"You are quite welcome."

He made to approach me, but I took a step back. "Why did you bother? Do you plan on feasting upon my blood?"

He raised a brow to my question. "You know?" He asked.

"Every creature knows of every creature."

His ghostly eyes slowly glided up and down my body. His brow creased as he tried to venture a guess as to what creature I was. "Not a vampire." He said. The man approached me closer and sniffed at the air surrounding me, "And not a werewolf."

"Getting warmer."

"A witch."

I nodded my head. "And from what I know, vampires *love* witch blood. Because we taste *so* sweet."

He made to take a step toward me but found he couldn't come any closer. His brow raised questionably. His hand pressed against the invisible barrier between us. "You think I am to harm you?"

My hand wrapped around the silver medallion that hung just below my breasts. "One can never be too cautious around a blood thief."

He nodded his head in understanding. "I cannot fault you for being cautious. My kind does not have the best history."

"No creatures have a clean history, each of us carry the blood shed from our ancestors."

His eyes regarded me with curiosity, tilting his head. "You talk wise for someone so young."

"I am no fool, *vampire*."

"It appears so." He began to step into the shadows, his pale face being masked by the darkness. "I bid a goodbye, young witch."

THE VAMPIRE

I did not understand why I helped the young woman. Humans never interested me, I never cared for them, not after what happened. But there was something about this woman, something different that drew me to her. Something that seemed to whisper to me, pulling me toward the woman. Her purple hair eliminated beneath the flickering streetlights.

Her dark dress trailing behind her. The silver chains of her necklaces glinting in the light, tangling together.

I made toward the woman as a man began to rush behind her. She turned around; annoyance written upon her pale face. Her dark lips curving in disgust at the sight of the sweat covered human. My ears listened to their conversation and it seemed as though the man was rather persistent.

When I saw him reach for her, his grubby hands grabbing her, I felt a spark of anger inside me. Something that never happened before when it came to humans. Confused by that sudden anger, I hurried over to the woman. The man raised his hand into the air, the woman did so as well. And it was then that I felt something strange flicker, like a light in the darkness, something stirring in the shadows. Something began to stir in the woman.

Quickly, I snatched the man's arm and flung his heavy body to the ground. The concrete rumbled beneath him. The fear in his eyes sparked that animalistic desire deep within me. My tongue ran itself across my fangs, they thirsted to bite into his flesh. I thirsted for his blood.

Then, the smell of the sweetest flowers crossed my senses, I was reminded of the woman. Hiding my fangs once more, I told the man to leave the woman alone. But, like all humans, he was foolish and refused to give up without a fight. He made the mistake in trying to attack, for I caught his fist within my hand, ready to crush his bones in my grasp. But, the scent of piss stained the air as the man wetted himself with fear.

Once the man was gone, I turned to face the woman I had saved. For the first time, in hundreds of years, the appearance of a mere human stole my breath. Her eyes were a lovely shade of blue, like sapphires glistening in the light. Her skin was smooth and milky. And though her hair was an unnatural color, it fell down to her waist in messy waves.

And when she spoke, her voice sounded with music. She seemed wise beyond her youthful years. A strange sense of familiarity nipped at the back of my mind, but I wrote it away as I realized that I had misjudged this woman. She was no human, she was a witch, brewing with magic deep within herself. I could feel it stirring about within her, wishing to be set free.

I found myself wishing to be closer to her, to touch her milky skin, but I was blocked from doing so. Her witch magic protected her from me. Knowing, she wanted nothing more to do with me, or my kind, I said farewell to the fair witch. And as I disappeared into the shadows, a bite of regret nipped at me when I didn't ask the woman her name.

THE WITCH

The rest of the walk to my apartment was without incident, thankfully. Though my mind remained on the mysterious vampire who helped me, though I could have handled the situation on my own. He was not after my blood, didn't once try to attack me and drain me dry. His eyes were clouded with concern... and curiosity.

What had made him help me?

Turning down a well-lit alleyway, there was a turquoise painted door toward the end. Approaching it, my feet stepped on the maroon *Stay Away* doormat. Reaching into my bag, I rifled through it trying to find my house key. My keychain jingled out of my bag, a mass of keys and charms, and I stuck the house key into the lock. The knob clicked and I turned it, entering my home.

The strong scent of dragon's blood incense wafted through my tiny apartment. Kicking off my boots, they landed with a soft thud on the wooden floor. Swinging my satchel off my shoulder, I tossed it on the narrow table beside the door. Then, my hands reached behind my neck, unclasped the silver chain that the silver medallion hung from, I placed it on a hook that was drilled into my door. No vampires would be allowed to enter my home. My hands set to work latching and locking all five of locks. A witch always made sure her home was intruder-proof.

My apartment was small but homey, every inch of it was a piece of myself. The artwork, the tapestries, the antique furniture, all of it spoke of me. Candles were situated throughout the apartment, scattered along shelves and tables. With a snap of my fingers, tiny flames blazed to life upon the candle wicks.

The wooden floor was cool against my bare feet, my body was exhausted, ready to rest. But there was something I had to check on first. Continuing down the entry hallway, I passed by the doorway to the kitchen and living room and the doors that led to the bathroom, and my room. At the far end of the hall hung a black tapestry with the zodiac constellations printed upon it.

My hand pushed it aside to reveal a door with a window, the glass being bulletproof. Peering into the window, I made sure that no one had disturbed my shop. Though, I could protect my home from werewolves, vampires, and even my own kind if needed, it was hard to ward off delinquent teenagers. Thankfully, nothing had been harmed.

The tapestry covered the door once more as I stepped away and ventured toward my room. The room was lit by candles, a warm glow radiated through the room. Though, I had light fixtures, I preferred the natural light that emanated from a flame. Taking a seat on the wooden chair, with the purple pillow, I found myself staring into the large mirror attached to my vanity.

My hands set to work, unclasping my many necklaces, and placing them on branches from the brass tree necklace holder. I removed my two rings; one of them silver banded with a large onyx in the center, it was my mother's, the other was a mood ring that the bartender, Cindy, had given me on my first open mic night at the bar. I placed them on separate fingers on the porcelain hand beside the brass tree.

I set to work brushing through the tangles in my purple hair, in the candle light it seemed as though my hair was almost black with a hint of purple. Setting down the dark wooden brush, I began to weave my hair together in one, long braid. Standing from the chair, I untied the strings on the front of my dress and slipped it down my body. I searched through my chest of drawers, my fingers hooking through the silver hoops and pulling the first drawer open. I changed underwear and slipped on a pale nightgown.

Finally, I lay my body to rest on the plush mattress of my bed. The silky turquoise, purple, and black sheets wrapped around my body. Though it was midsummer, I kept my house cold with magic. The sheets were cool against my skin and my eyes slowly closed with exhaustion.

Just as I was drifting away, I noticed that my sleeping buddy was not with me. "Pax." I called tiredly for my cat companion.

A meow sounded down the hall as he made his way to my room. I heard the *pat pat* of his paws on the wooden floor. The bed creaked as he leapt onto the mattress and crawled up beside me. He curled into a ball and his purring aided me to sleep.

Chapter Two

Strange Dreams

THEY SURROUNDED ME. Monsters. Blood thieves. The ancient ones. Their black eyes focused only upon me. They were the only things I could see clearly. The monsters' faces were a blur, the place a blur. Like a haze had cast itself around me, fogging my vision. My heart thundered within my chest, my pulse roaring within my ears.

A pain shot through my stomach; vomit raised in my throat. My mind became dizzy. The room was spinning, my vision leaving me. My body crumpled to the floor and that's when the vampires pounced. Fangs sank into my skin, sucking the blood from my veins, draining me. I couldn't think, couldn't see, and barely could breathe.

I was dying.

A shouted roar reverberated around us, vibrating my bones. The monsters glanced up, hisses sounding from them. Voices began to speak angrily, shouting, cursing. But I couldn't understand them, my hearing was leaving me as well.

Suddenly, the ground beneath my body began to tremble and my attackers fled, disappearing.

Gentle, strong arms lifted my body up, I stared upon my savior, but their face was a blur to me. Though I couldn't understand their words, I knew the person was saddened by my coming death. Then, they bent down and a pain pierced my neck.

A voice whispered to me, calling me back from my dreams and bringing me to the world once more. Slowly, my eyes opened, and I was met with the face of a young woman. Her skin was transparent like glass, her long hair floated around her in the air, her grey eyes starring upon me attentively. The woman's dress was tattered and frayed.

When she cocked her head to the side, her hair moved like water. "Are the dreams back?" Her voice echoed quietly.

"I'm beginning to think I'm foreseeing my death." I rubbed the tiredness from my eyes until stars began to flicker in the darkness of my mind.

"Don't say such things, it's possibly a nightmare and nothing more."

My hands flopped back onto the bed and I glanced at my ghostly companion. "Catherine, witches can have prophetic dreams. And this dream has come to me several times too many to be written off as just a bad dream."

She drifted across the room and situated herself on top of the black chest of drawers. Catherine began to trace a ghostly finger along the filigree silver patterns that decorated the edges of the top drawer. "If the dream proves to be true, you'll have me to guide you in the afterlife."

Pax finally awoke and uncurled from his ball, stretching out his sleeping limbs. He set to work licking one of his white paws and running it over his little black head. My hand reached for my companion and I scratched him behind the ears. "Good morning, Pax."

He blinked his emerald eyes at me and continued with his morning bath. Tossing the blanket off my body, I approached my vanity. Catherine's ghostly face appeared in the reflection. "At least I'll have one friend in the afterlife. But, death will have to wait, I have a shop to open in thirty minutes."

My fingers set to work, undoing the braid in my hair, allowing it to fall down the length of my back in crinkled waves. Deciding that my hair looked decent enough, I began to apply my makeup. With just a glance at the small tube of black liner, it lifted from the vanity, the lid slowly twisted, and the wand popped out of the tube. It drifted toward me and began to paint dark wings across my eyelids. While it worked, I applied my lipstick. Today, I would wear a dark maroon. My lips were turned from a soft pink, to a deep brown-plum-red.

"You know, in my time, you would be burned just for looking like a witch. They used to say that when a witch was burned, her soul was as well so it couldn't possess another's body." Catherine remarked from the chest of drawers.

"Sad times. Did you ever befriend a witch?" I asked.

She closed her ghostly lids as she began to reminisce of the past life she once had. "I did but she met a cruel end. Funny how that now I find myself friends with a witch once more."

"Well, you don't have to worry about a village chasing me with pitchforks. Times have changed. But for the better? I cannot truly say."

"Times now are better than they were when I was alive, Natalia."

"Perhaps." I said as I stood from the chair.

I ventured from my room and opened the purple painted door to the bathroom. My finger flicked the switch and a blinding light flooded the room. Right beside the door was the sink. The small mirror was attached to the turquoise wall above it, black beads draped along the sides of the mirror, little stars hanging from the ends.

The faucet turned on; water began to pour into the sink. Glancing upon my reflection, my hand lifted toward my face. My fingers hovered just before my maroon lips, and with a gentle motion, my lipstick peeled from my skin. The dark lip shaped lipstick floated in the air before me, hovering above my fingers.

With a gentle blow, the lipstick drifted through the air and fluttered about through the room. Now, I could brush my teeth without worry of ruining my lipstick.

Once my teeth were cleaned, my eyes wandered through the small room searching for the fluttering lips. With a whistle, they drifted toward me and the lipstick caressed my lips once more.

When I had returned to my room, I found Catherine floating over my bed. Pax was swatting at the ends of her frayed dress, such a silly creature. Catherine's ghostly giggles echoed around the room, her face beaming with happiness.

"If animals and creatures of the supernatural couldn't see me, I'd be quite lonely in this world." There was a faint sadness in her grey eyes, but it vanished quickly.

I approached the chest of drawers and began to pick my outfit for the day. "May I ask, why haven't you crossed over?"

Catherine was silent for a moment, causing me to glance over my shoulder. Her eyes had grown distant and vacant, any emotion had left her transparent face. "Perhaps because something holds me here to this world."

"Your death perhaps?"

A sigh escaped her, and she seated herself at my vanity. "I fell down a well. That's all I remember."

My fingers brushed against the satin fabric of a purple skirt. Tightening my hold on it, I pulled it from the drawer. "Maybe it was no accident." I closed the drawer.

She peered into the mirror; her brow creased as she searched deep into her old memories. "I cannot think of anyone who would wish to cause me harm." She let out a sad sigh. "Perhaps I'm stuck here forever."

My chest tightened. But, I wouldn't be here forever, not unless I used to spell to make myself immortal. A part of me wished to do so, but another part was far more curious about life after death. I couldn't bring myself to say it, to speak those words. And there was no guarantee that I would be trapped in this world after my death.

"I know what you are thinking, Natalia." She said. Her grey eyes staring at me from the mirror. "I've been your friend since you were six and now, you're twenty-three. I have many more years with you before I have to worry about such things."

Trying to lighten the mood, I twirled around to face her fully, and placed a hand on my hip. "I blame you for my old way of speaking."

Her face brightened as her lips curled into a smile. "Just two weeks after being your friend, you were speaking like me. It was quite silly to hear a six-year-old in this day in age speak that way."

I approached my closet and slid the door; it covered the other. Dresses and shirts of all styles and colors filled the closet. "My caretaker thought it was definitely strange."

My mother had died when I was four, I do not know how, and no one has ever told me. My father has never once been in my life, no one knows where he is or even if he's alive. I was placed under the care of an old family friend, she has long since passed. She was a kindly elder woman and though she thought I was a peculiar little child, she loved me none the less. Mrs. Warner never knew of my magic or my ghostly friend, she was completely naïve to the magical world.

Catherine giggled. "It was quite fun to play with the old woman. I would hide small trinkets of hers and watch her search curiously for them. I showed her mercy when it took her longer than thirty minutes to find the hidden items."

"Yes, I remember that. She always thought it was me hiding her things." My hand brushed along the different fabrics of the shirts, trying to decide which one to wear.

Finally, one caught my eye. A black shirt with sleeves so long that they passed my hands and billowed. The ends of the sleeves tapered into points. The neck line dipped into a low V shape and black strings laced up at the bottom of the V.

Grabbing the skirt and shirt, I tossed them into the air and there they hung, waiting for me to slip them on. I changed out of my nightgown, it dispensed itself into the black wicker laundry basket in the corner of the room. Approaching the clothes, I grabbed them from the air and slipped them on.

I faced my ghostly companion that was waiting by my bedroom door with eyes filled with excitement. "Ready to open the store?"

Her pale face beamed with happiness. "Oh, yes! I just adore your little store!"

Walking down the hall, the dark tapestry waited for me. Catherine, too impatient to wait, disappeared through the wall, she would be waiting for me on the other side. With a giggled laugh, I moved aside the tapestry, and opened the door.

THE VAMPIRE

After my encounter with the young witch, I found that my mind could not stop thinking of her. The witch's hauntingly beautiful face seemed to etch itself into my mind, bells seemed to ding, bells of familiarity. But I couldn't understand why. I had not met the witch before that night, never seen her before.

So, why would it feel as though we have met before?

I stood before the drape covered window, my hand reaching for the crimson fabric, and moving it aside. The tall windows loomed over me as the moon's light filtered into the darkened room around me. Bracing my forearm against the glass, I rested my head against it. My jaw clenched as I remembered the witch's sweet, alluring scent.

Something deep inside me, something menacing began to thirst for her blood, the sweet nectar in her veins. My hand balled into a fist, the veins rising to the surface of my skin. No. I couldn't allow the thirst for blood to control me, not again, never again.

Light footsteps sounded in the room, a sigh escaped me, but I didn't face the visitor. "Hello, mother." I said dryly.

"Where were you the other night, Roman?"

I lowered my arm from the window and stuffed my hands into the pockets of my trousers. "If you must know of my whereabouts, I was out feeding."

A gentle gust of wind whispered beside me as my mother moved across the room and stood before the window. Her ghostly eyes did not glance upon me, only out toward the darkened sky. Her blonde hair was pulled away from her angular, slim face.

"You know how I feel when you venture out alone, Roman. Especially when you do not tell me where you are going and when you will return."

A scoff sounded from me as I shook my head. "But, you would prefer me to be alone than with a werewolf."

Her eyes snapped over in my direction, her brow furrowed, her cherry coated lips pressed into a flat line. Anger blazed through her eyes. "That *creature* you call a friend is *our* enemy, lest you have forgotten."

"He is not an enemy, mother." Taking a step back from the window, I turned my back to the angry woman.

"You will not walk away from this conversation, son." Her words hissed from her lips.

"Oh, but I will. I'm not a child anymore and you have no control over me." I glanced over my shoulder, "Lest you have forgotten, *mother*."

THE WITCH

Catherine drifted through the small shop, her pale grey eyes taking in every oddity that lined the shelves. Oddly, her favorite items were the bleached skulls of animals. Her particular favorite was the fox skull. Each item came to me, or found me, already dead, freed from its skin. I did not harm animals, nor would I ever.

She then drifted to the other side of the store where the shelves of crystals, herbs, and grimoires could be found. "Perhaps, back in my time I would have loved to learn about magic."

"Did your witch friend not tell you of it?"

She glanced at me for a moment, a sadness in her eyes but a smile on her lips. "Though I loved and cherished her as a friend, I feared her magic. I was taught and raised to fear it. So, I never learned of her world, truly." She continued glancing at the crystals, her hand reached for them, to touch them, but it passed through them. "I am glad now, that I can learn more of your world, the magic in it."

Once I had made sure I had enough money in the register, I approached the door, flipped the closed sign to open, and unlocked the door. "If you lived in this time, you would love being a Wiccan. It's the closest that humans come to being witches."

Catherine gazed upon me with curious eyes. "I know some of the young girls that come in here are wiccan. But, I don't truly understand what that means."

I stood beside my ghostly companion, my hand flipping through the pages of the grimoire that was on display. A grimoire of healing. "They are humans that believe magic exists in their world, they wish to find it, learn of it. And I have come to find that humans can tap in to magic, but just a tiny bit. Enough to use charms of protection, smaller spells, or even see ghosts, simple things like that. But nothing more."

Her eyes brightened. "Ah, I would have loved to learn of magic!" And then, she grew saddened once more. "I wish people never feared it in my time."

"I cannot blame them, not entirely. Not all witches are kind."

"But my friend was." Catherine spoke softly.

The bell dinged above the door as a young girl entered my shop. One of the human wiccans. Her midnight hair fell just a little past her shoulders in soft waves. And I found that the whites around her hazel eyes were bloodshot, her dark makeup smeared, and trailing down her cheeks.

"Anne," I approached the young girl. "What happened?"

She made to wipe at her nose with the sleeve of her grey sweater, but I stopped her, led her to the counter, and handed her a tissue.

"My parents..." She wiped her nose. "They found my books, crystals, and sage."

Catherine moved beside me; her pale hands clasped over her chest. "They yelled at me; said they would not have a devil worshiper in their home." Another set of tears began to fall. "I tried to explain to tell them, tell them it wasn't related to the devil, but they wouldn't listen." She blew her nose into the tissue, "They burned everything in the fireplace and made me watch. And after it had all burned, they made me clean it out of the fireplace."

Hatred began to seethe within me. Humans were still fearful, and fear brought out the worst in a person. Handing the girl another tissue, I placed a tender hand on her shoulder. "Stay here, I'll be right back."

Disappearing through the door and into my home, I entered my room and slid open the closet door. Standing on the tip of my toes, I reached for the top shelf. My hands found themselves on a small chest. Small enough to fit into her satchel bag and big enough to store sage, crystals, and a grimoire.

Returning to the store, I took the girl's shaking hand in mine, and led her around. "Show me what your parents burned."

She pointed to a bundle of sage. I grabbed it and placed it inside the chest. She gazed upon me curiously, her brow raised. "What are you doing?"

I smiled, "Replacing everything your parents destroyed."

Her eyes brightened with gratitude, a wide smile spreading across her lips. "Thank you so much!"

"It's not a problem. Show me what else."

After several minutes, the chest was almost full. Quartz, amethyst, and topaz crystals were piled beside bundles of sage, and tall white candles. At the bottom of the chest was a grimoire for charms of protection. Little did she know that the chest itself had a charm upon it.

Anne carefully held the chest in her arms. "Thank you, so much." She bit her bottom lip. "But what if my parents find my stuff again?"

A smirk tugged at the corner of my lips. "Don't worry about that. Nothing will be harmed."

The young girl thanked me several more times and left the shop, a happy skip in her step. My heart lightened, knowing that I had helped her and made sure that her parents would never do something so foolish again.

"What a truly nice thing you did for the girl, Natalia." She peered at the door, "What charm did you place on the box?" She raised a brow at me, a grin playing on her lips.

"Nothing too complex, Catherine. Just the chest can never be burned or destroyed in any way and Anne is the only one who can open the chest, besides me, of course."

"Clever." She smiled.

Chapter Three

The Werewolf

THE VAMPIRE

MOTHER. THE DAMNED woman hated anything and anyone that wasn't of our kind. Even killed them without second thought, no remorse. The night I walked away from her, she chased after me, yelling my name like a fool. As if I was a child. But she held no control over me and hasn't for the last five hundred years. My mother was a sickness. A plague that never seemed to go away.

Always lingering, watching, waiting.

Buzz.

My phone vibrated in the pocket of my dark jeans. The screen was bright, the name *Good Boy* appeared on it. A laugh escaped me at the ridiculous name I had given my werewolf friend. The name he gave me was no better, *Blood Sucker.*

Sliding my thumb across the screen, I read the message.

Good Boy: Mom giving her little boy a hard time again?

He knew I was to visit my mother tonight and knew the visits were never pleasant.

Of course, meet me at my place.

Good Boy: Yes, master.

A laugh escaped me once more as I sent back, *Good boy.*

This place was my sanctuary. A safe haven I could escape too. No one knew of it except my friend. It was far away from my mother and the rest of my pestering family. Years ago, I stumbled upon an abandoned factory, and years ago, I made it my home.

A few short hours later, the door to my apartment swung open, the rusted steel groaning in protest. A man stood at the threshold; his hands stuffed into the pockets of his worn jeans. His onyx hair a mess of tangles at his shoulders. His brown eyes glanced at the old door.

"I see you still haven't fixed the door."

My arms crossed over my chest. "I prefer it that way; it alerts me when someone is breaking in."

A scoff sounded from the man. "Who would come to this decrepit place? Except for us two loners, of course."

I extended my hand toward the brown leather couch, Aron bowed sarcastically and fell onto the leather, draping his arm over the back of it and his other onto the arm of the couch. "So, what's the old broad whining about this time?"

I leaned against the wall. "Same as always. Hates me not living at the house and still hates you, of course."

He grinned, white teeth gleaming, canines exposed. "Ah, such a lovely woman she is."

My eyes glanced over to the open windows, night had fallen across the world, blanketing it in its darkness. A woman's face began to appear before my eyes, purple hair stretching across the star covered sky. Brilliant blue eyes taking the place of the moon.

"Roman?" Aron's voice caused my attention to break away from the sky, the witch's face disappearing. "Something else seems to be on your mind."

I shook my head, shaking away the thoughts of the woman. "It's nothing."

The werewolf sighed and stood from the couch. "Alright, we're leaving."

My brow raised at him. "Leaving?"

"I need a drink and I think you do too."

Aron marched out the door and I followed after him.

THE WITCH

Evening was approaching as the sun slowly set below the horizon. The sky was painted in hues of oranges and reds, the clouds dispersing. Closing time was near, excitement began to bubble inside me. Tonight, once again, I would be singing at the bar. I found joy in singing, it felt as though my soul was set free whenever a song whispered from my lips.

The store bell dinged as two dark skinned women entered my shop. An instant smile found itself upon my lips as I watched the two women. They approached the counter, smiles on their faces as well.

The first woman, the tallest of the two, spoke to me. "Ah, Natalia, it is a pleasure to see you. It has been some time since we last visited your little shop."

"A pleasure to see you too, Tasha. Did you enjoy Mardi Gras?"

A sigh escaped her smiling, crimson coated lips. "Perhaps we went a little overboard on the drinking, but, yes. It's always an entertaining experience."

Glancing over at the over woman, I found her eyes fixated on my lips. When she found me looking at her, she smiled instantly, and signed the word, *Hello.*

Signing back, I said, "Hello, Sasha." I spoke while I signed, Sasha read lips as she read hands.

The two women were twins. Tasha was mute at birth and Sasha was deaf. With magic, Tasha learned to speak but Sasha refused healing magic, she preferred being deaf. It was part of her, she had told me once, and she would never change it.

My eyes wandered to gaze upon their hair. Both of them wore braids, Tasha's went down to her waist and Sasha's just a little past her shoulders. I noticed that purple and green weaved through their hair.

Meeting their eyes once more, I asked, "Did you need anything today?"

Tasha glanced toward the sage, "The usual and I'll need a bag of wooden runes, I seemed to have lost mine at Mardi Gras."

The women wandered over to the shelves and I began to ring up her items on the register. When she came back, she placed a bundle of sage atop the glass counter.

Leaning down. I unlocked the sliding door. "Which bag would you like?"

Her brown eyes examined the colorful array of bags lined on the top shelf. "The purple one, please dear."

Scooping up the bag of runes, I placed them on the counter next to the bundle of sage. "It'll be five dollars."

Tasha raised a brow at me as she reached a hand into her beaded purse. "Always too generous, Natalia."

"Only to my favorite customers." I winked.

Tasha handed me a five and I placed it in the drawer of the register. "Do you want me to bag these?"

She shook her head and took her items from the counter. "No thank you, I'll put them in my purse." Once the items were tucked away, she headed toward the door, "Thank you dear, have a blessed night."

Sasha signed, *Have a blessed night.*

The bell dinged above their heads as they left my shop.

Catherine joined me by side. "Time to sing?"

Glancing at her, a smile crossed my lips.

THE VAMPIRE

The bar was in the slums of the town, a little run down, but people still seemed to enjoy themselves here. Forgetting the flickering lights, broken bar stools, and a few bugs that scurried along the floor. A thick haze filled the small bar, heavy from the smoke of cigars and cigarettes. It bothered my heightened senses, causing a headache to form.

Aron stepped beside me, a cocky grin on his face, and slapped me on the back. "The place will grow on ya." He chuckled.

I glanced uneasily toward the bar where a man had passed out, his hand still clutching the half drunken glass of beer, and drool dripping from his opened mouth.

"I won't get my hopes up." I said as I followed my friend to the bar and took a seat beside him. The bar stools creaked and groaned beneath us and for a moment, I thought they would give out.

Aron motioned to the bartender, holding up two fingers and nodding his head once. The blonde woman set to work filling up two shot glasses of clear liquid. She approached us and set the small glasses down atop of napkins.

"Enjoy." She spoke in a thick southern accent.

Immediately, Aron grabbed the glass and downed the liquid. Shaking his head, he slammed it down on the counter. "That's the good stuff." He grinned. "Your turn."

Glancing uneasily, into the clear liquid, I lifted the glass to my lips, and downed it. It burned my throat and coughs sounded from me. The alcohol tasted bitter, stale, even. Aron laughed and patted me on the back.

"I thought vampires could hold their alcohol better than that."

"We prefer the type that doesn't taste like you fetched it from a sewer."

He waved a hand at me, dark hairs poking out from the sleeve of his leather jacket. "The prissy shit doesn't give ya a buzz, either."

Meeting the eyes of the bartender, he held up two more fingers, ordering more of that wretched alcohol. When she set the glasses before us, I slid mine in front of him. He took it and downed it in an instant. I shook my head at my friend as he ordered more, not quite understanding how he tolerated the drinks.

The bar door swung open and instantly the smell of flowers aroused my senses, drawing forth my attention. My eyes searched the crowded, hazed room, and I found the purple haired witch. She moved through the room with fluid grace, holding her head high. I watched as she took the small stage, the bar growing silent as she reached for the microphone.

For a moment, I thought our gazes had met, my body growing stilled as her striking eyes took in the bar. She took in a breath and then, she began to sing.

Her voice commanded the room, gently. It was soft and light. Swirling through the air, tangling with it, as it moved throughout the bar. Everyone was hushed as they watched the young witch sing her song. Even Aron, who never had any care for music, was quiet as he watched the woman. His brown eyes focused solely upon her.

I began to wonder if she had bewitched us with her magic but, no, she hadn't. We were bewitched by *her*, her voice, there was no influence of magic or spells, only her.

Once her voice had trailed away, the wind taking it, she stepped down from the stage. And the warmth that had once filled the room, slipped away and the cold crept back in.

Aron turned around, facing the empty glasses before him, "She's what drew me to the place a few years ago." He began to say. "I was just wandering down the street one night and I heard this voice, followed it, and found myself here."

My eyes focused on her as she approached the bar counter. The bartender, whose name was Cindy, smiled and complimented the woman's singing. Then, the witch left, disappearing into the night.

"Do you know her?" I asked, intrigued.

Aron shook his head. "Nope, not even her name. She never stays after a show." But, I sensed there was something he was keeping from me.

Standing from the bar stool, he glanced at me curiously. I patted his shoulder. "I'll return, save me some sewer water."

His laughing sounded from behind me as I rushed toward the door in search of the witch. The crisp, night air filled my lungs. It hung heavy with moisture. I followed the scent of flowers down the side walk, into the night.

THE WITCH

As I walked along the sidewalk, I hoped that the man wouldn't follow me tonight. Not after his encounter with the blood thief, hopefully, he was scared off for good. The night air felt cooler, though it still hung heavy with moisture from the summer day. My hand reached into my bag and gripped my house key, my fingers fumbling with the keychains.

Behind me, footsteps sounded along the sidewalk. A sigh escaped me as I rolled my eyes. Perhaps, the man wasn't scared off. Quickly, I whirled around on my heel to face the man, but it wasn't him that I was facing.

Reflexively, my hand reached for the silver medallion that hung from my necklace, my thumb rubbing across the runes engraved into it, runes of protection. Immediately, the magic set to work and formed a barrier between the blood thief and I.

There was a wounded look upon the vampire's face, but it vanished quickly. His ghostly eyes took me in.

"Why are you following me?" My voice sounded with warning.

He gave me another once over before meeting my gaze. "You sing beautifully." Though he sounded awe-struck, his face remained calm and collected.

I arched a brow to him. "So, you're stalking me?"

"It was merely coincidence that I visited the same bar you sing in." He seemed offended.

Like, how could he, an immortal being, stalk a witch, a mortal? How dare I suggest such.

"Excuse me, *blood thief.*" I practically hissed the words. "It just seems too coincidental to me."

His cold eyes regarded me, seeming as though he had nothing to say. The vampire took a step toward me, but that was all he could take before he reached the barrier.

He reached toward it and traced his fingers along it. "What's your name, witch?"

"Why do you care to know?"

His eyes locked with mine, his features softening, the smallest hint of a smile tugged at the corners of his lips. "Curious, perhaps I would like to know the name of the woman who has a talent for singing so I may compliment her properly."

My hold tightened on the medallion. Every bone in my body screamed for me to leave, return home. But, something else whispered, *stay*.

"You confuse me, ancient one. You save me and don't drain me dry, then, you seem offended that I think you stalk me, and now you wish to pay me compliments." I took a step closer to the edge of the barrier. I realize now that he is much taller than me. "What is it that you want from me?"

His hand lingered upon the barrier before it fell away. "Your name and that is all."

"Natalia." I said.

The vampire began to disappear into the shadows of the night. "Natalia," he seemed to purr my name, "I do hope to hear you sing again."

And then, he was gone.

Once I had returned home, I placed the medallion of protection from vampires upon the hook of the door. My hand reached for the silver circle, my thumb tracing along the runes carved into it.

My mind began to wander to the blood thief. Why had he followed me tonight? Just for a simple compliment, there had to be more to it than that. Perhaps he thought he could catch me off guard, unaware. And drain me dry. But, if he wished to do that, then why bother stepping in and terrifying the man so much so that he pissed his trousers?

My brows creased together as I tried to come to an explanation for his actions. Blood thieves never bothered saving lives or paying compliments, so, why was he?

"Natalia?" Catherine's voice startled me, and I whirled around to face her, her grey eyes focused upon me.

"Yes?"

She cocked her head to the side, her hair rippling like waves in the air. "Something troubles you."

I shook my head and stepped around her, "It's nothing." I said before changing the subject. "I need to sleep; my aerial dance class begins early tomorrow."

Chapter Four

Lullabies

THE NIGHTMARE HAD haunted me once more. A cold sweat drenching my body. My breathing heavy. I took in my surroundings, reassuring myself that I was alive, I was safe. My hand reached for my neck, but my fingers only brushed bare skin. Releasing a breath, I shook my head.

It's only a dream.

Though, I knew it was more than that, much more.

Glancing at the clock, it read six. I would be there fifteen minutes before seven, allowing me an hour of free dancing before the other students arrived. Tossing the blankets off my body, I made toward the bathroom. Classes would begin at eight, giving me some time to get ready.

Once I took a shower, my teeth and hair brushed, I returned to my room. I dressed in my aerial clothes, clothes that were light and allowed me to move with fluidity and grace. Nothing that would weigh me down or get tangled in the massive ribbon ropes. Slipping on my favorite pair of black leggings that shimmered, I reached for the black, short sleeved crop top and slipped that on as well.

As I wove my purple hair into one, long braid, Pax brushed against my legs purring his morning greetings. A smile tugged at my lips as I reached down and scratched behind his ears.

Lifting my head, I glanced at the ghostly woman who lingered at the door. "Are you accompanying me today for the class?"

A smile tugged at her lips. "Of course."

I walked along the quiet sidewalk, the sun rays bathing my body in their heat. Catherine silently followed beside me, her eyes taking in the sights around her, though she has seen them many times before. Soon enough, our destination was in sight.

Miss Lola's Dance Class.

A pale-yellow building with a fluorescent pink sign. My heart always fluttered with warmth at the sight of the small building. This was one of my few happy places. A place I felt I could allow my soul to be set free.

Catherine could hardly contain her excitement and rushed ahead of me, disappearing through the wall. A giggle escaped my lips as I approached the glass double doors. Turning the golden handle, I stepped into the cool air of the dance room. The sweet scent of roses filled my senses as I breathed it in. Gazing around, I found my own reflection staring back at me from the mirrors that lined along the walls.

Before walking in any further, I slipped off my silk, black shoes, and stepped onto the cool hardwood floor. Ribbon ropes of varying colors hung down from the high ceiling. It was like a maze of colorful fabric. My ghostly companion danced around the hanging fabrics, a smile on her pale face.

"Miss Natalia." Startled by the sudden voice, my head faced toward the small hallway to the right side of the doors.

Standing there was Miss Lola herself. She was French and in her late forties. Her brown, silver streaked hair was pulled back into a tight bun. She was a short woman of slender build. Her face was angular, with sharp cheekbones. Her hazel eyes were focused upon me. A smile twitched at the corner of her thin lips.

"Good morning, Miss Lola."

"Arriving early for dance? One of my more willing students, I must say."

"I take great pleasure in dancing; my excitement gets the better of me sometimes."

She motioned toward the ropes, "Nothing wrong with excitement, my dear."

Eagerly, I approached the turquoise rope that hung from the ceiling. Wrapping the ribbons around my arms, I lifted my feet off the ground, hoisting my body into the air. My muscles began to burn as my arms held my body up. Holding tight to the ribbons, I flipped.

My head now angled toward the ground and my feet above me. Hooking the backs of my knees on the ropes, I unraveled the ribbon from one arm and twirled the turquoise fabric over one of my legs twice, securing myself in place. Then, I spun. The room slowly turning. Straightening my free leg and keeping my other hooked, I poised my head and angled my arms in a delicate position while I turned.

Gripping the ropes once more, I lifted myself up. Twirling my leg, the ribbon wound around it. Then, bending my knee, the calf of my leg rested beneath me, almost like a seat. My other leg was stretched outward. One of my arms was positioned above me, the ribbon wound around it, and my other arm stretched out with my leg.

For the next hour, I did several different positions and moves, feeling the strength and burn in my arms and legs as I worked my muscles. Sweat began to form on my forehead and coated my body in a thin layer, but I didn't mind. I took pleasure in the exercise, feeling as though I were floating.

Miss Lola always allowed me to do this before each class, working and strengthening myself. I was one of her favorite students, though she never liked to admit it out loud. In her class I was the only one who seemed to truly appreciate the art and dance.

Once the hour had come to an end, that's when the other students arrived for morning class. None of them questioned why I was dancing with the ribbons; this wouldn't be their first time walking in and seeing the purple haired woman hanging by the ribbons.

After my aerial class, I returned to my home. I took a shower and dressed, ready to open my store. Passing through the door from my home to the shop, I flicked the light switch and a warm golden glow washed over my shop. With a snap of my fingers, flames danced on the wicks of candles that were scattered about my shop. Approaching the door, I unlocked it and flipped over the sign.

Returning to the register, I watched as Catherine drifted through the shop as she did every day, humming a song to herself.

I closed my eyes and listened to her haunting voice. It was beautiful. It echoed with age, speaking of long forgotten times. And I found myself being swayed into the land of dreams.

The air rustled the tall grass, making it sway against the breeze, making it appear as though it were a green ocean. The branches above my head rustled as the wind crept through them.

My eyes searched the meadow once my ears caught the sound of voices. I was not alone. Two people stood in the center of the meadow, a man and a woman. Their backs were facing me, but I knew that the two were more than just friends. Their body language gave them away. The gentle way the woman laid her hand on the man's arm. The light giggles that escaped them.

Their hands found one another, their fingers entwining. It was then that they turned to face each other. But I found that they had no faces. Even so, they leaned in close as if to kiss. And where lips should have been, smooth skin met smooth skin. The woman's black hair was swept away in the breeze, obscuring the view of the two lovers. As if my eyes weren't meant to witness this.

"Natalia?"

When my eyes fluttered open, I saw Catherine's ghostly face before me. Her eyes were studying me with a curious look, her hair floating around her.

Stretching my arms, I let out a yawn. "Did I doze off?"

"That you did, perhaps my singing is to blame." She giggled and it echoed around the store hauntingly.

"Perhaps, but I do enjoy your singing Catherine. It's beautiful."

Though she couldn't show it, I knew she would be blushing now if she could. "Always so gracious with the compliments, my dear friend."

Ding.

The shop bell sounded above the door as someone entered. Rising from my chair, I placed a smile on my face to greet the visitor. But my smile did not find my lips. Instead my brows raised as I took in the man that approached the counter.

"Aron?"

A wolfish grin crossed his mouth. "Long time no see, Natalia."

THE VAMPIRE

Mother, always nagging, always demanding. Always needing to know where I have been and what I have done. Why do I continue to subject myself to her interrogations? Perhaps because if I don't visit her, she'll hunt me down until the end of the world.

Another night where I leave her behind in a fury as I walk out of another argument. Her voice chased after me, screaming, like a thousand damned souls crying out from the depths of hell.

As I soared through the sky, trying to clear my head, I found that the witch wove her way into my thoughts once more. Her voice haunting me as it has been these past days. Like a haunting lullaby, it tried to sing me to sleep, into a deep slumber. And some nights, I allowed it. While other nights, I gazed toward the stars and listened.

Somehow, I found myself above the bar she sang in.

I listened and couldn't find her voice. Lowering from the darkened sky, I entered the bar to find no one upon the stage. Approaching the counter, I found the blonde bar tender there serving drinks.

"Need a drink, sweetheart?" Her southern accent was heavy rooted and pained my ears.

"Is Natalia not singing tonight?"

She placed a hand on her hip. "Like I tell the other men, I never reveal her singing schedule. All of you are just some thirsty dogs."

I wished to make a remark, but I kept my mouth closed as I left behind the smell of the bar. Deciding there was nothing left for me here, I returned to my home. The door creaked open as I entered and there, I found Aron stretched across the couch.

"I wondered where you were. Figured mommy got to you." He sat up and ran his hand through his shaggy hair.

I stepped further into the room, ready to make comment, but stopped. I sniffed the air. The scent of flowers. In a flash I stood before him, rage seemed to nip at me.

"You visited the witch."

He stood quickly. "She was at the bar, calm down Roman."

"Don't lie to me. She wasn't there tonight, and neither were you."

He stuffed his hands in his pockets. "She was last night, that I'm not lying about. We both know scents stick around for a while."

I turned away from him and approached the window. "I apologize." Though I sensed he was hiding something from me.

THE MOTHER

The crimson, thick liquid swirled within the wine glass. My nails tapping on it, the sounds of it echoing in my quiet room. I stood before the window, my eyes staring out toward the sky. My anger and frustration still lingered, boiling within me. My *son* has been stubborn, more so than usual. Arguing and pushing more and more.

My nose crinkled as I thought of the mutt, he called a friend, that *dog*. Only my son, only he would befriend our enemy. Ignorant, foolish boy.

And not only that, the scent of someone else has been clinging to him, and his mind. I would know the smell of a witch anywhere. Their blood had a certain scent to it, a sweet earthly smell of flowers. My mouth watered at the thought of draining that creature dry.

"I shall find you, little witch. And I shall enjoy drinking every last drop of your blood."

THE WITCH

Tonight, I would not be venturing to the bar. Tonight, my voice will not whisper through the microphone. Tonight, I lay in my bed. My mind replaying that strange dream I had earlier within the day. Something pulled inside me, tugging, seeming to yell something. But I couldn't understand what it was trying to convey. My head began to ache as I thought too much on it, the faceless couple.

Did the dream symbolize something?

Did it have something to do with my past or future?

Or did it mean anything at all?

I glanced over at Catherine who was perched on my dresser like she always was whenever I went to bed. Her eyes met with mine. "Having trouble sleeping?"

"Perhaps."

Pax leapt onto the bed and curled up beside me, immediately he began to purr as my hand brushed through his soft fur.

"Why didn't you tell me where you acquired the werewolf claw necklace from?" A question I knew she would ask.

"I have told you and if you weren't wandering around that night, you would have met him before."

"You told me a werewolf came to you injured and needing healing three years ago. What you *failed* to tell me was how handsome he was." She seemed to swoon. Fanning herself with her ghostly hand.

A laugh escaped me. "He wasn't that handsome, Catherine." Although, he quite was.

"If I were still alive, I would have asked him to wed me." She fell silent for a moment after she realized that she would never be given that chance. Such a mortal thing to wish for and never receive. "What does the necklace do? I know it isn't some pretty piece of jewelry."

"It protects me from other werewolves. If a werewolf gifts you one of their claws, that means none of their kind can harm you. It means you have been accepted and earned one of their kind's trust."

She nodded her head. "You seem to have a necklace for everything, Natalia."

"It never hurts to be safe and have a few friends."

"Alright, enough chatter, sleep, dear friend. It is late into the night."

"Sing me a lullaby?" I batted my lashes.

Catherine smiled sweetly, "Of course."

As her voice sang me to sleep my dreams were once again focused on the faceless couple.

Chapter Five

Healing

THE WOLF
THREE YEARS AGO

I WAS LEANED AGAINST the side of the bar, a cigarette hanging from my mouth. The smoke coiled within the air and dispersed. It was quiet and dark, how I preferred it. No noise of the day, no cars or crowds of people. Taking another drag off the cigarette, I inhaled the nicotine and released it.

As I tipped the ash off the end, my ears prickled. I listened. Light footsteps, so light human ears wouldn't have heard them. They were moving fast.

Blood suckers.

Instead of running, I waited.

Soon, five figures emerged from the shadows. They approached me slowly. I took another drag off the cigarette. Smoke curling within the air.

"Let me guess, the queen vampire's dogs have been sent after me?"

A woman stepped forth, her midnight hair fell well past her shoulders, sweeping across her breasts. "We have orders to kill you, *dog.*"

I flicked the cigarette at her, landing before her polished black boots. "The queen couldn't kill me herself? I'm beginning to think she's afraid of me. That I might scratch that perfect face of hers."

The vampire snarled and stomped on the cigarette. "She needn't concern herself with mutts like you."

"So, she concerns her dogs with killing a simple man like me?"

The vampire revealed her fangs as she snarled, her slanted eyes turning as dark as her hair. "Prepare to die, dog."

I shrugged my shoulders and winked at the vampire. "I don't plan on dying today."

With that, I took off down the sidewalk. They were behind me. Taking a sharp turn, I disappeared down a dark alleyway and headed toward the cemetery. Leaping over the iron fence, I shifted. My black paws dug into the dirt beneath me as I made my way toward the other side of the cemetery. I didn't bother looking back, I knew they were there. Some running others perhaps flying.

Once I reached the fence, I leapt into the air once more, but something slammed into my side. A sharp pain pierced the side of my throat as the damned vampire began to suck the blood from my veins.

We were sent rolling across the ground, turning up dirt and grass. I was able to kick the blood sucker off and tear my teeth into their shoulder, pulling away skin from bone. The creature shrieked, piercing my ears. It leapt away from me and I ran into the thick forest of trees.

I wove my way between the old trees, leaping over fallen ones and roots that emerged from the ground. Above me, the vampires leapt from branch to branch.

Keeping my eyes ahead, I saw the glimmer of streetlights. Running toward the lights, I kept along the side of the road until I came across a line of shops with alleyways separating a few of them. My nose caught the scent of something sweet, flowers. And there walking along the sidewalk was a purple haired woman. But she was not just any woman.

Snarls and hisses sounded closely behind.

Heading toward where the woman disappeared down an alley, I found her standing before a door.

Her eyes found me.

Shock, fear, and confusion mixed within her blue gaze as her hand reached for the many necklaces hanging from her neck.

I shifted before her and found that my neck throbbed in pain. My hand reached for it and came away dripping with blood. Glancing behind me, I found the vampires.

"There isn't enough time to explain, please can you heal me?"

She peeked her gaze around me and took in the sight of the vampires. "You try anything, werewolf, and I will have your skin."

With that, she opened her door and we disappeared inside her small home. The witch led me down a hall, moved aside a tapestry, and opened a door that led into a shop. She pointed toward a chair and commanded me to sit. To that I laughed but did what she wished.

She began to inspect my wound that now burned like fire. "Mind telling me why five vampires were after you?"

"Let's just say, the queen vampire doesn't like dogs."

The witch began to make a salve, mixing together odd things that I couldn't tell what they were. Before she applied it, she gently cleaned the wound and wiped away the blood.

"You're lucky, werewolf, if you had found me too late, they would have killed you or this bite would have."

I winced as she applied the salve. "Our bite is just as poisonous to them as their bites are to us."

The witch wrapped a bandage around my neck. "I know werewolves can be quick healers but after a bite like that, it may take some time. For now, though, the bite won't kill you, but it will hurt like hell while it heals."

I stood from the chair, "May I know the name of the witch who took in a stray like me?"

She smiled, "Natalia."

I bowed my head. “Thank you, Natalia. Now, I would like to return the favor.”

She raised a brow. “There’s no need.”

“I offer you one of my claws, I’m sure you’re aware of what that means.”

Her eyes widened. “Are you sure?”

“I am.”

THE WITCH

The faceless woman stood alone in the meadow. The gentle breeze playing with her dark hair. A giggle of ghostly laughter escaped her. My breath caught in my throat as she turned to face me, but it was not me that she saw.

The faceless man brushed past me, a chill running along my spine. He too did not notice me. They embraced one another and the man picked up the woman and twirled her around. And I’m sure if they had faces, there would be smiles upon them and looks of love in their eyes.

Once he set her down on her feet once more, she stepped back from him. She held out the palm of her hand and snapped her fingers. A crimson rose appeared. Her fingers gently traced along the silky edges of the flower, careful to not prick the thorns. Though the man had no face, I could tell he was in awe of her magic.

Their faces came close once more.

I awoke in my bed, Pax sound asleep beside me, and Catherine nowhere to be found. Rubbing the sleep from my eyes, I got out of bed and began to get ready for the day.

Once again, I was in my shop, Catherine humming beside me. My mind couldn't focus on anything except the strange couple. Who were they? Why did I dream of them?

"Are you going to tell me what you're thinking so hard on?" Catherine spoke.

A sigh escaped me. "Just a strange dream and nothing more."

"Another dream of you dying?"

I shook my head. "No. It's nothing, really."

She regarded me with questioning eyes but didn't press the matter further.

The shop bell sounded, grabbing my attention.

And entering my shop were my favorite customers, and friends. The twins approached the counter and I found that their braids no longer had the colors of Mardi Gras woven through them.

"Hello, Natalia." Tasha spoke.

"Welcome to my shop, once again. What are you in need of?" I signed while I spoke.

"Oh, we were just in the neighborhood and thought we would stop by, perhaps browse the shop for a while. If you don't mind, dear."

"Browse as long as you wish."

"Thank you, Natalia."

Sasha placed a hand on her lips and moved it forward toward me.

The twins walked about the shop. Tasha being more interested in the herbs and grimoires while Sasha took a liking to the dried skulls and crystals.

While they browsed, I once again found myself thinking back on that dream. I wouldn't have had it twice now if it didn't have a meaning. I just needed to find the meaning, but how?

I didn't notice that Sasha had approached the counter, a look of concern in her eyes. *What troubles you, Natalia?*

Tasha was lost within a grimoire.

Instead of speaking, I signed. *I have had a strange dream, more than once. The same one.*

Her brows creased. *What is within the dream?*

A man and woman, they have no faces, and they are lovers.

She remained still for a moment. Then, she grasped my hands and closed her eyes. Being deaf, allowed Sasha a special gift, being able to read more into people's emotions, reading more into their energies, being more open to them than hearing witches.

When she opened her eyes, they studied my hands, confused. Her brow creased. Dropping my hands, she signed, *It is visions from a past life. But whose life it is, I cannot read. There are too many confusing voices whispering, too many energies. It is hard for me to read.*

Can you tell me why I am having visions of someone else's life?

She shook her head. *The message is unclear. Perhaps it is only for you to reveal the answer.*

Thank you, for your help, Sasha.

She smiled. *Always.*

Tasha approached the counter and placed a grimoire of speaking and summoning spirits down. "Do not worry, I refuse to summon any negative spirits. It is merely to speak with lost family and friends."

Though us witches could see spirits, many of them found it hard to grasp onto their ghostly beings. So, we reach out to wandering spirits with spells and charms, to aid them in manifesting into their ghostly form.

I nodded my head, placed the grimoire in a bag, and slid it across the counter. Tasha raised a brow. "Always too generous, Natalia." She grabbed the bag. "Thank you, have a blessed night, dear."

Have a blessed night.

And then, the twins were gone.

Catherine floated beside me. "You asked her about the dream, what did she say?"

"Even she had trouble reading it. All she could find was that it was someone else's life. Why I was having that dream, she couldn't say. Only that I could reveal the answer."

She cocked her head to the side. "How strange."

"Strange indeed."

The walk to the bar was quiet, save for the sounds of the buzzing lights and bugs flying within the air. The summer heat was finally fading off, soon autumn would present itself upon the world. My boots clicked along the sidewalk, my dress swaying in the gentle breeze behind me. My necklaces rattling together. My fingers toyed with the end of my purple braid, twirling it around my fingers. Soon enough, the bar was in sight. Swinging open the door, I stepped inside the hazy, smoke filled room.

Immediately, Cindy smiled and greeted me, saying the mic was ready whenever I was. I returned the smile and approached the small stage. And then, silence filled the small bar as all eyes fell upon me. Without realizing it, my own eyes were gazing across the bar, searching the crowd for the ancient blood sucker. My hand grasped the mic and I began to sing.

THE VAMPIRE

Tonight, the witch was here. Her voice filled the bar, silencing all other voices. Everyone was entranced by her, including myself. My eyes never wandered away from her, I watched her body gently sway to her own song, how she would sometimes close those blue eyes of hers as she grew lost within the music.

And before she began to sing, I could have sworn that her eyes had searched for me. The way she stood there in silence for a moment, the way her gaze washed over the crowd of people. It tempted me to step forth from the dark corner I was hidden in, but I stopped myself.

Many nights I have found myself here, in this rundown bar, searching for her, wishing to hear her voice. I would have sworn she placed a spell over me, but I knew she hadn't. Something about this witch drew me to her.

And then, her song came to end. Silence falling over the bar. And the warmth that was once in the room, seemed to fade away as the witch stepped down from the stage, taking her song with her.

THE WITCH

As always, Cindy complimented my singing as I left behind the bar. I dared a glance over my shoulder before I stepped into the night. I walked along the lonely sidewalk with only the mosquitoes accompanying me.

But as I made my way along into the night, I found a figure looming in the darkness before me. It was leaned against a building, the streetlight barely able to reach the person as they stood in the shadows. I stopped in my tracks and my hand reached for the silver necklace, my thumb rubbing across it.

"Who's there?" I called out to the figure.

They shifted and stepped into the golden, flickering light. A sigh escaped me as the ancient blood sucker approached me. "Why are you here?"

"Hello to you as well, Natalia."

My eyes narrowed. "What do you want, vampire? Stalking me again?"

He stuffed one hand in his pocket and placed the other against the barrier that separated us. "Did I not tell you before that I enjoy hearing you sing?"

I matched his gaze. "You were in the bar."

A grin tugged at the corner of his lips. "So, you were looking for me."

I looked away from him when I felt a blush rise to my cheeks. "Don't flatter yourself, blood thief, I like to know when I'm being stalked so I can prepare to defend myself."

He tapped at the barrier with his index finger. "Doesn't seem to me that you need much time preparing, Natalia."

"If you are done pestering me, I'll be on my way now."

I moved around the vampire and began my walk home.

"Wait." Though he didn't shout, I could feel the eagerness in his dark voice.

I stopped and glanced over my shoulder. "Yes?"

He made to approach me once more, his hands reaching for the barrier. "Must you always have this barrier between us?"

I hardened my face. "Yes, because your kind are blood thieves, especially thieves when it comes to witch blood."

"Have I ever tried to harm you?"

"It's hard to try when there's a barrier separating us."

"And what must I do to earn your trust, Natalia?"

I arched my brow. "And why do you wish to earn it, vampire?"

He was silent for a moment, as if he questioned it as well. Returning his hands to his pockets, he took a step back, "Apologies for troubling you tonight, Natalia. Beautiful singing, as always."

Then, he stepped into the shadows and disappeared.

Chapter Six

Mother

THE VAMPIRE

I STEPPED INSIDE THE room to find her sitting before a roaring fire. Her ghostly eyes dancing with the reflection of the flames. Her golden hair cascading down into her lap and within her hand, she held a wine glass. It was filled to the brim with freshly spilled blood, it stained her pale lips.

"Hello, Roman." Her voice was dry as she greeted me, her eyes not bothering to fall upon me.

I leaned against the wall beside the fire. "I've come for my interrogation, mother."

She sniffed at the air and that's when she faced me. "Who is the witch?" Her words sounded with disgust but also thirst.

"I suppose I can't have witch friends, either." Though I wouldn't call Natalia and I friends as of now.

Mother set her cup down upon the round, oak table beside her red velvet chair, and stood. But she did not approach me, instead she stood before the roaring flames, her gaze staring deeply into them.

"First, you befriend a dog. Now, you befriend food." Her eyes met with mine. "Is the witch female?"

I stood straighter. "And why should that matter, mother?"

She returned her stare to the fire. "Do you remember the witch you fell in love with all those years ago, son?"

My heart ached as though an axe were taken to it – cleaving it in half. Never, did mother speak of her unless she wished to truly hurt me. My hands balled into fists. "I will never forget her, mother. Or the way those humans murdered her."

"I'll never forget how you savagely killed every human who played a hand in her death." She approached me then, looking hard into my eyes, "That was the only time you ever made me proud."

Her words were like a slap in the face as she walked out of the room, leaving me behind with the sounds of the crackling fire.

THE MOTHER

After I left Roman behind in the room, I ventured down the stairs where two of my guards stood. One male and the other female. They bowed low before me once I reached the bottom of the stairs.

"Rise."

They did as I commanded.

"I have a job for you, both of you."

"Whatever you ask of us, our queen." The woman with long black hair like silk answered, my prized guard.

"My son seems to have found himself a new friend. A witch. Find her, but don't approach. Only observe and report back to me."

They bowed once more. "Yes, our queen."

With that, they ventured out into the world on the hunt for a witch. I had a feeling Roman has already left the estate, they'll be following close behind.

THE WITCH

As soon as I opened the door to my small apartment home, Catherine was there, waiting, arms crossed over her chest.

"Is something the matter?" I closed and locked the door behind me, placing the silver medallion on the hook.

"Who is he?"

I turned to face her, "What?"

"I know you're keeping something from me, Natalia. It never takes you this long to walk home from the bar, and it has happened more times than one."

A sigh escaped me. "Just a blood thief who has a habit of stalking me after every show."

She raised a brow as a grin tugged at her lips. "And what is his name?"

"I call him blood thief. That's what his kind is."

"Is he attractive?" She batted her lashes.

I hadn't given it much thought. He was a handsome man, there was no denying that. But a monster lurked beneath that too perfect face.

I shrugged my shoulders. "I suppose he is, for a vampire."

Catherine twirled around within the air, giddy with excitement. "Natalia has taken a liking to a man!"

I couldn't help the laugh that escaped me. "I swear you can act like such a child."

"Will you be seeing him again?"

"If I do, it won't be by my choice."

Catherine continued to pester me about the vampire, asking question after question. Turning into the bathroom, I closed the door in her face, knowing well that she could just pass through it if she wished. But, she didn't, she left me alone.

With a snap of my fingers, my makeup peeled off my face, turned into liquid, and swirled down the drain in the sink. After brushing my teeth, I entered my room to find Catherine giggling at Pax who swatted at the ghostly bottom of her frayed dress.

Seating myself before my vanity, I began to brush the tangles from my hair and wove it together in a braid. I removed my jewelry, piece by piece. Placing my rings upon the porcelain hand. My mother's ring glinted up at me and it made my heart ache for a moment. Though she died when I was quite young, I do have few memories of her. Faint, memories. Sometimes she would appear in my dreams, sometimes her laugh would echo about them.

The ring and an old grimoire are all that I have of my mother. The grimoire that taught me magic through my childhood years. The book was falling apart at the seams now and I kept it safely stowed away.

"You miss her, your mother." Catherine appeared beside me; her eyes fixed on the ring.

A sigh escaped me. "I knew her only four years of my life, but yes, I miss her."

"My mother passed when I was ten, giving birth to my youngest sister. I understand the pain of a lost mother."

Rising from the chair, I dressed myself for bed, and lay my body to rest.

THE VAMPIRE

Across the street was the bar, voices echoed from it, drunken laughter, pointless conversations. Men staggered through the doors, wandering through the streets aimlessly. I shook my head at them. And while I stood here, I realized how strange this was, how mad it seemed to be waiting and watching for Natalia.

And perhaps there might be something wrong with me, but something that also pulled me to this woman. Making me want to know her, to befriend her. As I watched the bar for any sign of the witch, I felt a light breeze beside me. I didn't bother a glance at the vampire beside me.

"Hello, Sakiya."

"Hello, Roman."

I tilted my head to gaze upon the short woman. Her dark hair was pulled back into a low ponytail, her bangs sweeping straight across her dark brown eyes.

"I suppose mother has sent you to follow me."

She nodded her head, her gaze never meeting mine, only staring at the bar across from us. "You suppose correctly."

A sigh escaped me as I turned my attention to the bar once more. "What's her reason this time?"

She crossed her arms over her chest. "She ordered us to find the witch woman you've been seeing, watch her and report back whatever we learn."

A vein in my neck began to throb. *"Mother."* That word came out as more a growl, a curse. "That damned woman must know everything about my life and then ruin it."

"I remember when she ordered me to kill that wolf friend of yours."

"But you didn't."

A grin then pulled at her lips, her emotionless expression fading away. "Just scared him a little and let the others do the rest. I do hope he's forgiven me since then."

A chuckle escaped me. "I think if anything, it made him more attracted to you, Sakiya. He does admire a feisty woman."

There was a glimmer of mischief in her eyes. "Perhaps I should pay the wolf a visit, it has been some time."

"He would like that, I would think. Just don't let my mother catch his scent on you."

She began to disappear into the shadows. "I'm always careful, you of all people should know that, Roman. I've been your friend since the beginning."

"Thank you, Sakiya."

"Always." And then, she was gone.

THE WITCH

The monsters surrounded me. Their faces and voices a blur, a roaring of noise that rattled my eardrums. My vision was fading, leaving me. In and out of seeing, in and out of darkness. I found myself losing balance, my legs giving out beneath me. Down I fell, it seemed, into eternal darkness. Laughter echoed loudly. The monsters were mocking my pain. Finding joy in seeing me become nothing but a limp corpse.

My throat burned as if acid had been forcefully fed to me. My stomach feeling as though it were turning on itself, devouring itself. My limbs had gone weak, paralyzed. I couldn't move. I was frozen on the ground as the monsters swarmed all around me. And then, they lunged.

My heart rapidly beat against my chest. Panic had taken over me. I sat up in my bed, trying to calm my breathing. Gazing around me, I found that I was safe within my room. Pax meowed and crawled over to me, nudging his head against my cheek.

My fingers scratched behind his ear. "I'm okay, Pax."

"The nightmare is back." I heard Catherine say.

"Nightmare or my future, or perhaps both."

"Natalia..."

I shook my head and wrapped myself in the warm blankets. "Goodnight, Catherine."

She let out a sigh, "Goodnight, dear friend."

And then, I returned to my nightmare.

THE VAMPIRE

The rain pelted against the glass window; lightning danced between the stars that scattered across the dark night sky. Thunder roared, rattling the place I called my home away from my mother.

I haven't seen her since I learned of her orders. Sakiya though has sought me out on some nights, telling me of what she has revealed to my mother about the witch and what she has withheld from my mother. Sakiya was putting her life in a dangerous game and she knew it well. She has done this since the very beginning of my long life, five hundred years we have shared as friends but acted with disdain toward each other in front of mother.

The door creaked open.

"Knew I would find you here." Aron tossed his body upon the couch, it let out a groan.

"It seems that I'm always here."

"Have you invited that little witch to your lovely home yet? Or have your balls still not grown?"

A smile cracked. "I wouldn't even consider Natalia and I friends."

"So, become friends. Simple enough."

I turned my head to face the werewolf. He had one arm stretched across the back of the couch, the other laying on the arm, one leg resting atop the other. "It is not that simple."

He shrugged his shoulders. "Then, make it simple."

A scoff sounded from me. "How? She refuses to let me near her. She hates my kind."

He raised a dark brow. "If she truly hated your kind, would she even give you the time of day?"

"I suppose not."

"The next time you visit the bar, why don't you ask her somewhere? Doesn't have to be a fancy dinner. Maybe a stroll through the cemetery. Your kinds seem to enjoy those types of places, amongst the dead corpses."

I leaned against the wall beside the window and crossed my arms over my chest. "Since when have you begun to give romantic advice? I haven't seen you with a woman in quite some time."

His face turned serious, losing its playful grin. "And I could say the same to you, Roman."

My own smile faded away as I returned my gaze to the stormy night. "You know why."

The couch groaned once more as he stood and approached the window, his brown eyes flashed with lightning. "You need to move on from her death, Roman. You refuse to allow yourself to be happy for even a damned second. Her death was not your fault, I know it and you know it."

"I'll never love another the way I loved her."

"Because you haven't given another a chance. Almost five hundred years. I'd say it's time for you to love again."

I glanced at him. “I can’t say that I like this soft side of you, may I ask you to return to being a sarcastic prick?”

He tilted his head back and loud laughter echoed from him.

Chapter Seven

The Cemetery

ONCE AGAIN, THE vampire had been at the bar. This time, I spotted him while being on stage. He was there, lingering in the back of the small crowd, his eyes fixated upon me. And my gaze never ventured away from his. When the performance had arrived at its conclusion, the vampire approached.

Words were not spoken between us as we walked side by side towards the doors, he opened one for me, and we stepped into the night. My hand found itself around the silver medallion and the shield draped around me like a curtain of protection.

He regarded me for a moment but did not address the matter of the barrier. "Your singing was beautiful as always, Natalia."

"Thank you. Now, if that's all you wish to say to me, I'll be leaving."

"There's more I would wish to say."

"Then, say it, vampire."

His eyes held mine. "Would you like to accompany me somewhere?"

I raised a skeptical brow. "Somewhere you can drain the blood from my veins?"

His finger tapped the barrier. "It would be rather hard to accomplish that with your barrier between us."

I rolled my eyes, "Where would you like me to accompany you?"

And then, he flashed a smile, a smile that caused me to lose any expression I had. The smile softened his hard features. Made it seem as though he was just an ordinary human, not the vampire he was that has lived a long, long life.

And I hated that.

"Follow me."

So, I did. Foolishly the sheep followed the lion to its slaughter.

He led me down the sidewalk, walking side by side, as closely as the barrier would allow. The walk was minutes spent in silence, the vampire not giving any hints as to where he was taking me. My mind began to race with thoughts, perhaps this wasn't such a good idea to follow the blood thief, but another part of me whispered that this had been the right choice.

Soon enough, we stood before tall, black iron fenced gates. They loomed over us like ghosts. Above the giant gates was a sign that read, *Cemetery.* Nothing more and nothing less. The cemetery was given no name to mark it. Leaving it with no name seemed as though it was a place that was meant to be forgotten.

And it appeared as though it had been.

"Is this a joke about the death you wish to grant me?"

His eyes hardened. "I do not wish death upon you, Natalia."

The vampire approached the iron gate door, lifted the latch, and the gate groaned with a haunting creak, echoing within the quiet night, hopefully it didn't disturb the dead. Arousing them from their long slumber.

He stepped aside, holding the fence door. "After you, my lady."

I took a hesitant step toward the cemetery, met gazes with the vampire, before entering the place where the dead rested. The gate creaked shut behind us as the vampire closed the latch on the them.

"No one comes here anymore, leaving their dead forgotten." He spoke as he led me down the stone path that was overgrown with weeds that webbed across it and between the stones.

"Why do you?"

His eyes wandered across every headstone we passed. The dates ranged from the 1500s and ending at the 1700s. There were few family names, most of them being the same. Perhaps, this was a private family cemetery, or once was. This cemetery had been built before burying the dead in the ground was no longer permitted here.

"I have my reason."

Ahead of us was a small hill, at the top beside the path, was a tall willow tree. Its branches were long and swept across the ground like a haunting hand fetching wandering souls.

"Why bring me here?"

"You shall see soon enough, Natalia." There was a darkness in his voice – but different than the usual shadows that haunted his words. This darkness was one of a great sadness. A heartache that weighed heavily upon his heart.

We walked up the hill, and the vampire paused before the ancient willow tree. He disappeared into its jungle of branches and I followed behind him. Passed the branches, there was the trunk of the tree, and beside it a small headstone. The vampire stood there, his back to me. He was silent. Only the gentle wind and the rustle of branches spoke to me.

Approaching the vampire, I stood beside him. I stared into his face and there, within his ghostly eyes, I found so much sorrow that it caused my heart to ache. Sorrow that no human could handle, sorrow that seemed as though he has carried it for several years. Decades or centuries even.

His eyes never glanced over at me, they were glued to the headstone before us. The vampire knelt onto the ground and brushed his fingers delicately over the carved name, as if he was scared his mere touch would cause the aged stone to crumble beneath his fingers.

Stepping closer, I could read the name upon the stone;

Alexandria Meriwether

December 14th, 1497

October 20th, 1517

"How did she die?" My voice asked tenderly.

His fingers curled into a fist, still resting it upon the stone. "She was a witch that never caused any harm. She was burned alive. They refused to bury her, so I did."

My chest tightened. I heard the anger and sadness in his voice. And I felt his guilt, too. The vampire blamed himself for her death.

"Who was she?"

"The first and only woman I have ever loved, or possibly ever will." And there, the heartache sounded. His voice cracked.

"I'm truly sorry for your loss." But it was then I realized, just how long of a life he's lived.

Silence draped itself around us. The vampire remaining knelt before his past lover's grave. It felt as though I was not meant to be here, not meant to see him in this way. As if I were intruding on something that wasn't meant for me to see.

He stood and finally faced me. His eyes meeting mine, revealing to me every emotion he was feeling, allowing me to see him exposed. His heart lay bare, soul open and flooding into the world.

"Why did you bring me here?"

A heavy sigh escaped him. "I wish for you to trust me, so I brought you to the place that leaves me the most vulnerable."

Not knowing what to say to the vampire, my hand reached for the medallion. My thumb sliding across the silver and the barrier fell away. If he was to be left vulnerable, then I shall be too. I stepped toward him and took his hand in mine.

And here, I broke the one rule witches never broke; never let your barrier fall.

"Thank you, for sharing this with me. I know it couldn't have been easy for you to do."

His gaze fixed on our hands; his fingers were so cold against my own. His thumb gently stroked my skin as he gave my hand a tight and gentle squeeze.

"Roman." He spoke quietly, "My name is, Roman."

"You have earned my trust, Roman. Now that you have it, can you tell me why you wished to have it?"

He held my hand longer as his eyes met with mine, a smile returning to his lips. "To be friends. That is what I wish."

"Then, your wish is granted."

As we left the headstone behind, I began to feel it tugging me back.

THE VAMPIRE

There was no hiding it from Aron. As soon as I returned, he smelt the witch Natalia on me, her floral scent attached to me. A wide, wolfish grin spread across his face.

"I smell that you have grown some balls." He laughed. "How did it go?"

The old, rusted door closed behind me as I seated myself on the other end of the couch. "I did as you suggested, took her to a cemetery."

His eyes squinted. "Do not tell me it was *the* cemetery."

I nodded my head. "I thought it the only way to earn her trust. To allow her to see me at my most vulnerable."

He raised a dark brow. "Did you earn it?"

"That I did."

"So, now you have two friends that your mother wishes dead."

"I'm assuming Sakiya told you of my mother's orders?"

He winked a brown eye. "She told me plenty, if you know what I mean."

A chuckle escaped me but then, reality began to settle over me. "Mother will have her killed. What have I dragged her into?"

Aron placed a hand on my shoulder. "If her dogs can't kill me, then they won't be able to kill her, either. Witches are ones not to mess with and refuse to die easily."

His words gave me little hope.

THE WITCH

The black-haired witch waited for her lover in the meadow, just as she always had. The tall, green grass swaying in the wind around her. Her hand brushing along the top of it, and if she had a face, there would be a smile found there upon it.

Then, he appeared, just as he always did. Except when I gazed upon him, he now had a face. A gasp of shock escaped my lips as I stared upon the man, the vampire.

Roman.

The two embraced and his lips met with her smoothed skin.

When I woke, I found it hard to believe. That my dreams have been about the vampire. About *Roman* and the woman, she had to be the lover he lost. The dreams now made sense, but I couldn't understand why I would be having them, over and over.

"Another nightmare?" Catherine asked from the dresser.

My gaze met with her confused one. "It's him." I said. "The dreams of the faceless couple. The vampire is the man and the woman is the lover he lost."

Her eyes sparked with interest. "Now that you know who they are, do you know why you are having the dreams?"

I shook my head, but a thought occurred to me, "I do not think they are dreams, Catherine, I think they are memories. Sasha told me it was someone's past life, that someone being Roman."

She cocked her head to the side, causing her hair to sway. "But why would you have his memories?"

My brow creased as I bit my bottom lip. I remembered the cemetery. How saddened he was by her death, how I felt drawn back to the grave. "Perhaps, I am to help him move on from her death? That has to be it."

"And how will you help him?"

I shook my head, "I don't know."

Perhaps I could start with being his friend.

Chapter Eight

Chased

WHEN NIGHT SETTLED over the world, I closed my store. Stepping through the door that led into my home, I latched it and the black tapestry concealed the door from view. It was then that my stomach began to howl with hunger, and I made my way toward the kitchen. Opening the fridge there was nothing to be found except a half gallon of milk and a few yogurts – nothing that would satisfy my appetite. Shouldering my satchel, I decided to make my way to the corner store.

"I'll be back soon, grabbing some groceries!" I called down the hallway to my room where Catherine was with Pax.

"Be safe!" She answered back.

Then, I entered into the night.

Hurriedly, I made my way down the sidewalk toward the little store two blocks away. It was quiet. Not a soul to be found wandering along the sidewalks, no cars passing by on the street. Only the lamp lights buzzed above my head.

Turning around a corner, the store was in sight. I walked faster, I hated being out this late at night. Why I decided to do my grocery shopping now? My stomach growled its answer.

As I passed a dark alleyway, I heard footsteps. My eyes glanced over but saw nothing stirring within the darkness, but I felt something staring back. My walking fastened.

So close the store was.

I wanted to break into run, needed too. But, something dropped from the night sky and stood within my path. A dark figure lurked ahead and another behind me. There was no running in those directions. To my left was a brick wall but to the right was an open street an alleyway that led toward a forest.

Instead of running, I flew toward the alley. But only one dark figure lunged. Once I came to the end, I took a sharp turn and shot into the stars. The figure halted at the end, their head glancing to the left and right.

I didn't waste a moment longer, I aimed myself home. The wind whipped through my purple hair, roaring against my eardrums. My hand reached for the necklaces that danced within the air but none of them were the one I was searching for. The silver medallion remained at my home, upon the hook on the door. I cursed myself for leaving it and hoped I would make it home alive.

But, I hoped too soon.

A body slammed into mine, strong arms wrapped around me, and down we fell. Plummeting through the stars, the earth coming dangerously close. I fought against my captor's hold, wiggling to where I could face them. And I was not surprised to be staring into the face of a blood thief, their smile revealing their fangs that wished to drain the blood from my veins, their eyes as dark as the night, no white to be found within them, only complete darkness.

"Hello, little witch." He purred.

Bracing my hands against his chest, I summoned my magic. "Goodbye, blood thief."

A strong force surged from my palms and freed me from the vampire's grip. He was sent flying backwards, far away. Twisting in the air, I was able to catch myself before the ground met with my body.

My hands began to tremble. I had summoned the magic too fast and too much at a time. Not giving it time to release and unbottle within me. I had forced it to explode from my depths without giving my body a chance to ready itself for the power.

Glancing up into the sky, I found no sight of the vampire but there was another. But where the other was, my eyes couldn't see. My feet lifted off the ground once more as I hurried my way home.

But I knew the blood thief would be back, perhaps he was watching me now. Stalking me like a predator does to its prey. And I couldn't lead him to my very doorstep.

Whirling around, I headed back in the direction of the grocery store and toward the forest. Now, I could sense the vampire following me, keeping his distance. I would not be an easy kill. I dove into the maze of trees.

Before the blood thief could spot me, I hid myself behind a tree, my eyes watching, waiting. And then, he appeared. Slowly making his way down into the forest, wary. His eyes searching for me. He came close to my tree.

I held my breath.

Slowly, he passed by. Here, my scent would mix with the other earthly scents, masking me. Making it hard for the predator to find its prey. The vampire stalked ahead, almost disappearing within the dark shadows. Stretching my arm before me, I exposed the palm of my hand. Before the vampire was an aged tree. The branches that hung from it came alive with my magic. They moved like serpents as they coiled around the vampire's arms and legs, trapping him.

The blood thief began to laugh. It was a low chuckle at first but then it turned into howling, maddened laughter. "A nice trick, little witch, but your branches cannot stop me."

With barely any force, the vampire broke free, the branches snapping apart and falling to the ground like broken bones. The vampire whirled around, a crazed smile on his face. He was craving the thrill of the hunt.

"Come out come out wherever you are, little witch."

I moved around the tree, concealing myself from his sight. I kept my breathing steady and quiet so his ears wouldn't find me.

"I will find you, witch, and I'll enjoy drinking every drop of your sweet blood."

The vampire began to move forward, straight toward the tree I was hiding behind. Soon, he would find me.

THE VAMPIRE

The door burst open, Aron and I quickly got to our feet, ready to face whoever the intruder was. But once we laid eyes on them, Aron and I exchanged confused glances.

"Sakiya? Why are you here?" I asked.

"Your witch," she spoke, "she's in danger."

My stomach dropped; my hands curled into fists. "What do you mean?"

"I was keeping an eye on her but someone else appeared. One of your mother's other guards. I couldn't help her or else it would expose me as a traitor, and I wouldn't be much help to you dead."

"Where is she?" A growl sounded within my voice. That darkness – that monster – awakening.

"Follow me."

Without another spoken word, we followed Sakiya from my home. My heart pounded within my chest. I had only just befriended Natalia and I was not going to lose her.

Hold on. I'm coming.

THE WITCH

I raced between the trees, he was too close behind me, too close for comfort. Sweat began to drip from my brow. My magic was absorbing every bit of energy I had. But, I couldn't stop. Not now. If I did, death would come for me.

Turning around, I flew backwards, facing the vampire. I aimed my hands at the ground and thrust them upward. Tree roots erupted and snatched at the blood thief, wrapping around his ankles. And though they didn't hold, they slowed him down, enough to put distance between us.

"I wonder how much longer you'll last little witch. I see you growing tired and slow. Give up, allow me my drink of victory."

I gritted my teeth. *"Never."*

The distance between us was growing shorter. Glancing down briefly at my hands, there was other magic I could use but that other magic would drain the last bit of energy I had. And I didn't know how much longer I could keep up this chase, the flying was slowly draining me as well.

I muttered a prayer to the earth and aimed my hand at the vampire, so that my fingers were spread apart directed toward the blood sucker. A crackling rushed through my veins like a wildfire and lighting emerged from between my fingers, moving towards the tips, and shooting toward the vampire. A blast of crackling light rushed toward him. His eyes grew wide as he tried to dodge. One bolt struck him, and a screech sounded from him.

The blood thief lost control of his flying and went tumbling to the ground, rolling across the grass, smoke sizzling from his body. My brief moment of victory came to an end as my head began to grow dizzy, my thoughts blurring, my vision blackening.

And then down I fell, my body slamming onto the unforgiving ground. I lay there crippled with pain, unable to move. My breathing was coming out in heavy rasps as I struggled to catch it. My eyes stared toward the sky that was a blurry mess of stars mixed with darkness, the tree branches seeming like hands reaching for me. Wishing to cradle my body close and protect me from harm.

Footsteps approached me and a figure stood tall over me. "That was a fun game, little witch." He knelt on one knee. "You even got me one good time." His hand brushed aside my hair from my neck, the perfect spot for drinking my sweet blood. "Now, I drink my victory."

Weakly, I tried to raise my hand, tried to summon my magic, but my body refused. My energy was gone. My body exhausted beyond its limit. My hand fell back to the ground as the vampire lowered his fangs to my skin.

Closing my eyes, I took in a breath, and prepared for my coming death.

But, his fangs never pierced me. The vampire was sent flying as something hurtled into him, a dark mass. The vampire shrieked and there was the sound of a low growl. Gentle arms lifted my body from the ground and cradled me against a strong chest. I tried to peer into the face of my savior, it was nothing but a blur to me.

"You're safe, Natalia. You're safe."

And then, darkness became me.

THE VAMPIRE

I had brought her back to my home. Gently, I had laid her body upon the couch and draped a blanket across her. Already, bruises were blooming across her pale skin, covering her slender arms. There were small cuts on her cheeks, her purple hair tangled, her bottom lip bleeding. Her clothes tattered and torn. My heart ached at the sight of her, to see the witch in this state. But all these bruises and cuts meant she put up a strong fight. Aron was correct, witches were not ones to die easily.

Sakiya approached and began to clean away the blood, cleansing her wounds. Being careful with the wetted rag. She took a brush to her hair and removed the tangles, then, she exchanged looks with Aron and they left me alone with her. The door creaking shut behind them.

My hand reached for hers, her knuckles bruised. My thumb gently traced along each of her fingers. "You're safe." I whispered to her, hoping she could hear me. "You're safe." I said, as if to reassure myself that she was alive.

I took in a breath as I stared upon her sleeping face. I only had myself to blame. If only I was there, this would not have happened. I shook my head. It was Alexandria all over again. My hand clutched Natalia's a little more tightly. I had almost lost her, almost lost a friend.

THE WITCH

The lovers were within the meadow once more and I beneath the willow tree as always. Their hands clasped together, their laughter echoing around like phantoms of the past. Roman's face seemed weightless, as if his long life was not reflecting within his eyes. There was only love within his gaze, a fiery love for the woman before him. It was fierce and bright. His hand cupped around her cheek, his thumb gently stroking her fair skin. His other hand brushed her dark hair behind her ear. Words echoed around, in the sound of a woman's voice. The words, I love you. And he spoke them in return.

My eyes fluttered open, adjusting, as I peered into the face of Roman. Relief washed over his features and I felt something squeeze my hand. My eyes wandered down to find his hand holding my own.

"Where am I?" My voice rasped; my throat dry.

"My home, Natalia. You're safe." He glanced over his shoulder, "Aron, a glass of water, please."

My brows creased. Aron? Footsteps echoed and the dark-haired man with a wolf's grin stood beside Roman, holding a glass of water in his hand.

"Aron?"

"Hello, Natalia." He smiled kindly.

Roman glanced between the werewolf and I, confusion playing upon his face. "You know him?" He asked me.

Aron handed me over the water, the vampire released my hand so that I may drink. The werewolf answered for me. "It's a long story."

"Do tell it." Roman said.

So, Aron told him.

The vampire raised a brow, his arms crossed over his chest, anger seemed to flicker within his eyes. "Why lie to me? You told me you didn't know her, not even her name."

Aron put his hands in the air, surrendering. "At the time, I didn't think it was important to tell you exactly what witch had healed me, you didn't know of her then."

"But, I know of her now, you lied at the bar."

"I was going to allow Natalia the pleasure of introducing herself to you."

Once I had finished my glass of water, I spoke, "I didn't know you two knew each other."

Aron slapped his hand on Roman's shoulder. "Too long I've been stuck with this blood sucker."

Finally, a smile began to crack on the vampire's hardened features. "Too long I've been stuck with this dog."

And though they made jabs at one another, I could see the true friendship the two had. It caused my heart to warm and placed a smile on my face.

Roman returned to the side of the couch, sitting upon the table before it. His hand never reached for mine. "How are you feeling?"

My eyes glanced down upon my bruised arms. "Sore but okay." I met with the vampire's gaze, "Thank you for saving me." I paused and peered at the werewolf, "Both of you."

"I enjoy any chance I get tearing into one of the queen's dogs." Aron grinned. "But you are welcome, Natalia. Just returning the kindness you showed me not too long ago."

I smiled at him.

"What did you do to the vampire?" Roman asked.

Aron leaned against the wall, crossing his arms over his chest. "I didn't kill him, but I did give him one hell of bite. I do wonder if he returned to your mother alive."

"Wait. You said the queen's vampire." I returned my gaze to Roman, "And then he said your mother."

Shame then presented itself in his gaze, along with hatred. "My mother claims herself a queen."

"But that would make you..."

He shook his head. "Please, don't say it. I am not that nor will I ever be."

My hand reached for his to comfort him. So much pain he carried within himself, the emotions I could feel turning inside him like a storm. Burden, grief, guilt, sorrow. So many and I wondered how he was able to conceal all these, to hold them. His blue gaze lingered upon our hands, his fingers gliding across my own.

Aron spoke from the wall he was leaned against. "I'm glad Roman has found himself a woman friend that's more at hand, I'm not too good at comforting him." He chuckled.

Roman's lips twitched into a small smile. "Your form of comfort includes taking me to a bar and forcing me to drink sewer water."

"And a place that has a woman who sings like an enchantress." Aron added with a wink toward me.

"She has indeed enchanted me." Roman said with a faint squeeze of my hand before he let go of it once more. The vampire stood, "I suppose it's time to return Natalia to her home." He glanced at Aron. "Since the sun is out, I can't escort her. Will you?"

The werewolf bowed, "It would be an honor."

Roman helped me to stand from the couch, offering his hand to me, and Aron escorted me home.

The werewolf walked me all the way to my door, handing me my battered, torn satchel. Which, he carried over his shoulder during our walk. He bowed and left, disappearing from the alleyway.

As soon as I stepped foot into my home, Catherine and Pax rushed to me. He meowed as he brushed against my legs, purring, happy to see me home safe and sound. Catherine asked a hundred questions, fear and concern showing on her face, along with relief.

Her ghostly fingers reached toward my bruised arm, a chill rushing along my spine at the contact. "My dear friend, what happened to you?"

I placed the satchel on the small table and made sure to lock the door behind me. There, the silver medallion hung. "A blood thief tried to drain me dry."

Her arms opened wide, as if to embrace me, but fell back to her sides when she realized she couldn't. "I am glad to see you safe, and from the looks of it, it seems as though you put up quite the fight."

I began to make my way down the hall, "As much of a fight as I could, at least. The werewolf and vampire had to save me once my magic had drained my energy."

Catherine clasped her hands together and held them against her cheek as she batted her ghostly lashes. "So, your vampire came to your rescue. How romantic." She said awe struck.

Opening the bathroom door, I stepped inside. "He's a friend and nothing more."

Catherine winked, "Just a friend?"

When I closed the door before her, her laughter sounded on the other side, causing a smile to form on my face. Facing the mirror, the smile vanished as I took in the sight of my bruised arms and face. Cuts traced along my cheeks, arms, and knuckles. Purple and green bruises seeming like a strange painting upon my skin. Stripping off what remained of my dress, I stared upon my naked reflection, there I found more bruises.

Reaching deep within me, I began to unbottle my magic. My energy had returned, allowing me to summon upon my power. It untwisted and overflowed within my being, racing through my veins with warmth. I felt as it made its way across my body and slowly, my bruises began to fade. The cuts slowly closing, the skin weaving together once more. And nothing remained upon my skin, no trace of bruises or scarring to be found.

Chapter Nine

Family

THE VAMPIRE

ONCE MORE I found myself standing before the crackling fire. My eyes watching as the flames performed their dance. My ears listening to their song as they popped and sizzled atop the logs. Mother was nowhere to be found within the room when I arrived. So, I waited for her to make an appearance. I began to grow impatient, my fingers tapping upon my arms that were crossed.

Then, footsteps sounded on the other side of the door. More than one pair of feet approached the room. I turned my attention toward the doors and watched as they opened.

First, my mother entered. And the person that followed behind her caused my stomach to drop into my depths. The woman had a harsh blue gaze, worse than mother's. Her blonde hair was cut short to frame around the hard angles of her face. Her lips pressed into a thin line. When the two women stood side by side, they were the same height, and some might mistake them for sisters.

"Why is grandmother here?" My tone was harsh as I spoke, my arms falling to my sides.

Grandmother narrowed her gaze upon me. "Still as ungrateful as ever, Roman. I've traveled far to visit, and this is the welcome I receive?"

A sigh escaped me. "If you dislike me so, then why bother visiting, *grandmother*?"

I felt the hatred in her eyes. "Perhaps because I had hope that your ungratefulness and selfishness has gone when I visit, but I see neither has left you."

I glanced behind her, "I see that grandfather isn't here." Then, I snapped my fingers as if remembering something, like it had just come to me. "Oh, that's because he left you. Like how my father left us."

A hiss sounded from mother. *"Enough."*

Grandmother and I both silenced our remarks and glanced over at mother. She straightened her shoulders and cleared her throat. "She has a reason for her visit this time, I have called her."

"Why?"

Grandmother wrinkled her nose. "I have heard troubling things, Roman." She sniffed at the air. "First being, you have befriended an animal. The second being, befriending a witch." She approached me, her low heels clicking against the floor. "One is our enemy, the other food. Must we teach you how to kill and feed again, Roman?"

My lips curled back, revealing my fangs. "Do not threaten them and do not threaten me, *grandmother*."

"You will learn our ways, *grandson*."

THE MOTHER

We sat before the fire, mother beside me in the other chair, a wine glass with blood held within her dainty hand. The liquid stained her lips in crimson, as it did mine.

"Does he always leave? Does he always speak to you in such ways, my daughter?"

My nails tapped on the glass within my hand. "Always. Roman has caused trouble lately, leaving the house, befriending such fowl creatures."

Mother shook her head, disappointment showing itself within her eyes. "I thought I raised you better than that. I thought I raised you to be stronger than this. Yet you allow your child to walk over you." She took a sip of the blood. "You, disappoint me, *Celeste*. I should have never handed over the title of queen to you, I see now that it was a mistake." She took in a breath and shook her head once more. "But, there's no taking it back now."

My hand tightened around the glass; I could feel it giving away beneath my grasp.

She set the glass down upon the table between our two chairs and stood, straightening her white skirt. "I'll figure out how to handle the situation with, Roman. We'll fix him and have him under control, as he used to be before I left all those years ago." She glanced at me from the corner of her eyes, failure was all I could see in them.

Failure in raising my own child.

"Yes, mother."

THE WITCH

Before me was the willow tree. The moon's light poured down upon it, the gentle breeze of the night caused its branches to sway. The meadow was empty and silent of any souls, the woman nowhere to be found waiting for her lover to join her.

As I stood beneath the willow atop the small hill, I heard something. It came whispering along the wind. The sound of sorrow and ultimate heartache. A figure appeared, walking toward the tree, something held within their arms. As they approached closer, I found that it was Roman. A body was held within his arms, but it was wrapped in cloth, hiding it from wandering eyes.

My heart raced within my chest as panic began to consume me. It seemed as though we were gazing into one another's eyes as he approached the tree. He stopped in his tracks an arm's reach away from me and I could have sworn he saw me.

Within his eyes, there were too many emotions, they overpowered me as I tried to read them. It felt as though I had taken his grief on myself for my own heart began to ache with the very pain he felt. His gaze was lost, the whites of his eyes reddened, he was broken.

Roman gently lay the body upon the ground and began to tear the earth up with his own hands. Digging a grave. My gaze drifted from Roman, to the body, to the willow tree. And I realized that this was the same tree he took me to in the cemetery. And the grave he was digging was his lost lover's.

Sobs sounded from him as he continued to dig into the earth.

Thunder rumbled overhead and rain began to fall from the clouds that scattered across the sky. The dirt turned into mud and still he dug. The vampire drenched in rain and heartache.

I lay there in my bed, my eyes staring toward the ceiling. My hand clutched over my chest as my heart still ached from the dream. The sorrow of that loss, to see Roman in such a state, had struck me deeply.

THE VAMPIRE

My anger had blinded me, all I could see was red, all I could feel was heated rage coursing through me. My mind raced with the image of Natalia laying on the ground, barely holding on to life. To the vampire that almost sucked the very life from her veins. To my mother and grandmother.

A snarl escaped me.

I needed something to calm this rage. Something.

Glancing down upon the town below me, I saw a lone figure walking along the side of the road. There were no other souls to be found. Quietly, I landed behind the man. And without any thought, my fangs pierced into the man's neck. Blood began to pour as he cried out in pain. But I heard nothing anymore, felt nothing, saw nothing but the bloody neck before me.

The thick liquid swept across my tongue as it made its way down into my throat. It was warm and tangy, nothing of sweetness mixed with this man's blood. But still, I craved it, devoured it.

As the man's legs gave out beneath him and he lay on the ground, I realized what horror I was causing. I wasn't going to stop; I was going to feed until there was nothing left of him. My eyes gazed upon my now blood-soaked hands. I was becoming the monster mother wished me to be. I was becoming the monster Natalia feared I would be.

Gathering the man into my arms, I soared into the sky.

Once the hospital was in sight, I set him by the doors and didn't leave until a nurse came out and screamed for help.

Chapter Ten

A Tangle of Memories

MY DREAMS NO longer seemed to be my own. Haunted by memories from Roman. The only time my dreams were once again mine, was when the nightmare decided to visit me. Reminding me of a future that could be. The near death to my short life.

Many times, I awoke in the middle of the night, my breathing heavy and sweat beading upon my brow. Catherine seemed to grow more and more concerned but stopped questioning me whenever I awoke. Because the answer had become the same; it was only a nightmare and nothing more. But we both knew that not to be true.

My eyes watched in horror as Roman hunted down the people who played a hand in his lover's death, one by one. The deaths were not quick and painless but slow and filled with agony and screams that rattled my very eardrums.

No longer could I recognize the vampire. His eyes had gone completely dark, any life in them had vanished and only vengeance was left behind. Snarls and growls had escaped his throat like a wild beast. Blood painted his face, clothes, and hands. Dripping down his chin. His fangs piercing and tearing apart throats, hands disemboweling his victims.

I grew sickened at the sight, but I could not tear my eyes away from the scenes playing out before me.

By the end of it all, a pile of victims lay at his feet. Limbs lay apart from their bodies, littering the blood-soaked earth. I could feel my stomach sickening. And then, his gaze had met with mine. Or so I had thought.

A woman had stepped through me, a shiver rushing along my spine. Her blonde hair fell down her back. She approached Roman and stood by his side, a pride filled smile snaking across her lips at the sight.

"Wonderful job, my son."

When I woke with a terrorizing scream, Catherine snapped. "You refuse to speak of your nightmares, but I see how they drain you every night, Natalia." She hovered over my bed, her ghostly eyes narrowed with anger and worry. "Tell me of these nightmares."

A heavy sigh escaped me as I wiped the tears away from my checks and sat up on the bed, bringing my knees to my chest, and wrapping my arms around them. "Every night, my dreams are troubled. It's either the dream of my death or dreams of Roman's painful memories."

Tonight, the dream was filled with bloodshed. Of bodies being struck down to the earth, long gashes distorting their frozen, screaming faces. Crimson raining through the air and painting Roman's face.

My breathing became shuddered as a shiver rushed along my spine. "Tonight, there was so much blood." My voice was a hushed whisper.

She seated herself on the side of the bed, "What occurred?"

"Roman killed so many people. I could feel his emotions, his rage and heartache at the people who burned his lover. Their bodies were mangled and deformed. He was covered in their blood. Bodies laid before his feet."

Her ghostly hand seemed to reach for mine but stopped just before my fingertips. Catherine's eyes flickered with sadness. "I wish I knew how to make these dreams cease so you may have a peaceful night of rest, my dear friend."

"Perhaps there is a way to make them stop." I said, an idea forming in my mind.

Her eyes flickered up to meet with mine, "What do you mean?"

"Sasha and Tasha may be able to help me with these dreams, make them stop."

"Are you going to, uh…" she creased her brows as she tried to think of the word she was searching for, "Email her?"

"Tomorrow, see what advice she has for me."

Catherine smiled, "Good, I hope she can help you."

THE MOTHER

The fire roared within the fireplace, the flames sizzling and crackling angrily against each other. The logs giving away beneath the hungry fire, causing ashes to burst with a glowing red color. The heat radiated through the room, warming my skin. I breathed it in, allowing the heat to fill my lungs.

Knock. Knock.

"Come in."

A woman entered my room, my most prized guard. My little samurai, I liked to call her. She bowed before me, her dark hair curtaining around her face. A smile curled at my lips, she never failed to deliver information. "What news do you bring for me, Little Samurai?"

She stood and her eyes finally met with mine, I could see the irritation flicker within them at my nickname for her, which caused my smile to widen.

"I've spotted the witch speaking with Roman, she seems to keep a barrier around herself against vampires."

My brows creased, "Troubling news, that will make it hard to come near the witch."

"Is there anything you wish for me to do, my queen?"

I smiled at her and trailed my fingertips down her cheek, "Always so eager to aid your queen, my Little Samurai. For now, you may rest. I shall call for you when I need you."

She bowed her head, "My queen." And she left the room.

THE VAMPIRE

The door swung open and Sakiya entered the room, immediately, her and Aron's eyes met. A grin began to play across the werewolf's lips, and I could begin to sense the tension building within the air.

"What brings you here?"

She broke her gaze away from Aron and glanced at me. "What else would bring me here, Roman?"

I raised a brow, "What has my mother done now?"

She approached the couch and Aron scouted over to make room for her but instead she sat down upon the arm of the couch and draped her arm over the back of it, behind Aron's head, leaning her body towards him.

A wide wolfish grin spread across his face.

"Not so much what she has done but what she can do."

I crossed my arms over my chest. "What do you mean?"

A sigh escaped her, "You do know I have to give her some information or she'll grow suspicious of me. I told her I saw the two of you together, but she keeps a barrier up against vampires."

"You didn't tell her where she lives or where she sings?"

Sakiya rolled her eyes, "Yes, Roman, I told your mother *exactly* where your witch lover lives."

"She's not my lover but thank you."

She nodded her head. "But, you do know your mother will ask and I will have to tell her, and if I don't then someone else will."

A sigh escaped me as I approached the window and rested my forearm against the cool glass, pressing my forehead against it. Defeat slowly began to claw at me. "I know."

Silence fell around the room and footsteps sounded behind me, followed by a strong hand clasping my shoulder. "Natalia is strong, you know this. The little witch can pack quite the punch, as we saw."

My jaw clenched. "She won't be strong enough against my mother." I met Aron's gaze, "None of us are."

THE WITCH

The following morning, I stood in my store. It was a quiet day, no one has come and gone. No one paying a visit to my little shop. Catherine floated beside me, not saying a word, but I knew she was waiting for me to send an email.

With a sigh, I stepped toward my store's computer, situated next to the old timey register. Pulling up my email, my fingers began to type upon the keyboard, quiet clicks sounding softly through the empty shop. The sisters tried persuading me to upgrade my store computer and phone, but this was much cheaper.

Hello, it's Natalia. I was hoping you could stop by my store today. I need your help.

Then, the email was sent.

Several minutes passed and there was a *bing* sounding from my computer. An email from Sasha.

On my way.

Was all she sent. She would be here soon.

"Do you think she'll be able to rid you of these dreams?" Catherine asked, her ghostly head leaning over my shoulder, her eyes reading the computer screen.

"I hope so."

Minutes slowly passed, anxiety began to claw at me as I nibbled on my fingernails, my eyes watching the door. Until, finally, it swung open and a heavy breath escaped me. Sasha made her way to the counter as I walked out from behind it.

What's wrong, Natalia?

It's the dreams. Can you make them stop? I signed back.

Her brows creased. *Explain them.*

They are memories from Roman, a vampire. But they are too much, some so heavy with sadness that I feel it affecting me as well. The nightmares of vampires murdering me. I wish for them to stop.

Sasha said nothing more and motioned toward my hands. Extending them to her, she grasped them and closed her eyes. She took in a deep breath as her face hardened. I watched as her eyes flickered beneath her lids, her forehead slowly creasing, her lips turning down into a frown.

Then, I felt magic flicker within the room. Our clasped hands began to warm, and a glow emanated from them, golden and bright. It seeped between our fingers like molten sunshine. A breeze lightly whispered through my hair and played with the bottom of my skirt.

And when Sasha's eyes suddenly fluttered open, a loud gasp escaped her as she dropped my hands from hers. She took a step back from me and leaned against one of the tables. Her breathing was heavy and hard.

The magic I felt had vanished, our hands no longer beaming with sunshine, no more whispers of a gentle breeze.

When Sasha had regained her breathing, her eyes met with mine and slowly she began to sign, *You are the reincarnation of Alexandria Meriwether.*

And then, it felt as though the world had disappeared from beneath my feet.

Chapter Eleven

A Past Life

MY BREATHING WAS hardly a whisper against the silence that had draped around us. My hands trembling as I signed to Sasha, *What? How can I be her?*

You were Alexandria in a past life, Natalia. You were – are – Roman's lost lover.

I took a staggering step backward, shaking my head. *No. It can't be. It's not possible.*

Reincarnation is possible, you and I both know this.

All witches knew this.

But still, I shook my head. *How?*

Your soul wished to be reborn, perhaps to be reunited with your past lover. She approached me, *I couldn't understand before, but now, it makes sense. That was why you were seeing his memories. They were trying to unlock your lost ones.*

So, why haven't they unlocked?

Perhaps because they are too deep within you, you must dig them out.

My eyes flickered down to my trembling hands. *How do I do it?*

Sasha's hands gently grasped my own, her brown gaze locking with mine. *I can help you.*

You can unlock my memories?

She nodded her head. *But it won't be a comfortable process.*

THE VAMPIRE

I felt it, like an ache within my heart, but something deeper within me. As if something had awakened and whispered to me. I heard it within the air, within my head. But whatever it was saying was unclear. But something had occurred, though I couldn't tell what.

THE WITCH

Catherine approached then; her eyes wide. "That's amazing." She said almost breathless and then a sadness flickered across her face, "But also terrible."

Suddenly, the shop felt too small, the air too heavy. I was being closed in. I needed to leave. *To run.*

Pushing past Sasha, I dashed for the door and disappeared into the gloomy day. Catherine's voice calling after me. My feet hurried down the sidewalk, unsure of where I was going, I allowed my feet to lead the way.

My mind had been consumed by a whirlwind of a thousand whispering thoughts. Of things suddenly making sense. But now, I shook them from my mind. Not wishing to hear them. It was too much.

Thunder roared overhead, shaking the ground. Lightning flashed and rain began to pour down upon the earth, like a heavy waterfall.

The droplets pelted against my face, but I blinked them away, aware of my makeup now melting down my cheeks in black streaks. But I didn't care. I didn't bother with magic, with forming a shield. That was the last worry on my mind. My hair had become soaked and tangled from the wind and rain. My toes squishing in my boots. My clothes clinging to my skin heavily and coldly.

I kept running unaware of where my feet had taken me until I finally broke myself from my thoughts and gazed around. I was beneath an old willow tree within a cemetery, standing before a headstone.

Finally, I crumbled.

A cry escaped me as I fell to my knees within the mud.

The willow branches brushed against my trembling body, as if to comfort me. The rain still fell, but not as heavy. I raised my head from my hands and peered at the headstone before me. Through blurry, tear filled eyes. My gaze glided across the name carved into the stone. What once was my name.

My hand pressed itself into the mud, my fingers curling into it. Just beneath me lay my former body, or whatever remained of it. My tears fell and mixed within the mud, some splashing on the back of my hand.

"Why?" I asked the air. "How?" I asked the headstone.

Knowing that neither one held the answers I desperately sought.

I shook my head.

I always felt older than what I was, as if I had an old soul. And now, I learn, that I do. How many lives have I lived? Just how old am I truly?

There were so many questions, so many things I didn't understand. And then, something else came to mind; would I tell Roman?

If so, how would I tell him? Just blurt it out in a mess of words? Or ease it to him? There was no easy way to say it. That I am Alexandria and Natalia. Or should I even tell him? How would he react?

Would he wish to be lovers now?

My chest warmed at the thought. But I shook my head.

I hardly knew him, but at the same time, I knew him once long ago.

My hand clutched itself over my heart.

Taking in a breath, I had decided.

It was time to unlock my memories.

To remember.

Chapter Twelve

Unlocking Memories

THE FOLLOWING DAY, I called Tasha. The store phone rang against my ear for what felt like an eternity. My teeth chewing on my bottom lip, my foot tapping uneasily. Until, the ringing had stopped as Tasha answered. "Hello, it's Natalia."

"Hello, dear. How are you? Sasha told me what had happened." Her voice sounded on the other end of the phone.

"That's what I'm calling about, actually. Can you and Sasha come to my store after I close." My fingers tightened around the phone as I said, "I'm ready."

"We'll see you tonight, dear."

And then, the call ended. Now, there was a long day of waiting ahead of me.

Catherine was beside me, "Are you sure about this, Natalia?"

Closing my eyes, I took in a steadying breath. "I am."

THE VAMPIRE

"What do you wish to nag about now, mother?"

She stood beside the fire, the flames dancing within the reflection of her angry eyes. "You have become so disrespectful towards your own mother. A woman who birthed you into this world."

"I respect you birthed me, but I do not respect the monster that you are and that you are trying to make me into one." I snarled.

Her face hardened as she approached me. "I want you to stop seeing this little witch of yours."

A chuckle escaped me. "You cannot control what I do, I am no longer a pathetic child afraid of his mother."

She reached for me, one of her nails tracing down my cheek. If she added just the slightest bit more pressure, then blood would seep from my broken skin. "Then I will have to get rid of the little witch myself, Roman."

Anger began to burn like a fiery rage within me, my fangs revealed themselves as I shouted, *"You will not harm her!"*

And for the first time, I saw a flicker of fear in my mother's eyes. Fear of me. She took a trembling step back, her hand falling from my face. Those ghostly eyes of her widened with shock as she gazed upon me.

Heels clicked softly against the floor as someone else had entered the room. “Now he is shouting in your face. What sort of pathetic mother allows their son to do these things?”

Grandmother stood an arms-reach away from us, disgust painted upon her face as her eyes glanced between the two of us. Immediately, mother became like a small child beneath grandmother’s harsh gaze. She bowed her head in submission.

“Roman, you will listen to your mother. For if you don’t, then you will have me to deal with. And I promise you, you do not wish for that. Do I make myself clear?”

“I do not listen to monsters.”

“Then you have forgotten what being a vampire means. *We are all monsters.*”

I shook my head. “I will never be one. Not again.” Then, I left the room behind me. Along with two snarling beasts hidden beneath human skin.

“I don’t see why you continue seeing the old hags.” Aron said from the couch.

“At least I’ll know what they plan on doing to Natalia if I continue seeing them.”

He shrugged his shoulders. "They want me dead; they want her dead. What's more to know, Roman?"

A sigh of defeat escaped me as I slouched beside him on the couch. "I wish I could protect her. But I can't."

"Sakiya and I are willing to help protect her, you know this."

My head fell into my hands. "We can't go against my mother; she'll send all her guards after us. We might as well call ourselves dead now."

His hand clapped me on the back of my shoulder. "Always looking at the negative." Aron rose from the couch and approached the door, "I'm going to the bar, there's too much dread in the air here, dampening my mood. Perhaps our songstress will be there tonight."

A laugh escaped the werewolf as I lunged from the couch and followed him out the door. My heart leapt at the thought of seeing her, hearing her beautiful voice. It gave me hope, something I haven't had in many, many years.

THE MOTHER

Her eyes never left me. They weighed heavily over me, her gaze bearing down. I felt myself shrinking beneath her eyes and I hated the way she made me feel. She was no longer the queen here, I was. And I should not fear this woman, she should fear me. I could feel her judgment, her disappointment, and possibly even her hatred. But the feeling there, was the same.

My whole life, I have hated this woman that now stood over me. Since I could speak, she trained me into a monster, prepared me for the position of queen. And now, she was threatening to rip the title from my very grasp.

A scoff escaped me as I began to think that perhaps this is how Roman feels. Perhaps this was something that ran within our family's blood. Hatred for the women who raised us, turned us into something we wished not to be.

But now, I appreciated the long hours and unforgivable punishments. Because it formed me into the monster that I am today. The *queen* I was destined to be. It made me stronger, lethal, and feared.

"Why do you smile like a fool?"

I finally met her gaze, "Because, there is one thing that I am thankful for, *mother.*"

She arched a brow. "And what's that?"

My gaze returned to the fire. "For turning me into what you are."

And though I didn't glance at her, I knew there was a smile on her face. She was proud of what she had done to me. What she had turned me into.

"Now, what do you plan on doing with that disrespectful son of yours?" And then I knew, the frown had returned.

"You seem to have better ideas than me, mother."

"Kill the witch."

THE WITCH

My little store was closed early. I could no longer wait. Anticipation and fear had been clawing at my very soul, my head pounding as though something were trying to force its way through. The little bell dinged above the door, and they approached me. Both having large bags hanging from their shoulders.

"Are you ready, dear?" Tasha asked.

I straightened my back and nodded my head, "I am."

With nothing else said between us, I led them into my home and into the living room. They began to unpack their bags upon the floor, spreading different items out across the black rug. Sasha began to place candles along the carpet in a circular pattern. They ranged in heights, some tall and skinny, others short and stumpy. They were white, black, and cream colored. She didn't light them, not yet.

"Natalia, please stand in the middle here." Tasha motioned toward the center of the candles.

Once I did so, Tasha and Sasha grabbed a bundle of sage each from their bags and lit the ends. Smoke curled from them and twisted within the air, the scent filling the room. They walked around the circle, fanning the smoke, twice. Then, Sasha stood in front of me and Tasha behind me, never stepping inside the circle of candles.

Sasha leaned down and grabbed two, golden bowls from her bag. She placed one down at her feet and the other floated from her hand and around the circle to place itself at Tasha's feet. They placed their bundles of burning sage into the bowls and tied their braids back. Then, with a nod of Sasha's head, they knelt before the bowls on their knees.

"Alright, Natalia, lay down." I heard Tasha say behind me.

I laid myself upon the carpet.

Tasha leaned down, but she never crossed over the candles. Her dark eyes held mine, "Are you sure, dear?"

"I am."

They met gazes and nodded their heads. "Before we begin, I must say, that this might be painful."

I took in a breath and nodded my head.

They held gazes and lifted their arms into the air and snapped their fingers. Flames blazed to life upon the candles' wicks, tall and flickering. Then, they began to move their arms side to side, guiding the smoke from the sage burning within the bowls.

The smoke began to pass from one sister, to the other. Swirling in a grey cloud before each one until they moved positions. Tasha was knelt before my feet and Sasha was behind my head. The sage smelled strongly now that the smoke was being passed over my head.

My mind began to feel light, as if something had been lifted from it. My being feeling as light as a feather.

"It's time." I heard Tasha say, but she seemed so far away.

From the corners of my eyes, I saw two hands a few inches away from either side of my face. Sasha's eyes met with mine as she leaned over me – taking her sister's place. A reassuring smile appearing upon her lips as she mouthed, *Close your eyes.*

I did as she said, and my world was encased in darkness. The only way I could tell that my soul had not left my body, was the smell of sage burning within my nose.

Suddenly, there was a faint flicker of light within the darkness. It grew and grew until it was blinding, unbearable. Heat washed over my being, sweltering. And my mind felt as though it were being torn in half by strong hands. I felt my voice ripping through my throat and breaking free from my lips. Sweat began to form and bead down my forehead, my hands becoming clammy. And the pain became more intense, my head felt as though it would burst.

I didn't think it would end until I heard a voice within my mind. *"Calm yourself, Natalia."* It wasn't Tasha's voice speaking to me. *"I'm here. We are almost to your memories."*

"Sasha?"

I heard a slight laugh, *"Yes, dear. As of now, our energies are merged, allowing me to speak to you within your mind."*

Then, there was a single stream of silver light ahead, and I felt as though I were being pulled toward it by a gentle force.

"What's happening?"

"That leads to your past life, Natalia."

Suddenly, I felt heavier. Glancing down, I saw my own hands and my feet were dangling below me. I saw the wisps of my hair floating around me. And when I glanced beside me, I saw Sasha. Her short braids were floating as well, and she had a smile upon her face.

"I'll be by your side." Her voice echoed around us and I felt her hand gently squeeze mine as we entered the silver light before us.

A PAST LIFE

Mommy held my hand as she led me away from our cottage. The sun was bright, and the wind was cool. My bare feet walked along the soft, grassy path. Mommy didn't say where we were going, only that she was taking me to a special place. My excitement bubbled up within me and I could feel my magic stirring.

"Calm yourself, my Alexandria. We cannot risk your magic being seen." She said in a stern, but gentle voice.

Tilting my head back, I gazed up at my mommy. There was a smile on her pretty face, a twinkle in her blue eyes. Her dark hair was tied back into a long braid, but a few wisps escaped.

Then we came upon a meadow where the grass was almost taller than me and swayed in the breeze. But toward the end of the meadow, there was a cliff. Mommy led me toward it, and we stopped at the edge. A small gasp escaped me as we over looked a vast lake. The water shimmered in the morning sun.

Mommy sat down at the ledge, her bare feet dangling over it. But she wasn't scared of falling. She leaned her head back and seemed to soak in the sun. A smile appeared on her face. The wind rushed through her hair.

My mommy was the most brave and beautiful woman on this earth.

Her eyes opened as she looked upon me, "I love you, my Alexandria."

I sat beside her, my feet dangling in the air. "I love you, mommy." I smiled back to her.

The memory began to fade, the colors turning to grey, the voices becoming muffled and distant. Darkness surrounded me again. I found my hand reaching for the ghost of my past mother as my heart ached. My cheeks were warm and wet from the tears that had fallen from my eyes as I watched the memory.

"Are you alright, Natalia?" I heard Sasha speak beside me.

I nodded my head and wiped away my tears. *"Just trying to understand all this. Seeing my past life, a past mother, is so strange. Because I can feel myself remembering as if it were yesterday."* My brows creased and Sasha gently squeezed my hand. *"I could hear the water below us, I could feel the wind, and I could smell the grass. I was there but I wasn't."*

"You once were."

Ahead of us, another path had begun to form, the light shining brightly. I glanced over at Sasha, searching for reassurance, for a guide. I couldn't do this alone and I knew I wouldn't.

She smiled, *"Come."* And led me toward the light.

The night was clear, like any other. The stars were bright against the darkness of the sky, shining as brightly as the moon. The air was cool against my skin. The breeze whispered gently through the grass surrounding me. All was quiet and peaceful.

My hands flattened against the earth, feeling it breathe, feeling the life growing, the energy flowing. The earth spoke to me, whispering like a long-lost lover. It spoke to my very soul. I breathed it in, connecting myself to the earth, attaching my energy, my magic, with its.

I felt my power awake and stir within my very being, swirling within my core, rushing through my veins warmly. It traveled throughout my body all the way down to my fingertips where it bled into the earth, feeding it. But the earth was not greedy, it gave part of its energy to me, as thanks for sharing mine with it.

I felt the dirt stirring beneath the palms of my hands. I opened my eyes to find flowers blooming around me, of all kinds. My fingertips traced along the silky petals, a smile playing upon my lips. The scent of floral fragrance surrounded me.

But my peaceful night has come to a halt when the presence of another approached. Quickly, I stood to my feet to face the intruder. A man stood not too far from me, but I sensed he was more than a man. My hands raised into the air, ready to defend myself against the monster.

Though I could not see his face clearly, I could see that he tilted his head in curiosity at my hands. And when he stepped closer, I hated to admit that he was beautiful, but of course, all blood thieves were.

"What do you want, blood thief?" My voice was anything but friendly.

Those blue eyes of his took me in, seeming to take in every detail of me. I could feel myself shrinking beneath his judging gaze. "Not your blood, little witch."

"Do not lie. I know you hunt our kind because our blood is like wine to you monsters."

"You label me a monster due to my kind without yet knowing me. Do you honestly think that fair when I have not passed judgement on you for your kind?"

A part of me realized the truth in his words but another part of me knew better than to trust the tainted words of a vampire. And yet, I found myself lowering my hands.

I straightened my back, "I ask again, what do you want?"

The man approached the flowers that were still blooming beneath the moonlight. He knelt before them and reached a hand toward them, his finger tracing along the petals of a lone rose.

"I watched you for a while. Your presence attracted me here when I felt your magic. You seemed so at peace." Those last words hung heavy. "I wished to know what true peace was, what it feels like." He turned those blue eyes toward me, and I found myself lost within them. "Tell me, what does it feel like?"

A sigh escaped me, and I turned toward the moon. "It isn't something you could easily describe, *vampire*. But it feels like a weight is lifted from you and a light begins to fill you."

I approached the vampire and knelt beside him; I was not afraid of him. Placing my hand against the earth, I closed my eyes, aware of his watchful gaze.

"Peace for me is connecting with the very soul of the earth, its essence. I can feel it breathing, I can feel the life around me. I feel light and warm and the darkness is gone. I breathe in and let go of my regrets, my sorrows, I set my soul free."

And once more, the dirt began to stir. A single white flower blossomed from the earth. I reached for it. “And that, vampire, is my peace.” I turned my gaze to meet with his, “What will yours be?”

His eyes turned away from mine and peered toward the moon. “I’m afraid I’ll never know, little witch.”

“Alexandria.” I corrected. “Nor am I little.”

A smile cracked the vampire’s hard features and a soft laugh escaped from him. “Roman.”

His laughter still echoed around as the memory faded away. It was haunting, almost, ghostly. My hand rested upon my chest; my heart rapidly beat there. My first encounter with Roman. The first time we had ever met. And just like the first time I met him in this life, I had been drawn to him in my previous one.

Sasha stood beside me, quietly. Her eyes watching me. Taking in a breath, I prepared myself for the next memory. Meeting her gaze again, I nodded my head, and we ventured forth.

Voices shouted angrily, screaming vile things, accusations. Spit was wet against my skin, my bare feet dragging along the cold earthly ground, the soles of my feet weeping with blood. I tried to walk on my own, to straighten myself, but the men holding me wouldn’t allow it. So, I held my head high. I wouldn't allow these people to break me, I wouldn't allow them to see my pain.

We arrived in the center of the town where everyone was gathered. A tall post waited for me, wood and timber gathered around it. I knew what this was to be, my end. But, I was not afraid.

They pressed my back against the post, pulling my arms behind me, and binding my wrists. The wood beneath my bare feet splintered my skin.

The village people gathered around, their hateful gazes upon me.

A shouted cry raised out above the crowd and a woman pushed herself through. Her tear stained face emerged, and it was then that I allowed a flicker of pain to show.

"Please, release my daughter! She is of no harm to anyone!" She tried to reach me, but two men tugged her back by her arms, and she fell to her knees.

Her eyes met with mine and then I could sense it. There was a spark within her blue eyes, and I could feel her magic stirring. Holding her gaze, I shook my head. Closing my eyes, I reached out with my magic, connecting it with hers. Our energies were one.

"We both cannot die on this night. And fighting them will only cause their hatred to grow." I spoke into her mind. *"Do not be saddened by my death, for I am not. One day, these people will learn, they will see the wrong they have done, and the regret that they must live with will haunt them."*

"I love you, my Alexandria. One day, we will meet again."

"And I love you, mother. Now, leave. I do not wish for you to see this."

Our connection broke and we once again beheld each other's gazes. Another set of tears rained from my mother's beautiful eyes. And though I felt my own rising, I refused to let them fall. I needed to put on a brave mask for my mother to let her know I was not afraid.

When a man lit his torch, that was when my mother turned her back, and forced her way through the crowd. She disappeared into the night. The man lowered the torch to the wood at my feet and flames ignited brightly.

"Let the witch burn!" Cheers erupted throughout the crowd as they watched the flames make their way toward my feet.

And though I could use my magic to flee, I refused. Something inside me told me this must be done, that this was not the end for me. So I listened, and closed my eyes. I blocked out the sounds of the people, I blocked out the pain, and only focused on my mother's face, on Roman's.

There was a smile on my face as the flames devoured my body.

My scream erupted around us. It felt as though my skin were burning, I could smell flesh cooking in flames. My nails scratched at my skin in a panic, my mind racing and unclear. My heart rapidly beat against my chest, feeling as though it would burst free. Thundering against its cage. Tears tracked down my cheeks in hot streams.

"Natalia." I heard Sasha's voice. I felt her arms around me, and I fell into her embrace. *"It is over, dear. The pain is long gone."* Her hand brushed through my hair gently as I wept onto her shoulder.

"It felt like I was living it all over again."

"It is over, dear. There is nothing to fear."

I pulled away from her embrace and dried my tears. *"Thank you, for being here for me."*

She smiled sweetly. *"Always."*

Ahead of us, another path alit. But it did not seem to lead to another memory. I felt myself being guided along the path, a gentle force pulling me forward.

"The rest of your memories will unlock in due time, Natalia. For now, your mind and body must rest."

I nodded my head and we merged into the light.

THE VAMPIRE

My hand clutched my chest, it felt as though my breath had been knocked from my lungs. My head erupted in pain as memories emerged. My heart raced as I was forced to remember her, how she died, how I buried her. My eyes stung but anger raised inside me like a storm. My nails dug into the wood of the bar, cracking and splintering it.

"Roman?" Aron clapped a hand on my shoulder. "What's wrong?"

I shook my head; I couldn't think clearly. My memories were drowning me. Her voice whispered through my mind, her laughter echoing, her face a phantom.

"Alexandria."

Chapter Thirteen

A Sign

PAX LAY ON my lap, purring as my fingers stroked through his fur. Catherine was seated beside me upon the bed. She listened to every word that poured forth from my lips. I told her of my past life, unlocking my memories. I spoke of my past mother, of my first meeting with Roman, and my burning. She devoured every word, every memory. Sadness softened her ghostly eyes.

"My dear friend..." Her words whispered like a ghostly echo within my room.

I took in a steadying breath. "Sasha said that my other memories will unlock in time. My mind needs rest for now."

"Have you decided on whether you are going to tell Roman?"

I shook my head. "Not now. I still need time to understand, to process all this. Someday I will tell him but today won't be that day."

"That is understandable, Natalia. But right now, I believe it best that that pretty head of yours gets some sleep."

A smile appeared on my lips. "I suppose so."

THE VAMPIRE

The rain pelted against the window, echoing around in the quiet space of my home. Lightning brightened the sky, flashing its brilliant light. The clouds roared, thunder rattling the earth.

Tonight, reminded me of the night I buried my lover.

Alexandria.

Something was whispering to me, tugging at me, my soul. I pressed my forehead against the cool glass and closed my eyes. "Alexandria, please, if your soul has found its way back, then I beg you to give me a sign." A sigh escaped my lips, "Please, my love."

I know there was only a small amount of hope, but I would cling to that hope with every fiber of my soul.

THE MOTHER

"My dear, Sakiya." I gazed down upon the woman knelt before my feet.

"Yes, my queen?"

"Tonight, go out and follow that little witch. I wish to know where she goes at night, where she lives, how she spends her time. And report back to me every location she stops at or even glances at. Do you understand me?"

She kept her head bowed. "Yes, my queen."

My hand reached for her and stroked her silky hair. "Such an obedient servant. Now, leave."

She straightened herself, bowed to me, and left the room. A smile curved like a serpent upon my lips. Soon that little witch will be mine.

"If only your son could be that compliant."

I was reminded of my mother's presence within the room. "He will be, soon enough. Once I get my hands on his witch, he'll listen to every word I say."

Her eyes hardened. "He should have been that way since the beginning." She made to walk past me but stopped beside me, her eyes only focusing on the door before her. "Do not disappoint me again." With that, she left the room.

Rage sparked inside me like a ravenous fire. A scream bursting forth from my lungs. I reached for the nearest object. My hands gripped the wooden chair and hurtled it across the room. It smashed against the wall, falling to pieces upon the floor, echoing throughout the room.

THE WITCH

While I slept, my dreams had turned into memories. Each one unlocking, one after the other, like a long movie. I began to remember being a child long ago, in my past life. Laughing and running through the tall grass, my mother chasing after me. But there was never a father to be found within my fleeting memories. And though a father was missing, I never seemed saddened by it. So young and already so accepting, moving past a parent who was never part of my life, much like now.

My memories began to morph, showing me lessons with my mother inside our tiny cottage home. Magic was alive within our home, all around us. There were smiles to be seen upon my mother and I's faces each time I perfected a spell or made an object move by command.

Now, I was shown times spent with Roman, late nights beneath the stars. I saw a night where we lay underneath the light of the full moon, our bodies bare and exposed, melded together. How love had been made on that night.

Then, those memories faded away as another emerged. I stood before a girl whose back was turned to me. Her long, blonde hair whispering in the wind. And when she began to face me, I was awoken from my memories.

THE VAMPIRE

The wall cracked and splintered, the sound of it echoing around. It groaned beneath my trembling fist. Anger had seized me, rage running rampant through my being. My vision saw nothing but darkness, hatred. It was burning inside me like an intense flame that could not be put out.

"I will not give her that information, Roman. Trust that." Sakiya's voice sounded distant, muffled.

I shook my head, removing my fist from the wall. "No." My voice hissed. "She'll kill you if you disobey her, you know that."

Her boots sounded across the floor as she approached me. "I know." Her voice held no fear.

I turned to face her. "I will not sacrifice an old friend. I will find a way to protect Natalia without anyone dying."

Aron stepped beside her, placing his hand on her lower back. "Bring the witch here. Your mother doesn't know about this place, it's the safest bet."

"Aron's right."

"She won't accept that. She would have to hide away for the rest of her life, locked away within these walls until my mother finds her, and she will." I turned back to the wall. "I cannot do that to her."

"Then you know what must be done."

A sigh escaped me. I always have known what must be done. "It won't be easy killing my mother. We might die before we even get close to her."

"Two vampires, a werewolf, and a witch. We might pack more of a punch than you think, Roman." Aron said.

"That's if she'll want to fight. It will be her choice."

"She's a feisty one, I believe she'll pick knocking your mother's fangs in."

THE WITCH

My store kept my mind occupied; the memories were presenting themselves more and more. Some mornings I would wake with headaches, a pounding behind my eyes. Keeping my mind elsewhere, helped put the memories at ease for a while.

It's only been three days since the awakening of my memories and I still wasn't used to believing that I lived long ago. And then I realized it has been quite a while since I've seen Roman.

My gaze found itself staring out the windows. I wondered if he was alright or if something terrible happened to him. My hand clutched itself over my chest.

No.

He's alive. If something happened, I would have felt it.

And so, I took comfort in that.

The sun was slowly setting, the sky turning orange from the sun's final rays of the day. Darkness was creeping onto the world. I flipped my opened sign to closed and locked the doors. Once the tapestry concealed the door that led into my shop, I turned around to find Catherine.

"I think it best that you get out of the house for a while." She spoke to me in her motherly tone of worry.

A sigh escaped me as I realized she was right. "To the bar I go, I suppose." This time, I remembered to wear my medallion and the wolf's claw, just in case.

"Be safe, Natalia."

"I'll try." And then I closed the door.

It's been some time since I've stepped foot inside the bar and the people had noticed my absence. Cindy caught my eye and a wide smile spread across her cherry lips. She dashed across the bar and wrapped her arms around me. Her perfume was strong but comforting.

"Dear, I've been so worried about ya. I'm glad to see ya back." She pulled back from the hug and brushed a strand of hair behind my ear.

I returned the smile. "It's good to be back, hope it's okay if I still sing."

"Well of course, Natalia. The mic is always yours."

"Thank you."

She smiled once more and returned to the bar, serving drinks. I approached the small stage, took the step up, and stood before the mic. Several eyes were upon me, the bar was more crowded tonight than any other. The thick cigar smoke obscured my sight, along with the bright lights aimed upon me. I tried to search through the crowd of faces, but Roman's was nowhere to be seen.

My hand reached for the medallion, my thumb tracing across it. Closing my eyes, the soft notes of the song began to escape my lips.

THE VAMPIRE

As the three of us walked through the town, a song had caught my ears. A voice that sounded familiar. I had stopped in my tracks and listened closer. The song had begun to speak to me, my soul. It rang familiar bells within my mind. A song that had once been sung to me, long ago. From the very lips of my lover.

No longer did I focus on anything else. Only the sound of that voice. I followed it, ignoring the questions of my friends. All I could do was run, my heart beating rapidly.

"Alexandria."

THE WITCH

The song had come from deep within myself, my memories, the very core of my being. I thought that perhaps if I sung it, Roman would appear. But still, there was no sign of him. Pulling the hood of my cloak over my head, I left the bar, and disappeared into the night.

I didn't know where I was going, I had sunk so deep into my thoughts, that I had begun to wander about blindly. Allowing the earth to guide me.

Where I would end up? I couldn't tell.

THE VAMPIRE

There was no sign of her in the bar, her scent nor her face could be found. The bartender Cindy had said she had left the bar a little bit ago and then told me to stop being such a thirsty dog.

I shook my head and hurried out of the bar. That was when strong hands had gripped my arms. I found myself staring into confused, worried, brown eyes.

"I might be fast but it's hard to keep up with a vampire. What's driven you mad, Roman?"

My thoughts were still buzzing with the sound of the song, it wove its way through my mind, echoing. "It's her."

He raised a brow. "Her?"

"Alexandria. She's back."

Aron shook his head with a heavy sigh, "Roman. She's gone. She's been gone a long time."

I broke free of his grasp. *"She's back."*

"Roman!"

His hands reached for me once more, but I was quick, and gone within the blink of an eye. No one would stop me. She was back, I could feel it, *I knew it.* And I would find her.

The song had led me here. The cemetery where my Alexandria was buried. My heart ached but also leapt with hope. Perhaps this was my sign. That she was back, and I had to find her, and I would.

I hurried past the headstones, ducked beneath the willow branches and knelt before her grave. My hand reached for the cool stone, tracing along her name.

The hope within me began to flicker and sputter out. A heavy sigh escaped me as I pressed my forehead against the stone. "My love, please, give me a sign."

As soon as those words left my lips, footsteps sounded behind me. Quickly, I leapt to my feet and faced the person approaching. My breath had caught within my throat, my heart thumped. And it felt like the earth itself had stopped.

A woman of purple hair and blue eyes stood before me. Her gaze locking with mine. Shock appearing upon her features.

"Natalia?"

Chapter Fourteen

Back Once More

MY MIND HAD BEEN quieted, not a whisper of thoughts could be found as I stared upon the vampire before me. His eyes were wide with hopefulness but there was also confusion to be found within his gaze. Roman cast a glance back at the headstone and his eyes found mine once more. I watched as he began to piece it together within his mind.

"You're her." He spoke softly.

I swallowed and nodded my head. Afraid to speak. Not knowing what to say, my mind blanking.

His brow creased. "How long have you known?"

I stepped past him and knelt before the headstone, pressing my hand against it. "Three days." I said. "I awoke my lost memories. They're coming back to me, slowly."

He knelt beside me, his eyes didn't meet mine, only gazing upon Alexandria's name. "What do you remember?"

"My mother. How I died." My hand left the stone and placed itself atop Roman's hand that rested upon the ground. "And, you."

His blue eyes drifted down to my hand. "Forgive me if I find this hard to believe. It just seems too good to be true."

My hand left his. "I understand, I'm still processing it myself."

"What of me – us – do you remember?" I could hear the eagerness in his voice, hope.

Through the willow branches above us, I could see the night sky. And though it was a cloudy night, the stars still shone through. "When we first met. The song I had sung to you." My cheeks began to warm at the thought of the other memory. "And when we first made love."

It was then that I could feel his eyes upon me, but I couldn't bring myself to meet his gaze.

"The memories come back to me piece by piece. Every day or night, I remember something else. Some memories are happier than others."

For a long while, we sat there in silence, but the sort of silence that was peaceful. Roman's eyes studied the stars, his face being hard to read, but his emotions spoke to me. Within the mixture of hopefulness and happiness, there was so much fear to be found.

"Forgive me." He said, breaking the silence. "I've spent so many years, hoping that one day, Alexandria would return. And part of me had begun to lose hope." His hand reached for mine and I did not pull away.

"And now, here you are, once again." He turned to face me, those eyes of his taking me in with great detail. "I do not expect you to be mine in this lifetime. Though it would be one of the greatest joys of my life, the decision remains with you." He brought my hand up to his mouth and placed a gentle kiss upon it. "Whether you wish to be lovers or friends, whichever choice, I will happily accept as long as you are part of my life, Natalia."

Gently, he helped me to stand, our gazes never breaking. "I do not expect an answer now, take your time."

My eyes drifted down to our feet, aware of the fact that his hand still clung to mine. "Part of me – the past me – wants nothing more than to leap into your embrace." I took in a shaking breath, "But the me now, needs time. To know you in this life."

"I understand, Natalia."

A sigh escaped him, and I was forced to gaze upon him. His brow had creased with worry, there was something else on his mind. "What's wrong?"

He squeezed my hand gently, as if afraid to let go. "It's my mother. She is beginning to track you, Natalia. She wishes to know where you live, work, where you visit most often."

"Why is she doing this? Why did she send that one vampire after me?"

"Because of me. Because you have spoken with me, because I claim you as a friend instead of my next meal."

"My home and store are protected with several charms and spells." I bit my bottom lip, "But she'll find me eventually, won't she?"

"Not if I can help it. I offer you a place to stay at my home. Neither her nor her followers know of it, you'll be safe there. Until we figure out what to do about her." His hand released mine. "That is also your choice, Natalia."

Taking in a breath, I said, "Give me a few days to gather my belongings."

He nodded his head.

"Oh, and we will be sleeping in *separate* beds, Roman."

A smile finally cracked upon his worried features as a chuckle escaped him.

THE MOTHER

"Have you gotten the witch *yet*?"

Mother had burst into the room, her patience coming to a thin end. I ignored her and tipped the wine bottle back, savoring the last few drops of it.

Her heels clicked against the floor as she approached. "Is that your solution to the problem? Drinking cheap wine in a cheap silk robe? What have you become?" She now stood before my vision. "A disgrace, that is what you've become."

I faced my mother, my anger blazing through me. "I have a vampire watching the witch, and she will report back to me where the witch lives and where she goes. And that's when the pest will be mine."

I turned my back to her and stormed toward the double doors. I stopped in my tracks when her voice followed after me. "If I were queen, this problem would have been solved immediately."

I flung open the doors, "But you are no longer queen."

"We shall see how much longer your reign shall last, daughter."

I glanced over my shoulder to find my mother's eyes fuming with hatred. "Don't worry mother, it won't end anytime soon. I promise you that."

The doors slammed shut before my mother could speak another annoying word.

THE WITCH

Roman had walked me home, to make sure that I had gotten there safely, and to be sure that no one would follow me. He placed a kiss upon my hand and bid me a goodnight and sweet dreams. I watched him until I could no longer see him, he had disappeared into the shadows and seemed to vanish from this world.

The following morning, assortments of items were floating about within my little apartment, sorting themselves into bags lined along the couch. Pax pounced around, swatting his paws at the floating objects, Catherine's ghostly laughter echoing throughout the rooms.

As my belongings packed themselves, I entered my store, today it was closed. Picking up the store phone, I dialed Tasha's number and waited for her answer.

Three rings later, her voice sounded on the other end. "Yes, Natalia?"

"Hello, Tasha. I was just calling to let you and Sasha know that I'll be out of town for a while. I was wondering if you two wouldn't mind keeping an eye on the shop for me while I'm gone?"

"Of course, dear. May I ask where you'll be going?"

I bit my bottom lip, hating to have to lie to a dear friend. "Visiting some relatives of mine, I won't be gone longer than a few weeks, possibly a month or so."

"Have fun, but not too much fun." Tasha purred. "Let us know when you'll be back."

"I will and thank you."

"You're welcome, Natalia."

Then, the call ended. There was a heaviness on my heart. For I felt a darkness lingering, waiting for me, in the very near future. Perhaps, my nightmare will become true.

Everything was almost packed. I checked all four bags, but I found that I was running low on some personal products. For a moment, I stood there and pictured what it would be like sending Roman to the store for feminine hygiene products and a smile formed upon my lips as I pictured his confused face. Deciding to spare him of that, I gathered my purse, placed my necklaces around my neck, and I ventured outside.

I pulled the hood of my cloak over my head since the sun had already set. I was breaking one promise to Roman; never venture outside alone at night. That was one promise he asked of me to keep while he walked me home the other night. But, I figured I would be safe enough. My aim was the small corner store and back to my apartment in no longer than fifteen minutes. That was all I needed to do. Get in, get out, and return without any troubles.

Taking a breath, I hurried along the sidewalk into the quiet night. The air was chilly, nipping at my exposed ankles from my shin length dress. The weather was changing quickly this year, the sun setting faster, the air growing ever colder, the sky always seeming to be gloomy.

The store was in sight and I hurried inside. The bell jingled above my head and the cashier greeted me with a smile. I quickly returned it and rushed down along the aisles, gathering the items I needed and as many as I could.

As I ventured down the last aisle, where the coolers where, I found a lone blonde-haired woman standing before the rack of wine. Within her hands, she held a bottle of red wine, those blue eyes of hers examining the label closely. But when her gaze lifted from the bottle and met with mine, that was when I felt as though the world had caved in beneath my feet. That was the woman from Roman's memory. The woman *proud* of the victims he slaughtered.

His mother.

The Vampire Queen.

Averting my gaze, I headed toward her, and walked past her with my head held high. She had no idea who I was exactly, as far as I knew, she has never seen my face personally.

As I checked out at the counter though, I could feel her eyes upon me, more confused than anything. I gathered my bags and hurried outside before she could piece together who I was.

I had returned to my apartment without incident. But Roman's mother's face still lingered in the back of my mind. Hurriedly, I removed my necklaces and placed them upon the hook on the door. Just in case she had figured out who I was and decided to follow me, and though I felt no one watching me during my walk home, it was better to be safe than sorry.

"Gather everything you need?" Catherine appeared from the doorway that led into the living room, Pax trailed behind her.

"I did, figured I would spare Roman the confusion of having to send him out to buy me things while I'm staying at his place."

Sadness flickered across Catherine's ghostly features. "How long will you be gone?"

I raised a brow to my old friend. "You think you aren't coming with me?"

Her eyes widened with excitement. "Oh, thank goodness! I would have gone insane here all alone!"

THE MOTHER

The scent was undeniable. A witch was here within this store and not but three feet from me. When my eyes found hers, I could have sworn I saw fear flicker within those blue eyes of hers. But if there was fear to be found, it had vanished within a second. The purple haired witch held her head high and walked right past me, her scent strong, causing my mouth to water at the mere thought of tasting the sweetness coursing through her veins.

But as I watched her wait to pay for her items, something flickered within the back of my mind. Something whispering of familiarity, bells trying to chime. It was when the witch had left the store that I had begun to fear the possibility of Alexandria still being alive.

I shook my head.

I had watched the witch burn.

She was long gone, never again to return to this world.

Chapter Fifteen

A Safe Place

THE NIGHT HAD arrived, the night I would be leaving behind my home and store. I did not know how long I would be gone but it already felt as though a part of me was missing, left behind within my home as Roman led me away.

He must have noticed the saddened look upon my face because his hand found mine and gently squeezed. “It’s not forever, Natalia.”

I nodded my head and faced ahead of us. “I know.”

“So, I get stuck with carrying everything?” Aron grunted behind us.

“I can take a bag or two if you would like, Aron.” I offered.

I had also offered before to use my magic and allow my luggage to follow behind us, but Roman insisted on me saving my energy in case we found ourselves in trouble during this move.

He flashed a wolfish grin, “No, dear Natalia, I do not expect that of you. That comment was directed more toward the blood sucker there.”

Roman didn't glance back at his friend but there was a grin upon his face. "We'll see you at my place." He gathered me into his arms and faced Aron, "And be gentle with her cat, I know how you loathe felines."

Before Aron could bark out another joke, Roman took to the stars. The wind whipped my braid through the air, a few wisps of hair freeing themselves from it.

I raised a brow to Roman, "You do know I am capable of flying, correct?"

A smile. "I like dramatic exits." His grip on me began to loosen, "If you wish to fly, I can let go."

Before I could answer, another memory presented itself upon me. A memory that was very similar to the moment I found myself in now. Roman carrying me across the sky, through the stars. Tender looks of love shared between us, sweet kisses passing on our lips.

When I snapped out of the memory, I found Roman's eyes watching me carefully. "Memories?" He questioned with a gentle voice.

For a moment, I did not answer. My hand reached for him, caressing his cold cheek. Flashes of that memory flickered before my mind, one second I was in the past another I was back in the present. The only thing that changed in the view I was beholding, was Roman's clothes, nothing else had changed about him, nothing.

"Only one." I whispered.

Not a single word whispered from his lips but within his eyes I found understanding. He knew of the memory I spoke of. His arms wrapped a little tighter around my body and the rest of the flight was spent in peaceful silence.

Roman landed swiftly on his feet before an abandoned factory that seemed to be in the middle of nowhere. Trees surrounded this place, covering it from the sight of wandering eyes.

He set me down on my feet and led me inside the dark factory. I kept close behind him on his heels. The steel frame of this place was rusted and old, creaking and groaning as the factory settled or the wind pressed itself against it. The shadows were taunting, confusing my eyes, playing tricks upon them. Making me believe there were evil spirits hiding away, waiting to strike. He led me up a steel staircase, each step I took caused the stairs to moan beneath the weight of my boots. My hand gripped tightly to the rusted railing.

We ventured down a long and narrow hallway until we came upon a door toward the end. He opened the door and stepped aside, "Welcome back to my home, Natalia."

I stepped inside and was greeted by a familiar sight. The small living room. My eyes wandered over to the couch I had awaken on once before, after that vampire attack.

I scanned the rest of the place. There seemed to be a kitchen area within the living room, set off into the corner. Only a few counters lined along the wall and two lone cabinets hanging above them. There was a fridge and a coffee maker, a sink between the two counters, and that was all.

When Roman entered, and closed the door behind him, another view was revealed to me. A short hallway that only had three doors. I assumed my room would be behind one of those.

"Aron should be here shortly." He said as he approached the curtain covered window and pulled them away, exposing the night sky. Allowing the moonlight to filter through.

I joined his side by the window. "Is it safe to leave him alone?"

"Another friend of mine will be with him, watching from a distance."

I nodded my head and gazed toward the moon. "You know," I began to say, "There's something I've been meaning to tell you."

"What is it?"

"Before I learned that I was – am – Alexandria, my dreams had turned into your memories. Every night, there was another memory." He remained quiet while I spoke. "And one, I would not call a dream but a nightmare." I felt him tense beside me. "The memory of you hunting down my killers."

"Natalia-"

I fully faced him, my gaze locking him in place. "Though the memory terrified me, seeing those bodies lay at your feet, the blood soaking your hands." My hands reached for his, only one, holding onto it gently. "I could see the heartache within those eyes of yours, saw it behind the mask of a monster. And I realized that if I had been in your position, I would have done the same." His hand began to tremble. "I do not fear you, Roman. I know that is not who you are, I have known you once before, and I knew then that you were no monster, but a man. A man whose heart was heavy with grief." I let go of his hand, reached toward him and wiped away the lone tear that escaped his eye. "I wished for you to know that."

His lips moved as he began to form the words, he wished to speak but stopped when the door swung open. I took a step back from Roman, my hand leaving his face. Aron entered the room, followed by a short woman with long, midnight hair.

"I'll take her things to the room." He said and disappeared down the hallway.

"Did anyone see you?" Roman asked the woman.

She didn't look at him, her gaze was focused on me. "No." She took a step closer. "So, this is the witch we've heard so much about." She extended her hand and a smile appeared on her face, "Hello, Natalia. I'm, Sakiya."

I shook her hand, her skin cold but silky. "Nice to meet you."

Finally, her gaze left me and ventured to Roman. "Do you have a plan? Or are we to stay locked away until our bones turn to dust?"

Aron returned. "And I'd prefer not to be dust, so if there isn't a plan yet, let's make one."

"For now, Sakiya will return to my mother and give her the information she asked for." My heart ached at the thought of that woman knowing where I live and work. "And Sakiya will report back whatever my mother plans after."

Aron moved a step closer to Sakiya. "Don't be gone too long, or I'll have to come find you myself."

A grin tugged at her lips. "You're an animal."

He wiggled his brows. "Would you have me any other way, my dear vampire lover?"

She made her way toward the door. "And would you, my dear werewolf lover, wish to be castrated if you call me dear again?"

As she closed the door behind her, Aron's laughter followed after her.

THE MOTHER

"Good job, my little samurai, I knew you wouldn't disappoint me." My fingers traced along her cheek. "Now, all that's left to do is to dispose of the witch." Something flickered within her eyes, it was gone quickly, leaving me to guess at what that something was.

"How will you dispose of the wretched thing?" Mother's voice spoke irritably from the fireplace where she watched us with close eyes.

My hand fell away from Sakiya's face and shooed her away. She bowed before she left the room.

"Her death will be a slow one, I promise you that, *mother.*"

She raised a brow to me. "And when shall she die?"

I reached for the wine bottle, plunged my nail into the cork, and ripped it free. "In a few weeks' time, there will be our annual masquerade. A celebration that even Roman cannot miss. The witch will be there."

"And how do you know this?"

A smile crossed my lips, "Because, once I threaten her life to Roman, he'll make sure she'll be there."

"A trick, toying with minds." Mother's lips seemed to curl in approval. "I knew you weren't completely useless."

My grip tightened around the glass bottle, my nails scratching it like a chalk board.

THE WITCH

The room was small, but homey. There was a four-post bed situated at the center of the wall it was pressed against, across from the door that led into the room. Beside the door was a small, wooden dresser. A black carpet covered most of the hard floor beneath it. Aron had set my bags along-side the wall on the opposite side of the door. Pax was curled on the red, silk sheets upon the bed.

The zippers upon the bags unzipped and the items within them eased into the air. The drawers on the dresser slid open and my clothes began to fold themselves and then putting themselves away within the drawers. My sage, crystals, makeup, and other assortments of items arranged themselves atop the dresser. One bag was left with a few more 'personal' items and I would fetch them when needed. The bags slid beneath the bed and my unpacking was finished.

I closed the door and faced the room. "Alright, show yourself."

Catherine faded into view, her ghostly hair fanning through the air. "Small but lovely." She said as she looked around.

"Why hide yourself?"

"I didn't wish for your lover to find the sight of me repulsive." I remembered her telling me once, a few years ago, that some vampires hated spirits. Mostly because it would be spirits of their victims that would decide to haunt them for eternity.

"He won't." I said.

"For now, I wish for you to only know of my presence. If that is alright."

I nodded my head. "Whenever you're ready for your grand unveil, just let me know."

After I had left my room, I ventured back into the living area and found only Roman remained. Aron apparently slipped away to the bar for a few rounds of drinks. Roman told me he did that whenever Sakiya had to leave and return to the queen, the drinks helped his nerves and take his mind off his fear.

I was seated upon the couch while I waited for Roman to make a pot of coffee, though I insisted on doing it myself. The smell of it brewing wafted through the small area and I breathed in that scent. It seemed to warm my soul, make me feel more at home.

A few minutes passed and he brought a steaming cup of coffee to me. "Thank you." I smiled to him.

He nodded his head and took a seat at the other end of the couch, giving me space. "You won't be locked away here forever, I promise you that, I'll return you home as soon as I can, Natalia."

"I know." I took a sip of coffee. Several minutes were spent in silence until I decided to break it. "How long have Aron and Sakiya been lovers?"

A chuckle escaped Roman as he ran his hand through his brown hair. "Lovers off and on for several years." He began to tell me their tale. "At first, Sakiya couldn't stand him but eventually his charm worked on her. They saw each other occasionally, whenever I was here, and they would visit. But then, one night, my mother sent Sakiya on the hunt for Aron.

She didn't harm him though, of course. But she kept away for a long time so that he would be safe. And now, my mother's focus has shifted to me, not Aron, and also to you."

My finger traced along the edge of the cup. "Why does she hate me?"

He leaned back on the couch and propped his elbow on the arm of it, his fingers scratching along his strong jawline. "Because she fears that I'll taint our bloodline, falling in love with a creature that is not of vampire lineage. She doesn't believe in mixing species. That, and your kind is also considered a food to us." He struggled getting that last sentence out, the vein in his neck throbbing.

"You never thought of me as food, not even that first night." I said as a hushed whisper.

His gaze found mine. "Never."

The weight of emotion in his gaze caused me to look away. "How long were we happy before... *it* happened?" I didn't wish to voice it, Roman knew what I was saying.

A long sigh escaped him. "A few months." Then, a reminiscent smile cracked the saddened features upon his face. "And it was several months before then that I cherished those moments of friendship. Where we shared our life stories together, where you showed me your magic, showed me your heart, laying your soul bare."

"I remember when you confessed to me." I stated, still tracing the cup ring.

"A rather embarrassing moment, if I recall."

A laugh escaped me. "I never knew a vampire could be so graceless, almost falling on his face because he wasn't paying attention as to where he was walking."

"Your beauty was too much a distraction to notice the hole in the Earth." He chuckled embarrassingly, remembering that moment as well.

I set the cup down upon the table before us and scooted a little closer to Roman, he watched me closely. "You are the light within my darkness, my hope within this hopeless world. I love you, more than I ever imagined loving another. You have become my heart and soul." I met his eyes and found tears forming within them. "Those were the words you confessed to me on that night."

He took a breath to steady himself. "And those words remain true."

His hand reached for me but stopped for a second, waiting to see if I would reject his touch. I did not move away from him, only closer. His fingers brushed against my cheek gently, as if he was scared, I would vanish, as if this was all a dream.

I had told him – told myself – that I needed time, time in this life to know him. But I did know him. Heart and soul and he knew me. Something was tugging me to him, and him to me. Something that could not be ignored or forced away. It was love that bound us, love that was eternal, love that has transcended lifetimes, and found its way back to its mate.

As our gazes held, memories began to awaken.

Nights laying beneath the starry sky as if they were our blanket from the rest of the world. Our voices speaking of our lives, our secrets, and fears. Fingers interlacing with one another. Bodies meeting in love and passion. Laughter echoing around us. Arms holding one another closely, afraid to let go. Words of love escaping our lips.

Roman's face leaned closer to mine and I did not back away. And when our lips met, my heart and soul seemed to explode as if they had been waiting for so long to be reunited with their other half.

Their mate.

Their match.

As the kiss began to deepen, his hand found the back of my head, his fingers tangling within my hair. My hand doing the same to him while his other wrapped around my waist and brought my body closer to his.

There was no denying what I felt for Roman. He was once my friend, my lover, my refuge. And in this life, he will continue to be. He was my safe place, a place for my heart to rest without fear of heartbreak. And I would be his safe place, for as long as I lived.

He leaned me back on the couch, now on top of me, his hand was braced beside my head, while the other gripped my side. My chest felt as though there was fire kindling within it, each touch, each sweep of his tongue, caused the fire to swell.

Roman broke the kiss, his eyes holding mine. "You once asked me what my peace would be." His hand stroked my cheek tenderly. I felt the emotions within him, strong and unyielding love. "You, Natalia. You are my peace."

Before I could answer, his lips found mine once more.

Chapter Sixteen

An Old Friend

THE YOUNG WOMAN stood before me, her back facing me. The wind rustled through her long, pale hair. Whispers began to echo around me, buzzing within my mind. And ever so slowly, the woman began to turn. My heart began to thunder as I waited to see her face.

A gasp escaped me, my hand covering my mouth, as I took in the sight of her beautiful face. She smiled brightly, her auburn eyes glowing from the rays of the sun, her golden hair bright.

"Alexandria." Her voice echoed my name.

"Catherine."

I woke with a jolt, my heart beating fast. Pax leapt down from the bed as I had startled him, and Catherine eased toward the side of the bed. And all I could do was gape at her with wide eyes.

Her hair swayed within the air as she cocked her head, concern flashing within those grey eyes of hers, eyes that were once auburn. "Is it the nightmare again?"

I swallowed and shook my head. "No." I whispered, hoping I hadn't woken Roman. "Catherine. We were friends in my past life." My eyes met with her questioning gaze. "Your witch friend that was burned, was me."

She blinked slowly, as if processing her thoughts. Then, her eyes widened as she realized. "How could I not have known, not have seen it?" She seated herself at the edge of the bed. She fiddled with her ghostly fingers. "I knew I was drawn to you for a reason, but I never knew the exact reason why. I should have pieced it together sooner, how alike you two seemed, well or should I say how alike you and your past self-seemed." Her gaze slid back to mine. "Did you happen to see how I..." She looked away.

"No. It was only a flash of your face and that was all I saw."

She nodded her head. "Perhaps one day I'll know how and why."

Knock. Knock. "It's Sakiya, may I come in?"

Catherine quickly vanished from sight. "Yes!"

The door swung open as Sakiya entered, her eyes seemed to search the room. "Thought I heard you talking to someone, figured Roman was in here."

"Sorry, I was talking to Pax." He was curled by my side, quietly purring.

A smile pulled at the vampire's lips. "Aron hates cats." She approached the bed, "May I?" I nodded my head and she sat on the edge of the bed. "I, on the other hand, love them." Her hand gently combed through his fur, causing his purring to grow louder.

"You know," She began to speak once more, "I'm surprised I didn't find Roman waiting outside your door like a lost dog. Or in here pestering you."

I arched my brow, "Why did you expect that?"

Her dark gaze fixed on the blank wall before her. "For so long, he grieved over Alexandria's death. Aron and I thought he would never move on from her. He seemed to always be searching for signs of her, to see if she would come back to this world. But after years, he had become a shell of himself, his grief eating away at him." Her eyes found mine, "And now, here you are, alive once more. And I can see the life returning to him, that fire within his soul kindling."

"How long did he grieve?" I asked.

"Too long." She raised from the bed and approached the door, "If he does become too much, don't be afraid to ask me to haul his ass elsewhere." She winked a dark eye at me before closing the door behind her.

This place was quiet, silence filling the empty air. Roman had left just moments ago and already; loneliness had begun to settle over my bones. I did not know why it bothered me now, I had been used to living alone with only Pax and Catherine. But while my cat companion slept and Catherine roamed from the apartment sometimes, the loneliness never seemed to bother me.

My hands ran along my arms, as I wandered down the hall and found myself in the main room of the apartment. Not a soul was to be found lingering here. With a sigh, I approached the window and pulled back the curtains, revealing the night and all its darkness. It did not soothe the loneliness I felt, it only seemed to echo it.

"Something troubles you, dear friend." I heard Catherine's ghostly voice whisper beside me.

"I do not know why but I suddenly feel so lonely. Even though I know you and Pax are here, I just cannot shake the feeling."

Her eyes drifted toward the door and then returned to peering upon me. "Perhaps it is because Roman has left."

I shook my head. "Part of me feels as though it is too soon to be in-love with him but..."

"Your past self tells you that you have always loved him." Catherine finished for me.

I nodded my head. "It's truly frustrating trying to find a balance between my two lives, nothing seems to equal out, my thoughts always combating each other, my heart yearning, my soul crying out." I rubbed my temples. "I could really use a drink right now."

Catherine's chuckle echoed beside me. "Though I am sure you wish to fall into blinded drunkenness, I do know of another way that will help you."

I raised a skeptical brow. "I'm okay with drinking but drugs are *completely* out of the question."

She smiled and shook her head. "Sing, Natalia."

"Right now?"

"I know it soothes your soul whenever you sing, that was why you frequented the bar so often."

I turned my gaze toward the night stretched out before me. Closing my eyes, my voice began to seep from my lips, the notes whispering through the air like hushed melodies. They drifted through the room, echoing my heart's emotions, my soul's turmoil. The song spoke of a lost soul finding its other half in a new life. And still, their love seemed to be doomed from the start. As I sang, I noticed that my cheeks had wettened as tears squeezed themselves from my closed eyes.

My mind was hazed, confusion fogging it. Who was I?

Who am I in this life?

Am I Alexandria or am I Natalia?

Which life holds the one true me?

The song continued to pour from my lips as memories flooded from the core of my soul. My past life began to reveal itself before the darkness of my mind. There, I saw a loving mother. There, I found Roman and I. And it was there that I witnessed my own death in a fiery haze.

My life now began to seep into the cracks forming within my past memories. I saw Sasha and Tasha within my store. Pax curled at my feet. Catherine sitting upon my dresser, ghostly laughter escaping her. A microphone was before me in a hazy bar. Roman could be found within these memories, too. And then, there was light. Bright but not blinding. It seemed to meld the cracks within my memories – my past lives – and formed them together into one.

One soul. One heart. One life.

As the song came to an end, the room was draped in silence, settling around me like a comforting blanket. My soul felt soothed; my heart had ceased its aching. A breath escaped my lips and the fog clouding my mind dispersed.

And when my eyes opened, I knew who I was.

I was Alexandria; I was Natalia.

I am me.

I am whole, not split apart by two lives. But stitched together by them to make me complete, they created me, shaped me.

I know who I am and who I was.

I am me.

Chapter Seventeen

A Plan

THE MOTHER

MY EYES WATCHED the night, it was dreary, a gentle rain pelted against the glass of the window. Lightning crackled within the darkened sky, thunder roaring from the grey clouds and shook the earth. Feeling its tremble beneath my feet. A creak sounded as the door opened to the room, determined footsteps marched toward me. I didn't need to face the person; I knew who it was.

"Leave us alone." Anger rippled within my son's voice.

My brow arched, "I'm assuming by 'us' you mean your little witch friend and yourself."

"Not just us, Aron too. Let us live in peace, mother. Don't you tire of these games? This hatred?"

I shook my head at my foolish son. "You'll never survive in this world, my son, if you think love and hope will carry you through anything." My nail tapped on the glass. “This world will eat you alive.” A screech sounded as my nail trailed down the glass. “From the inside out and it will not bat an eye as it does so.”

“This is truly my last visit, mother. You’re a monster and you’ll never change. Father saw it before I ever could.”

My head tipped back as laughter escaped my lips. “You call me a monster, son.” I finally turned to face him, my eyes meeting with his, “But you forget of the monstrous things you have done. What do you think your father would think of you now?”

His eyes narrowed upon me, “I do not claim to be an innocent, but I will never become what you are.”

My hand rested upon his shoulder, “Don’t you remember how you felt when you tore apart those people that had your precious Alexandria burned alive?” I began to circle him, slowly. “How you tore their limbs from their bodies? How you drained their blood? How you enjoyed the sounds of their screams?” My hand traced across his back to his other shoulder and I faced my son once more. “How you stood over their bodies and gazed upon the carnage with that hunger in your eyes? How revenge tasted upon your tongue as the taste of their blood remained within your mouth?”

“Enough!” A snarl ripped free from him and echoed within the room, his body trembling, the veins in his hands throbbing.

I simply smiled to him and turned toward the window once more. "I know this shall not be your last visit."

"It is, mother."

"Do you forget about the masquerade we host every year? You wouldn't wish to miss that, would you?"

"I could care less about that damned party." He growled.

"Oh, you'll wish to attend this one, my dear son. For this year, I have a surprise planned just for you."

"What do you mean?"

I smiled, "You'll see soon enough."

As Roman stormed from the room, my mother entered. He had run into her in his blinded, childish rage. But he didn't stop when she called out to him, yelling out his name as he disappeared down the hall.

"You have raised the most disrespectful child I have ever seen. It makes me regret ever leaving. If I had of stayed, he would never have turned out this way." She shook her head and seated herself before the fire on one of the two chairs before it.

A sigh escaped my lips as I could feel a headache begin to throb at my temples. Instead of joining her by the fire, I remained at the window, my back facing her.

"How are the preparations coming along?"

"The masquerade will be hosted on a different day this year."

"And what day shall that be?" I could hear the disapproval within her voice, she wasn't one for changing tradition.

"It'll hold a more significant meaning. To Roman and to the witch. October twentieth."

"Fine." And I knew she waved her hand dismissing the subject. "What else?"

"I have planned a special drink to welcome our little witch." A smile curved at the corners of my lips.

"Poison is a cowardly way out of killing someone with your own hands, I thought I taught you that."

The smile vanished. "It won't kill her immediately, *mother.* Only weaken her from the beginning, making her experience pain she has never felt before and then, her blood will be mine for the taking before she slips from the world."

That night after seeing that purple-haired witch in that store, it finally pieced together within my mind like a puzzle. Alexandria had returned to this world, too foolish to remain dead. I would kill her in this life and the next and the next after that. I would continue to kill her until she learned it was better to remain dead and forgotten.

A scoff, sounding almost like a chuckle echoed through the room. "It is a poison still, weakening her so there will be no true fight." My lips curled, my nails digging into my flesh at my mother's mockery. "But you are *queen*, do what you wish. For you have proven to be nothing but cowardly and utterly useless."

THE WITCH

Roman had returned, the door banging shut behind him, I listened to his pacing footsteps. My door creaked open as I stepped into the hallway and headed toward the man. His hands were clasped behind his back, his brow creased as he sunk deep into his thoughts. His eyes were clouded, he was trapped within his own world.

Taking careful steps toward him, I reached out a hand. "Roman?" My voice was gentle, my hand grasped his shoulder.

He turned his head to face me, blinking slowly, returning to the world. "Sorry if I disturbed you, Natalia."

My hand cupped around his cheek, "What troubles you?"

A sigh escaped him as he leaned into the palm of my hand. "My mother... I can't stop her. She won't stop." He stepped away from my hand and it fell to my side.

"Roman?"

He approached the door. "I'll return soon. Stay here, where she can't find you. I need to find Aron and Sakiya."

Before he opened the door, I pressed my hand against it. “Be safe.” My voice was a hushed whisper.

He leaned down and placed a kiss upon my lips and pressed his forehead against mine. “I won’t lose you again.”

With those parting words, he left me alone.

Chapter Eighteen

The Well

CATHERINE WAS ONCE more before me, but I wasn't truly there in body. I was merely an observer within this memory as I had been in the others. Her blonde hair glistened like starlight in the moon's glow. She hurried over to the well with a bucket held within each hand. She began tying the rope around one of the bucket's handles and lowered it within the never-ending depth of the well.

Everything seemed peaceful as she began to pull the bucket of water back up. She hefted it and set it upon the edge of the well and began to tie the other bucket handle. But, she stopped.

Catherine's amber eyes peered around at the darkened woods before her when the sound of a snapping branch echoed into the silence. That was when I noticed a dark shadow darting between the trees, too fast for her to take notice.

I tried to shout a warning, but I found I had no voice.

I watched as the figure leapt forth from the darkness and shoved Catherine over the edge of the well, the buckets falling with her. Screams echoed down, down, down. Then, there was the sound of a sharp crack and silence until her body fell into the waiting water at the very bottom.

I raced toward the well and came face to face with the murderer.

My eyes met with ghostly blue; their hue so similar to someone I know. Her blonde hair swept along the edge of the well, a grin tugging at the corners of her serpent-like lips. For a moment, I remained still, thinking she saw me, but no. She knew not of my presence as she glanced back down into the well.

And that was when I knew, who had killed my dear friend.

When I woke with a jolt, my eyes frantically searched my darkened room. Catherine instantly appeared before my vision, her ghostly eyes searching mine.

"The nightmare again?" She situated herself on the edge of my bed.

"Catherine..." My mind still raced at the revelation, "I know how you died."

She stilled, even her ghostly hair that usually moved like water, had halted within the air. Her eyes were wide and stared blankly. Slowly, she blinked. "What did you say?"

Tossing the blanket from my body, I seated myself beside her. "I saw how you died in my dream."

Her eyes drifted away from mine and she stared ahead at the blank wall before us. "How did I…" Her grey eyes closed as she collected herself and opened them once more, fixed on the wall still. "How did I die?"

"You were collecting water from a well and someone came up behind you and shoved you over the edge." My hands clutched the fabric of my sleeping gown. "I heard a crack and your screams ceased and I heard your body hit the water."

Her ghostly hair whipped about in the air as if remembering that traumatic experience. As if remembering tangling within the air as Catherine tumbled down the well. "Did you see who did it?" Her voice had become hushed.

When our gazes finally met, I told her, "The vampire queen."

She sat silently for a moment, her brow creasing as she thought. "But, why? I didn't know of her in the past life. I only knew…" Catherine shot into the air, her dress rippling like waves. "Roman." Her hands grasped at her grey hair and tugged. "How could I not have known? Not have pieced it together sooner?"

"Catherine, what do you mean?"

Her body drifted back down toward the bed. "I never saw him, never knew his name. But you spoke of him, often. Even revealed to me that he was a vampire." A chuckle escaped her. "She killed me because I knew what he was, what they all were." Her eyes found mine again, "Killed me because I was connected to you, because I had befriended you."

My gaze drifted down to my lap. "Your death was my fault."

"It most certainly was not!" Her voice reverberated through the room. "If I could go back in time and never befriend the village witch, I would not choose to do so. I do not regret a moment of knowing you in the past or in this life. Not one single moment."

"This village witch vows to end that vampire queen's life. Too many have suffered because of her."

Catherine reached her hand toward mine and did not stop. It passed through mine, a ghostly chill trembling along my spine. But still, her transparent hand remained. "Do not lose yourself, Natalia. Do not allow vengeance to consume your soul."

"I do not plan on losing another part of me by her doing."

THE MOTHER

I had returned to the little shop I had seen the witch in, the wretched thing that refused to remain within the ground. Sakiya walked beside me, my personal little assassin. My little Samurai. My most prized possession.

"What do you know of the purple haired woman that visits your store?" I had leaned against the counter; the older man took a step back from me. It only caused my smile to widen.

His brown eyes darted over to the woman standing beside me, weary of her. “I-I don’t know much about her.”

My nail scratched across the glass counter, “What do you know?”

A bead of sweat began to form upon his brow. He wiped it away using the back of his hand and straightened his circular spectacles. “She sings in a bar not too far from here, but she hasn’t been there in a while. And she runs a little store.”

“Interesting.” My voice purred. “That is all, I’m assuming?”

He nodded his head, his throat bobbing as he swallowed. “Yes.”

I straightened myself, my hand sliding off the glass counter. Turning to Sakiya, I nodded my head. Her eyes turned into pure darkness as she set her focus upon the older man.

“Thank you for your time. But I am afraid to say that your time has come to an unpleasant end, *human*.”

Sakiya advanced toward the terrified man.

“P-Please! I have grandchildren to take care of! I beg you!” He backed into a wall of shelves containing random knickknacks. They toppled to the floor, clattering against the ground. Others shattered and glass scattered like glistening crystals.

I tilted my head, “Isn’t that a shame?”

Sakiya leapt over the counter and stole the life from the old man. I watched in satisfaction as the life was drained from his veins. His screams did not last long before they turned into gurgles and then, nothing escaped the man at all. Sakiya raised and faced me. Crimson stained her pretty face, some matting into her midnight hair.

"Come, we have a bar to visit."

The air was thick with the scent of copper. Crimson pooled on the wooden floor beneath my feet. It repainted the walls, streaks of crimson splattered across them. Bodies lay scattered about the bar. Some toppling over from the chairs they had been seated upon. Others rested against the bar, their alcoholic drinks spilling onto the ground. The rest lay here and there, wide eyed staring up at nothing. Throats torn apart. It truly was a beautiful sight to behold.

This was how humans should be treated; disposed of. I would gladly have them all die at my feet if our existence didn't depend on the blood coursing through their disgustingly weak bodies.

I walked through the bar, enjoying the carnage, and stood over a woman who lay behind the counter. Her blonde hair was half painted in crimson. She twitched and gurgled, writhing at my feet.

Kneeling down, I brushed a strand of golden hair behind her ear. "I know you know the woman I'm searching for." My finger trailed along her cheek. "Do you know where I may find her?"

She gurgled, blood spurting from the wound in her throat. But her brows creased together. Her eyes hardening. Slowly, she shook her head.

I leaned closer to the woman, "You may think you are protecting her, but I already know where she lives. Though she wasn't home, I will find her, and I will enjoy killing her."

"Damn… Y-You…" She spat blood in my face before her head fell back against the floor and her eyes rolled into the back of her head.

THE VAMPIRE

It was a massacre. Not a single person breathed with life. All the bodies were soulless shells scattering across the floor. Blood wept from the victims.

"Have I ever told you that your mother is a heartless bitch?" Aron stood beside me, his hardened eyes looking upon the carnage lain out before us.

Sakiya stood beside him, still covered in blood. She said nothing. Only staring upon the victims whose lifeforce coated her lips and hands. She had not spoken since we arrived. Had hardly moved.

"On more than one occasion." Aron was more than right; my mother was a heartless monster.

"I had to do it." Sakiya finally spoke but her voice sounded so far away. Her eyes still upon the bodies.

Aron pulled her close to his side. "We know. She will pay."

"Not soon enough." Sakiya stepped away from Aron and left the bar. The door slamming behind her.

"This will hurt Natalia." Aron said.

My fists trembled by my sides. "This was meant to hurt her."

THE WITCH

My eyes gazed upon the ring that rested upon my middle finger. The colors shifted and changed, churning and whirling. Black began to surface and devoured the colors that wrapped around the ring. Violet and blue turned murky as the darkness mixed with them. Soon, it was nothing but a black band of my heartache.

Not wishing to hear anymore, I stood from the couch and returned to my room. Catherine uttered not a word; she had heard everything. Pax meowed and brushed against my legs. I scratched behind his ears.

Grabbing my long, hooded jacket, I slipped my arms through the black sleeves and clasped the silver buttons. The jacket reached down to my knees, almost concealing my body. Seating myself on the edge of my bed, I tugged my knee-high black boots on. The velvet fabric brushed against my fingers as I pulled the zipper up.

As I left my room, I approached the door.

"Natalia, it is not safe for you to travel alone." Roman braced a hand against the door.

Meeting his gaze, I said, "I am not alone."

And that was when Catherine made her grand unveiling. No one questioned her, none spoke a word. They only stared upon my ghostly companion.

"She cannot protect you, Natalia. Allow me to go with you, please." Roman's voice was pleading, his eyes cast with worry.

Taking a step toward him, I placed a kiss upon his lips. "I won't lose you again."

His hand fell away from the door, and I left this place far behind me as I ventured back into the world.

My hand slid into one of the pockets in my jacket, my fingertips brushed against cool metal. Pulling it forth, I draped the necklace over my head. My thumb brushed along the cool silver of the medallion and a shield fell around me, protecting me from any vampire that hunted for me.

My magic began to awaken from deep within my being. It filled my soul with its warmth and light. I felt as it rushed through my veins, burning brightly within me.

Then, my feet lifted from the ground and I took to the night sky.

Chapter Nineteen

Visiting Old Friends

I DRIFTED DOWN FROM the stars and landed before a small home just outside of town. Flowers and vines grew within the garden that surrounded the home, the vines creeping along the sides and nesting atop the roof. Standing before the oak gate, I raised my hand into the air. My fingertips brushed against the surface of the barrier guarding the home. The witches residing within would be alerted of my presence.

Then, as if a curtain was being pulled back, there was an opening within the barrier. I stepped through with Catherine trailing close behind me. The barrier sealed once more. The gate creaked open in welcome and I approached the door, that also opened on its own.

When I stepped inside the home, the door closed behind me and a pair of twins greeted me with welcoming smiles. "Welcome, Natalia and Catherine." Tasha wrapped me in an embrace for a breath before she stepped back.

Hello, Natalia and Catherine. Sasha signed.

"So lovely to see the two of you again." Catherine seemed to ease with comfort at the sight of the two witches.

"I've missed you both." I signed as I spoke.

Tasha smiled and draped an arm across my shoulders, "Come, let us have some tea."

I was led into their living room. Incense fogged the air, the smell of lavender and dragon's blood wafted into my nose. The scents weren't over powering, they mixed together in peace.

I seated myself upon the dark blue couch before the rectangular, oak coffee table. Catherine drifting down beside me to my left. The incense burners could be found resting atop the glossy wood. A dragon, with its jaw gaping open, exhaled the scent of dragon's blood. On the other end of the table was a thin, wooden incense burner with a stick of lavender incense stuck into the hole at the end of it. The wooden burner caught the ashes as they drifted down.

The room was bathed in a warm, golden light from the flames that flickered upon the many candle wicks within the room. There was a silver tray placed on the center of the coffee table and three candles were situated in a cluster on the center of the tray.

Two round, wooden tables were at either end of the couch I was seated upon. And brass candle holders held three red candles. The wax dripped down the sides of the slender, tall candles.

Tasha and Sasha returned to the living room, Tasha carrying a silver tray that held the tea pot and three porcelain cups. Sasha carried another tray that had an arrangement of porcelain bowls filled with little foods to snack on. They placed the trays upon the table before me.

Sasha seated herself on the dark blue chair facing one end of the coffee table and Tasha did the same on the other chair. My eyes watched as the tea pot lifted into the air and the three cups separated from each other as the tea was poured into them. The cups flew into our awaiting hands.

"What brings our favorite witch and spirit to our doorstep?" Tasha leaned back in her chair and sipped her tea.

A heavy sigh escaped me as I gazed into the tea, "The vampire queen wishes me dead and everyone connected to me."

For a moment, silence draped over the room.

Catherine did not utter a single word.

Tasha set her cup upon the table. "We heard the news of the old store manager and the incident at the bar. It had vampire written all over it."

My stomach couldn't bear anything, not even the slightest sip of tea. So, I set my cup upon the table. "My visit here is to warn you – beg you to leave town until she is finished for good."

"Oh, honey, did you honestly think we would let you face that monster alone?" Tasha let out a low chuckle. "Sasha and I are more than willing to lend our help." She stood from her chair and sat beside me. Her hands grasped mine, "Do not be afraid to ask for our help. We are here for you, dear. Always."

I glanced over at Sasha, she smiled and nodded her head. She understood, not just because she had been reading our lips, but because she is more sensitive than any witch when it comes to connections within people, the universe.

Tasha returned to her chair and I faced Sasha, *I wish to know how the village people found out of my secret. Can you show me?*

I can.

Sasha and I sat across from each other, our legs crossed, and our hands clasped together over the flame of a red candle. Around us, other candles formed within the circle. Their wicks dancing with flames that flickered in sync with one another. The incense began to burn more profusely, thickening the air within the room, their scents swirling together.

Sasha nodded her head to me, and we closed our eyes from the world. I felt her magic course between our shared hands. It filled me, warmed me. It touched my soul. From the darkness of my eyelids, I could see a faint, golden glow as Sasha summoned her magic.

And then, I was falling deep into the past.

Once more, I was an observer, a mere phantom to these people's eyes; for their eyes could never find me. My being was weightless as I soared over the village, the place I called home a lifetime ago.

My memory sparked at the familiar sightings, the familiar people.

The people that would soon burn me for my secret.

My soul was being led along the wind, tugged through the village until I came upon the largest home. This was where the richest man in the village resided, the mayor. My eyes wandered down to find a woman with golden hair glowing in the moonlight approaching the man's door. I lowered myself within hearing distance.

The door opened to reveal a heavy-set man in his sleeping clothes. His silver streaked; auburn hair mussed. "Can I help you? And, are you aware of how late it is, dear?"

As I ventured lower, a ghostly gasp escaped me as I peered upon the vampire queen's face.

A wicked smile curled at her lips. "I am aware, but this is a dire matter that could not wait till morning."

The man straightened his round spectacles. "Well, go on then."

"There is a witch living amongst us." The words dripped from her lips easily, dripped like poison. A promise of my death.

The man's brown eyes widened. "I beg your pardon? Did you say a witch?"

She nodded her head, too eagerly. "Alexandria Meriwether."

"Miss Alexandria?" He shook his head. "What a shame, she seemed like such a sweet girl."

She took a step closer to the man. "That is how they trick you. Making themselves seem innocent while a monster lurks beneath the surface."

A sigh escaped the man. I could see it within his eyes that it saddened him for what he was about to do to an innocent woman.

"Please, you must do something before she does something terrible!" She cried out, her eyes watering with false tears and fear.

He nodded his head gravely with a heavy sigh. "The witch must be burned."

The candles surrounding us were silenced as the flames dancing upon their wicks were blown out by a ghostly wind, when my eyes snapped open.

The vampire queen was responsible for my death. But, how could I not have seen it? A witch involved with the queen's son. It wouldn't have ended well, no matter what. And perhaps, it still would not.

And then I realized, Mr. Richards was not present during my burning. I did not see him amongst the crowd of cheering people, applauding the flames that devoured my body whole. Perhaps, the death of an innocent witch who never caused harm upon any living soul, was too much to bear for him. And knowing that he had sent me to my death, as if he lit that very fire himself, I wondered how he lived with that grief. That burden weighing heavily upon his shoulders.

"It was the vampire queen." I signed, "She told the villagers my secret."

Catherine lowered herself to the ground beside me. "She has killed so many, and for what purpose?" I could see the sadness surfacing within her grey eyes. I could see her falling into that dark pit of despair that I myself have known for too long.

Tasha's lips began to move but a sound did not whisper from her throat as we all gazed out the window.

Our ears listened closely to the utter stillness that draped over the world outside. Then, we heard the light footfalls of people approaching. It was then that the incense burning within the room began to shift into a red mist that drifted through the air. Tasha and Sasha shared cautious glances toward each other.

"What is it?"

Tasha stood and approached the door, followed by Sasha. "Vampires." She tossed the word over her shoulder as they stepped into the night.

I trailed behind them and stood between the twins as we took in the sight of the three vampires that stood a breath away from the barrier. One of them stood out amongst the group. Her golden hair unmistakable, that wicked grin playing upon her crimson coated lips.

"Hello, little witch." She glanced between the sisters. "Or should I say witches?" There was laughter within her voice.

"You are not welcome here." Tasha spoke.

The vampire queen raised a sculpted brow. "I am allowed wherever I please. I am Queen."

Tasha took a step forth, refusing to back down. "Queen of the dead. No queen of mine. You are unwelcomed here."

She tilted her head back as a laugh escaped her. "Oh, my dear, you'll be dead soon enough."

"No." I moved to stand before Tasha. "Leave them be. It's me you want."

"Brave little witch, aren't you? So willing to sacrifice yourself to save your friends. How noble." Her voice was coated with mockery. "Come, little witch. Come and play." Her finger beckoned me forth, her eyes dared me to cross over the edge of the barrier.

"Natalia. You will not face her alone." Tasha made to reach for me, but I took a dangerously close step to the edge.

The queen and I were within reaching distance of each other. If only I stretched my hand toward the barrier...

"You share her likeliness."

I blinked.

She laughed.

“Your mother, both of them I should say. Both fun to kill.” She traced a nail across her lips, smearing that crimson further down her chin.

“My mother…” I felt that familiar ache within my chest as my eyes drifted down to the other ring upon my first finger. The ring of my mother.

“I hunted down every woman in your family for generations to ensure that you were never reborn. But, I was too late when I found your mother. Your father was at least smart enough to hide you. But not smart enough to hide himself so cleverly.” A sigh escaped her, “I will admit that he wasn’t as fun to kill as your dear mother.”

All at once, I felt my emotions churning inside me. The rage mixed with hatred. The sadness mixed with despair. The heartache mixed with the darkness deep within me. They surged like a storm inside me, my magic responding to them, crying out.

I stared into the face of my parents’ murderer, Catherine’s murderer, Cindy’s, and my own. As I stared into her taunting eyes, I felt myself being pulled toward her. My hands itched with the need to end her life. To avenge those who were wronged by her doing, to find redemption for my shattered soul – my heart.

She took a step back and beckoned me to leave the protective barrier. “Come, Natalia, avenge your parents. Avenge your dead family. Avenge your past life.”

I took another step. The barrier just before the tip of my nose.

"Natalia, don't listen to her." Tasha stood beside me. "She is only taunting you. Do not fall for her tricks."

I met her gaze. "Even so, she won't leave this place until I do. I'll lead her away from here, you and Sasha stay here. I cannot lose more people that I care about."

Laughter erupted into the air. "Oh, don't worry my dear Natalia, we'll come back for your friends." Her tongue slithered across her bottom lip, "Vampires do love witches' blood. It's so *sweet.*" She seemed to moan as if she could taste our sweetness now.

Fingers entwined with my own. To the right of me, I met Tasha's fiery auburn eyes. To the left, Sasha smiled as she inclined her head.

Together. We would face the vampire queen together.

We stepped forth through the barrier. I felt as it tugged on our bodies as if pleading for us to return to its safety.

"I'll find great pleasure in killing you, little witch. Come, let us play."

The other two vampires spread out on either side of her, their eyes finding the twins. I was the queen's kill and no others. And she would be mine.

Within my being, I allowed my magic to erupt, breaking free of its prison in my core. It flared alive and coursed through my veins like molten lava. It was electric and fiery all at once. And I would use every ounce of it to bring the vampire queen to her death.

Beside me, I felt the twins awaken their magic as well. It sang through the air, mine meeting with it. When I glanced over at the women, I saw that their fiery eyes were bright with magic, golden streams of it flowing within their irises. And I knew mine were alive with magic as well.

Then, the vampires sprang into action, leaping toward the twins, their eyes turning into vast pools of darkness. Hisses echoed through the air as the vampires snapped at the twins with their fangs. Sasha and Tasha leapt into the air, dancing with the wind. Their hands were a golden halo as their magic shot forth toward the creatures.

A cry of pain escaped the male as the magic met with his flesh, it sizzled and smoked, melting away to reveal the white bones beneath the surface. A grin tugged at Tasha's lips. The vampire snarled and lunged at the woman. But she evaded the attack gracefully, twirling through the air.

My attention was drawn away from the twins fight as fingers snapped. "Your focus is on me, little witch. I wish to play before I drain the life from your pretty neck."

The skin upon my hands warmed as halos of golden light encircled them. "I refuse to die by your hands."

She leaned into a crouch, her eyes transforming into darkness. Her tongue slithered across her sharp fangs. "We shall see."

In a blur of motion, she lunged. My body lifted into the air, dodging the vampire queen's nails by a breath. She whipped around and launched herself into the air. I ducked and found myself beneath her. Raising my hands, I unleashed that golden light. Streams of molten light erupted into the darkness and aimed themselves at the woman. Her dark eyes went wide as she tried to escape my magic.

When her voice cried out, I knew part of the attack had hit its target. But only part. My eyes gazed upon her ruined leg, flesh breaking free and revealing bone. Crimson dripped down the length of her pale leg, raining down upon the earth below.

Her eyes were alit with rage, her lips pulled back thinly as a snarl escaped her. *"You'll pay for that, witch!"*

I was too slow as I tried to evade her attack. Her sharp nails had caught me across the cheek. They raked my flesh, peeling it apart. A burning pain encased the side of my face. A wetness began to drip along my jaw and down my neck as my wound wept with blood.

"I'll scar that pretty face of yours!"

She made to swipe at me again, but I thrust my hands before me, and a force of wind rushed toward the vampire queen and sent her tumbling backward through the air.

For a moment, I drifted there within the air, gazing upon my own hands. By now, my magic would be draining my energy. By now, I would be panting for breath, sweat dripping down my body. But I felt stronger than I ever have before. Perhaps since I unlocked my memories, I unlocked magic I did not know I had stored deep within my soul. A shouted cry found its way to my ears. My gaze drifted toward the twins ongoing fight.

Tasha had been tackled from the air, the two tumbling down toward the earth. Sasha's eyes widened as they watched her sister fall. Her brow creased as she thrust one hand forward toward the female vampire rushing at her. Roots erupted from the ground and tangled themselves around the vampire. She screeched as she struggled against the roots hold.

Then, Sasha bolted through the air in a blur, hands aglow with magic. She latched on to the vampire male's shoulders, her magic burning through his flesh. A howl of pain escaped him as he let Tasha go free.

The twins lowered to the ground. Tasha reached a hand toward her neck; crimson coated her fingers. Her eyes turned into slits. "They have stolen from me. Witches blood is a sacred thing and they have *stolen* it." She hissed.

Tasha would not be turned, not unless the vampire had bitten his own tongue and transferred his blood into her vein.

The vampires stood before them, the male having a cocky, bloody grin upon his face. "You are nothing but food, dessert, nothing about your kind is sacred."

Tasha straightened herself, Sasha's hands raised into the air, ready to unleash her magic. "Our magic is linked into our blood, our hearts. That is why it tastes sweet to you thieves. You drink what you cannot ever have, you steal because you shall never have powers like ours."

The air shifted around the twins. A faint, golden glow wrapping around their bodies. Their braids slithered through the air, their auburn eyes had shifted and changed as if mini suns had been hidden there all along.

"Your kind is powerless, *weak.* And that is why you hunt us, thieves."

The ground trembled beneath the women, the Earth responding to their powerful magic. Roots and vines erupted through the soil and danced within the air behind the twins.

Tasha turned her golden gaze upon me. She seemed no longer an ordinary witch. It was as if her very being, her soul, had transformed into something ethereal. As if she had become the embodiment of a goddess.

"This is the true power of us witches," She spoke to the vampires but kept her gaze locked with mine, "You hunt us not only because you cannot have our power but because you fear it. Fear what we become when we allow our magic to engulf us entire." Now, her words were directed toward me. "Awaken, Natalia. Not just your past life, but your magic. *Your soul.*"

My magic stirred at the command, seeming to beg to be set free – unleashed.

"She will not have the time to do so!" The vampire queen's voice reverberated through the air as she lunged herself at me.

Before her hands could reach me, a barrier draped itself between us, her claws met with magic.

"Go now, Natalia. We shall ensure they won't follow you."

I met Tasha's gaze again, "No, I cannot leave you to fight them alone. This is my battle as well."

She shook her head. "Your magic must be unleashed, too big a portion of it was hidden away with your memories. For now, go. We can handle ourselves just fine."

My eyes glanced over to Sasha. She inclined her head.

"We shall meet again." I took a step back.

Tasha smiled, "Of course, my dear. We do not plan on dying anytime soon."

As I lifted into the air and disappeared into the darkness, the vampire queen's screams chased me through the stars.

Chapter Twenty

Masquerade of Dreams

WHEN I HAD returned to Roman's home, the door flung open and instantly, I was wrapped in the embrace of my past lover. His breathing was uneven, panicked. He held me as if he would never let me go again, afraid he might lose me if he did.

My arms wrapped themselves around him, "I'm here." My voice whispered to him.

It was a long moment before he answered, his voice rasped, "I was terrified."

"I'm okay, Roman. I'm right here, with you."

He pulled his head back enough to stare into my eyes, the intensity I found within them held me in place, stopping my breathing for a moment.

His hand left my back and stroked my cheek tenderly, his touch so gentle as if he feared breaking me. "I'm aware of your strength, Natalia. But that night I found you laying there and that vampire so close to killing you, I had so much fear swelling within me." His eyes refused to leave mine, "I feared that I had lost you. And I knew I would not survive a loss like that again. It would utterly destroy me, and I would become a monster that would no longer recognize who I was, no one would."

My hand grabbed his and moved it from my cheek down to my chest and pressed it against my skin. His fingers lingered there above my heart, feeling its rhythmic beat. "I vow that you will not lose me, not in this life. Not ever. My heart and soul have been yours Roman, since that first night we met in the past and in this life."

With his other hand, he gently tilted my chin upward. He leaned down; his lips were a breath away from mine. "My peace." He uttered against my lips before pressing his own over them.

We had been too absorbed within one another to notice that Sakiya had approached us. Our lips broke free from their dance but Roman never let me go. His arms still wrapped me within their tight embrace.

And as her eyes wandered down to my other cheek that had been covered by my hair, that was when roman's gaze fell there as well. Delicately, he brushed the purple strands of hair that had concealed my wound. I flinched slightly as his fingertips had come in to contact with the scratches that marred my cheek.

"Natalia, what happened?" His voice was low and soft, but I could feel the anger awakening inside him.

My gaze broke free of his, "Your mother."

And at the mention of his mother, his hold on me had tightened and something roared to life in his ghostly eyes. *"What has she done?"* There was a growl in his throat, as if he fought that very monster, he feared he would become.

"She found me at the home of twin witches, my friends. She wished to kill me, kill them." I took my bottom lip between my teeth, "She'll never stop hunting for me. She'll kill me in every life if she has too until I cease being reborn."

"I won't allow that to happen. I will protect you, Natalia."

But I could see the fear and doubt lingering within his gaze. As if he were asking himself, *can I truly protect her?* And as his eyes flickered down to my cheek, it was as if they answered him in a mocking way. *No, you'll always fail.* They would say to him.

My hands found themselves upon his cheeks, forcing his gaze away from the wounds. "You did not fail me, do not think that for a single breath. We will stop her. We will."

"And do we have a plan in mind? Or are we going in blind?" Sakiya spoke up, crossing her arms over her chest.

Aron took a step beside her and wrapped an arm around her waist, resting his hand on her hip. "Going in blind sounds a bit more fun, don't you think? Leave room for a little surprise and excitement."

She cut a sideward glance at the werewolf. "Or leave us drowning in our own blood."

"See? Exciting." He winked a brown eye.

Sakiya shook her head, but there was a faint smile upon her lips. "So?"

Roman's gaze shifted over to the pair standing before us, "The masquerade." He looked upon me again, "That's where we'll face my mother."

"A room full of blood sucking thieves? Now that sounds really exciting."

Sakiya rolled her eyes as a scoff escaped her lips. "You must have a death wish, fool." She glanced over at Roman with a brow raised, "Both of you do. Do you honestly think we'll stand a chance against some of the oldest vampires we know?"

I could see the disbelief surfacing within Roman's face, but hope flared much brighter. "I believe we stand a chance. Many vampires are not happy serving beneath my mother's rule."

Aron cracked a wide smile of approval. "Thinking about starting a revolt at the party?"

"I am. And it'll be a party to remember."

Aron cracked his knuckles. "I'm ready to sink some teeth into those blood suckers."

Sakiya sighed and rolled her eyes. "You fools are going to get us all killed, you know that?" Then, a smile appeared upon her lips. "But I'm willing to fight and die if it means taking down the queen. She's ruled for far too long."

"So, when shall we be expecting to receive our gracious invitations?" Aron questioned.

Roman glanced back to me. "We won't need invitations."

Aron raised a brow, "Crashing the party as it begins?"

"Mother won't suspect Sakiya as a traitor. She will be expecting me and Natalia to be appearing as my guest." Roman approached the werewolf and clapped a hand on his shoulder. "You, my friend, shall be one hell of a surprise."

"Now, I do like the sound of that." He grinned his approval.

I was surrounded again. My stomach aching with crippling pain. Down to the floor I fell. The monsters had circled me, ready to devour my body and soul whole. Their faces were a blur, my ears ringing, head spinning. It felt as though I were suffocating, my heart then began to roar within my ears. My head echoed with the sound of the rushing beat.

A voice screaming out that morphed into the sound of a growl erupted through my deafened ears. The monsters stepped back; arms wrapped around my body protectively. The voice spoke to me, but I could not understand their words. I felt as their hand brushed the hair away from my neck...

I woke with a jolt, startled from my nightmare that had returned. My knees curled up to my chest as my arms wrapped around them. I had thought that the nightmare had gone but it came back to remind me of the death that would soon capture my soul.

Catherine appeared beside my bed; her ghostly brow creased. "It has returned." She spoke quietly.

I only nodded my head. But then, something formed together within my mind. The last piece of the puzzle fitting together.

"The masquerade." I breathed, my voice barely a whisper.

Catherine seated herself on the edge of the bed. "What?"

I met her grey eyes, "My nightmare. My future. That's when it shall come true." I cast my gaze away from hers. "That's when I'll die."

Her eyes widened, "You cannot go!"

I shook my head. "I must. If it means putting an end to the queen, then I'm going. I must see this through."

"My friend..." She looked as though she wanted to cry but could no longer do so. "Are you going to tell Roman? Are you sure there is no other way?"

Roman.

My heart ached. The tears began to burn behind my eyes. "He cannot know. He will forbid me to go."

"I wish you would remain behind, but I know you won't. You are beyond stubborn sometimes." She chuckled lightly but there was pain within the forced laughter.

"Hey, I'll have you to guide me in the afterlife. Teach me all about being a ghost and ghostly things." I smiled.

"Ghostly things? You sound like you did when you were ten. Always asking me to do 'ghostly things'." She returned the smile. Then, her gaze turned serious as she reached a ghostly hand toward mine, "Do not fear of being alone when death comes, for I will be here at the end of life, waiting with an offered hand."

"Thank you, dear friend."

THE MOTHER

"You have failed, again. Why am I not surprised?" Mother's fingernail tapped upon the wine glass she held within her grasp.

"Those witches are more powerful than any I have ever seen, *mother.*" My arm hung uselessly by my side, my skin and bone slowly healing. The muscles lacing together once more, the bone cracking and forming.

Mother's face hardened as she stared into the flames that crackled within the fireplace. "Vampires are the strongest creatures on this earth, and you have allowed yourself to be defeated by our *food.* Failure is all that I see here."

I approached the long, oak table on the other side of the room. It was situated against the wall with a crimson table cloth draped over it. An assortment of wines was lined across it along with a rack of crystal glasses. Ignoring the glasses, I grabbed a bottle of red wine and ripped the cork free, bringing the bottle to my lips.

"You act as though you are the most perfect creature on this earth, mother."

She turned her head around the chair and glared at me, her mouth set into a scowl. "You dare speak to me in that way?"

My free hand rested on the table, my nails growing in length. "It's an observation."

She stood from her chair, still holding that glass in her hand. "I am perfect because I make no mistakes, except for one; crowning you queen. That is my only failure."

My head tilted back as laughter escaped me. "Your only failure? That is possibly the largest lie I have ever heard."

Her grip tightened on the glass. "There is no lie there. And I suggest you cease speaking to me in such a way."

I straightened my back and raised a brow. "And what will you do if I don't stop? I am queen here, not you, mother. You gave that title away long ago. You have no power here. No rule here. Your words mean *nothing.* You are *nothing.*"

I could see her confidence waver as she backed down. "When that witch comes to claim your life, I will not be there to stop her."

"And you think she will not claim yours?" I approached my mother and whispered into her ear. "You will be granted no protection from my guards. You will fend for yourself. And the little witch will be mine to claim. Good riddance, mother."

Her mouth gaped open, "How dare you..."

And it was then that I had decided to truly cut ties with my mother. My nails lashed out and tore into her pale throat. My mother's eyes widened as her hands grasped at the spraying wound. Warm liquid had coated my face before she fell to her knees.

Crimson began to stain the wooden floor. She gurgled, trying to form words. I guessed she were cursing me, but I didn't care. I enjoyed watching the life drain from her, as it pooled and inched toward my feet.

She fell onto her back, her gaze meeting mine. I knelt beside her and brushed her golden hair away from her face. "Who is the failure now, mother?"

Her wound wouldn't have time to heal. My nails had cut too deeply. I smiled upon my mother's dying face. As I stroked my mother's pale cheek, I realized I should have done this long ago.

Knock. Knock.

I stood from the ground and straightened my clothes. "Come in."

The door opened to reveal Sakiya. Immediately, her eyes were drawn to the scene that lay before my feet. I glided across the room, stepping over my mother's corpse, and stood before her. My hands cupped her face, one of them staining her cheek with my mother's blood. I felt her tremble within my grasp.

"Ah, my dear Sakiya."

She lowered her gaze, "My Queen."

"Be a good little pet and find my son, tell him the masquerade will be hosted on a different date this year."

"What date shall I tell him, My Queen?"

I tucked a strand of midnight hair behind her ear. "October twentieth."

THE WITCH

Sakiya had left hours ago to return to the vampire queen. Hoping to gather any information that would aid us in our attack. I tossed and turned in my bed, sleep refusing to claim me. My mind had raced with a thousand thoughts. I wondered if the twins were alive but deep within my soul, I knew they were. They had to be.

It seemed my mind would not ease anytime soon. Sleep would continue to evade me throughout the night. With a sigh, I tossed the blanket off my body and swung my legs over the side of my bed.

Catherine gave me a questioning glance but said nothing. Opening my door, I stepped into the narrow hallway. My eyes drifted toward Roman's door. Steadying my trembling hands, I approached and lightly knocked upon it.

Within a heartbeat, the door opened, and there he stood, shirtless. Words had left me. His hair fell into his ghostly eyes. His sweatpants hung low and loosely at his waist. And though I had seen him naked before, made love to this man, he still captivated me.

"Are you having trouble sleeping?" His voice was raspy.

I nodded my head. "It seems vampires favor the late hours of the night, so I thought I would bother you."

He grinned and stepped aside, "You are never a bother, Natalia."

Once I had stepped foot into his room, he closed the door. We were alone within his bedroom. My eyes wandered about, there was only a bed, a dresser, and a door that led to I guessed a closet. And that was all. There was no window within the room. He was completely shut out from the world in here.

My room was much the same except for my furry companion and my ghostly one. Except for the window that allowed the sun to bathe me in its light.

"It seems so lonely in here." I whispered, my back still facing him.

I could feel him behind me, his breathing just behind my ear. His breath was warm against my hair. "Vampires tend to live lonely lives." There was a sadness within his voice.

Finally, I turned to face him. Our gazes meeting. My hand reached for him and cupped his cheek. He stilled at my touch. "But loneliness is not what you wish for, Roman."

He leaned into the palm of my hand, closing his eyes, and taking in my scent. "I wished for you." My heart ached at the pain in his words. "Every night and every day you were all I wished for, Natalia." His eyes opened once more, "And I had begun to lose faith, in hope. That you would never return." He closed the small distance between us, his hands resting upon my hips, his gaze devouring mine. "And then, you returned. My wish had finally been granted. You could be mine once more, if you wished it." Then, he stopped himself, "Do you?"

"Was there ever a doubt?"

He chuckled, "You did seem to hate me when we first met, my love."

Butterflies seemed to stir within me as he called me that. "I blame that on memory loss, forgive me." I batted my lashes.

His smile was soft. His hand reached out and brushed my hair behind my ear. "Always."

The tenderness in his voice – in his eyes – caused my chest to tighten. My hands found themselves resting on the back of his neck, my fingers playing with the ends of his hair.

Once more, memories played before me. Moments stolen beneath the stars. Wrapped in one another's embrace, smiling warmly at each other, fingers lost within locks of hair.

My heart seemed to cry out for those moments that had been lost, stolen from us all too soon. As I stared into Roman's face, I had decided that we no longer needed to wait for those precious moments. I no longer needed to hold myself back from him. My heart and soul knew him. And piece by piece my memories were returning to me. This man was my other half. My soul had searched for his after death and found him once more.

I once found myself disbelieving in soul mates, destiny, or fate. Before my past life memories had been awakened. But staring into his eyes now, told me that soulmates could be true. That our love was true and strong. And that together, we could survive his mother and whatever fight was thrown our way. We were strong apart, but we were stronger together.

"I love you." And the words that escaped my lips were the truest words I have ever spoken.

Roman stilled, his breathing almost silenced.

He had been waiting to hear my lips whisper those sweet words to him for so long. Thinking he might never hear them again. And now, here we were.

His hands slowly lifted from my hips and gently cupped either side of my face. His thumbs stroked my cheeks. And within his eyes, I found silver lining them. "I've waited so long to hear you say those words." His voice trembled. "I love you, my Natalia."

And then, his lips had greeted mine.

The kiss was different than the one we had shared on the couch. It seemed more intimate – as if we had finally allowed our hearts to greet one another again. My hands had found themselves in his soft hair, tangling with his locks. His own hands gripped my sides and hugged my body closer to his. I took a step back, bringing him with me. He followed my steps till the backs of my legs met with his bed.

It was only then that he had broken the kiss, his hand reaching for my cheek once more and gently stroking it. As if I were the most precious thing on this earth.

His eyes glanced toward the bed briefly before meeting with my gaze once more. "Natalia, I do not want you to feel as though you have to do this."

"I want too, Roman. I wish to share this night with you, to share my body with yours." Raising onto the tips of my toes, I placed a kiss upon his lips. "I wish to open my heart to you again. In this life. I wish to be yours."

"There is nothing that I want more in this world, than to have you by my side. I am yours, Natalia. All of me – everything I can give – belongs to you."

My chest ached with warmth. "Your love is the only gift I need."

"And that gift is yours."

Then, our arms tangled around each other as our lips met in a passionate dance. Our bodies fell back onto the bed.

I do not remember when or how our clothes had left us, but I felt his bare skin against mine. Warm and soft. I felt his hot breath in the nape of my neck where he had buried his face in my purple hair. My hands traced along his back, my nails just barely grazing his skin. His lips pressed against my neck and warmth blossomed at the spot.

My skin had remembered his – the feel of it against mine, the heat of it. Our rhythm was like a melody, gentle and paced. We took time savoring this moment, savoring each other.

As our lips met and I had melted into the kiss – into the taste of him, my chest had exploded in a fiery warmth. It spread throughout my veins and captivated my body.

The night had passed while we had made love.

A love that was sweet and gentle. We were brought together once more after too many long years and we wanted to take this time to savor the moment, each other. Because it seemed as though both of us believed this to only be a dream, that it couldn't be real.

But, it was.

Chapter Twenty One

Troubling News

THE WEREWOLF

THE DOOR HAD swung open and Sakiya had entered the room. The steel wall groaned as the door slammed shut. When those dark eyes of hers took me in, I saw the crimson marking her face.

I lunged from the couch; a growl had rumbled within my chest. My lips pulling back into a snarl. "What has the bitch done this time?"

As if remembering the blood on her face, she wiped it off with the back of her hand. "Where's Roman?"

Before I could answer, her head snapped in the direction of his door. She began to march down the hall, but I grasped her hand. She whipped around to face me, her bangs swaying before falling back into her dark eyes.

"*Let go of me.*" She snarled.

I shook my head, "Sorry, my dear vampire lover. But I cannot."

She raised a brow. "Really now? How about I break that arm of yours?"

"Whatever terrible news you bring, can wait till the morning."

She opened her mouth to speak but I covered her lips with my own. Her anger seemed to ease, and her body melted against mine as a sigh escaped her lips. When I pulled back, I grinned at her.

"You animal." She rolled her eyes.

"Feel better, my dear?"

She crossed her arms over her chest. "I hate it when you do that, Aron." But there was a faint smile upon her lips.

"You hate that I can so easily calm you."

She waved a hand in the air, "I really need to talk to Roman."

"And I believe that the news can wait, Sakiya."

Before she could say anything, her ears listened. Her gaze ventured down the hallway toward Roman's closed door. A sigh escaped her.

I took a step toward her and cupped her cheek. "Allow them this one night of peace, save the news for the morning."

A sigh escaped her as she nodded her head. "He's waited too long for her, I won't take this night from them."

My lips pressed against the crown of her head.

Then, I felt her hands glide up my chest and resting at the back of my neck. I looked down upon her and placed my hands upon her hips, bringing her body closer to mine.

"If they are allowed a night of peace, are we allowed the same?" Her eyes lingered upon my lips.

A smile flashed across of my face, "Would it truly be a night of peace, my dear?"

A light laugh escaped her. And for a moment, I was taken back by her beauty. By the way her face had eased and the pain she was hiding away had vanished. Leaving only that perfect smile of hers, that light within her dark eyes.

"You truly are an animal." As she said this, she took my bottom lip between her teeth and tugged.

A pleasurable growl had rumbled within my chest. "Would you have me any other way?"

"Never." And she placed her lips against mine.

THE VAMPIRE

Natalia was sound asleep, the black sheet draped across her pale body. Beneath her eyelids, her eyes fluttered as she dreamed. Light breathing escaped her, her chest slowly rising and falling with every breath. Purple hair splayed across the pillow beneath her head, some falling across her face.

Gently, I tucked the stray strand of hair behind her ear. Her skin was silky to the touch. It had been many years since I last felt her skin, how soft it was. Many years since I felt her body against mine, her lips, to have those beautiful blue eyes of hers staring back at me. Many years since I've heard the sweetest words escape her lips. My heart was filled with such joy when I heard her speak those words that I felt my knees would give out beneath me. Leaning down, I placed a gentle kiss upon her forehead and carefully moved from the bed.

Once I had dressed myself, I headed out of the room, closing the door behind me quietly. As I ventured down the hall, I found Sakiya and Aron waiting for me on the couch. I could tell by their faces that something was wrong.

"What happened?" The words were almost a growl.

Sakiya glanced at Aron and then back to me, a sigh escaped her. She stood from the couch and approached me. "It's your mother."

My jaw clenched. "What has she done?"

Her hands grasped mine. "What I'm about to tell you, will upset you. I need your word, right now, that you will *not* rush out of here in a fit of blinded rage." Her dark eyes narrowed, "Do I have your word, Roman?"

My body tensed. Slowly, I nodded my head.

Aron moved from the couch and stood before the door, making sure that I wouldn't run.

"Your mother has changed the date of the masquerade."

I raised a brow, "Why would that upset me?"

Sakiya cast an uneasy glance over her shoulder at Aron. He nodded his head, his arms falling to his sides, readying himself.

Her gaze met mine once more, hesitation appearing on her face. "October twentieth."

The walls trembled as a roar sounded through the air.

THE WITCH

A sound had awakened me from my sleep, causing me to tumble away from my ever-sweet dreams. My lids fluttered open; my hands reached for a body that was no longer there.

The sound erupted again.

I sat up in the bed. "Roman?" My voice called out.

The answer I received was another loud sound and voices shouting. Tossing the cover off my body – not caring of my naked being - I slung open the door and hurried down the hall. My eyes took in the sight before me. Sakiya and Aron had Roman by the arms. A terrible sound surged from him. It rung in my ears. It sounded like a caged animal crying to be set free, roaring at its captors.

And when they turned toward me, I took a step back.

Roman's eyes had changed into that vast darkness. Fangs had lengthened and revealed themselves. His face was contorted in rage, anger, as he tried to fight free of their holds.

Sakiya's eyes found mine. "Natalia, you do not need to see this."

I took a step forward. "What's happened to him?"

She shook her head, "Please, go back to the room. He wouldn't want you to see him like this."

Another step. "Why do you speak as though he doesn't understand?"

Aron answered, "Because, little witch, he can't."

My eyes glanced back at Roman, the beast that had been set free. My chest tightened. "What do you mean?"

"He's only been like this once before." Sakiya spoke as she struggled to keep her hold on him.

A snarl rippled through the air as Roman snapped his fangs at Sakiya. A growl answered him and Roman turned his gaze toward Aron.

"When you died, this is what he became; a beast blinded with rage." She finished.

I stepped closer. "What caused this?"

"His bitch of a mother." Aron answered.

Another step brought me a hand's reach away from Roman. His eyes met mine, but I could see that he did not recognize who I was. Who either of us were.

"She planned the masquerade on the day you died, Natalia." Sakiya answered, "As a taunt, a reminder."

My hand reached toward him, but he snapped at my fingers. I drew my hand back with a yelp. He glared at me with those dark eyes of his, I saw myself in his gaze. A terrified woman was all I appeared to him, possibly an enemy.

But I had told him once before that I did not fear him. And looking into his eyes now, I still held no fear. Straightening my spine, I stepped closer to him and reached for him once more.

"Natalia, you might not want to do that if you wish to keep those fingers." Aron said.

I raised my brow, "How else would you calm him?"

The werewolf shrugged, "I planned on knocking him out."

"Brute." Sakiya rolled her eyes.

This time, I held Roman's gaze. My hands reached for his face slowly. "Remember me." I spoke gently.

His lips pulled back as a snarl escaped him, his fangs flashed before my eyes. But, he did not bite at me.

"Remember me." I repeated.

My magic began to stir within me as I summoned upon it. Its fragrance filled the air as it draped around us. Roman seemed to ease a bit as he took in the sweet scent. My hands cupped his face within my palms. His breathing had slowed as he held my gaze. The snarls ceased.

"Roman." I whispered his name tenderly.

His black eyes blinked slowly as he began to remember. His face softened, the wrinkles of rage fading away, his fangs disappearing. And I found myself looking into eyes of blue.

A smile formed upon my lips, "There you are."

Aron and Sakiya released Roman's arms. His hands formed over my own. His fingers gliding across my skin. Roman closed his eyes and breathed in my scent. "My Peace." His voice whispered.

My heart warmed.

His hands dropped from mine and cupped my face. His thumbs brushed against my cheeks, his gaze holding me in place. Roman's eyes glanced at every aspect of my face, taking in every detail.

"I'm so sorry you had to see me in that way, Natalia." He shook his head, "I was a monster."

My fingers wrapped around his wrists, "You are no monster, Roman."

"My mother knows how to bring the darkness out in me." His lips brushed against my forehead, "But you know how to bring the light back."

My arms wrapped around his waist as I pulled him to me. My head nuzzled against his chest, his heartbeat against my ear. I felt his chin rest atop my head as his arms tightly wound around me. He released a heavy sigh, his breath warm against my hair.

"What are we going to do?" I heard defeat in his voice.

"I thought we were crashing the party?" Aron said.

I heard footsteps growing distant. "I'm going back to your mother; I have to tell her I delivered the news." She paused, "And how you took it."

There was silence for a moment before Aron shattered it. "I'm tagging along. There's something I need to do too."

"And what's that?" The door creaked open.

I glanced toward the couple; Aron winked a brown eye. "Werewolf stuff."

With a roll of Sakiya's eyes, they left.

THE MOTHER

The woman was knelt before my chair, the fire crackling behind her. Her midnight hair cascaded down her shoulders, her bangs hiding her eyes as her head was bowed.

"I have told Roman of the changed date, my queen."

My nails traced along the fabric of the chair arm. "Good. How did my dear son react to it?"

"He lashed out in rage."

My brow raised as a smile quirked at the corner of my lips. "Did he become the monster that he's meant to be?"

She nodded her head. "He was no longer Roman; he was a monster. The thing he became when she was killed."

Laughter erupted from my lips, causing the woman's dark eyes to glance at me. Leaning down, my hand cupped around her cheek. "You've always been such a devoted servant to me, my dear Sakiya."

She swallowed.

I smiled.

My lips brushed against her forehead before they moved down to her ear. "But, I know where your heart truly lies."

I heard her heart quicken its beat.

"That dog will be dealt with soon enough, but I'll allow your play time, for now. Soon it will come to an end. A bloody one." My lips lingered before her ear for a moment. I drew back, my fingers brushing her midnight hair behind her ear. A smile coating my lips. "Goodnight, my little samurai."

My hand fell away as she shakenly stood, "Goodnight, my queen."

Chapter Twenty Two

A Warrior

ARON AND ROMAN had left for the evening, venturing out into the darkness of the night. Into whatever danger would be waiting for them. I had watched their silhouettes disappear into the night; my heart ached when I could no longer see Roman's figure.

At my ankles, Pax purred and rubbed his head against my shin. His fur was soft against my legs. A smile tugging at my lips as I knelt down to pet my furry companion.

"You worry too much, even Pax can sense that." Catherine spoke from the couch, she hovered above the arm of it, ankles crossed.

I glanced over my shoulder, "Until the queen is dealt with, I'll continue to worry."

"Do you still refuse to tell Roman?"

I looked away from her then and gathered Pax into my arms, cradling him close. "You know my answer hasn't changed. I cannot change the future and I will not stay away from a fight that is also mine."

A sigh sounded from her, "I wish I had that sort of bravery."

Rising to my feet, I approached her with a smile. "You befriended a witch in a time where that would have gotten you burned alongside me. That, is bravery."

She smiled.

When the door opened, Catherine vanished, and Pax leapt from my arms. Sakiya strode into the room, her eyes distant. She seated herself on the couch, propping her elbow on the arm, and rubbing her forehead with her fingers.

"What's wrong?" I sat beside her.

She didn't look at me. "She must be stopped."

"What's she done?"

A sarcastic laugh escaped her, and I could hear the pain and fear within it. "What hasn't she done?" A sigh escaped her. "She knows about Aron and I and I wonder just how long she's known. How long she's known of the night I let him go free." She closed her eyes then, "How long until I can be free?"

"We'll stop her, Sakiya. We will."

Her eyes opened, and she glanced at me. Her hand falling away from her forehead. "Do you know how I came to be the queen's favorite? How I came to be a vampire?"

I shook my head, "No." Though, I always wondered.

Her eyes moved toward the window, her gaze growing vacant as she stared out into the night. "It was long ago, I was young then, still human when she had found me. Fifteen or sixteen, I cannot truly remember. I was becoming one of the best Onna Bugeisha in my village." A faint smile appeared on her lips, her eyes softening as she fell into her memories.

"Onna Bugeisha?" I asked curiously.

Her eyes found mine and her smile widened, "A female warrior." But that smile faded and her eyes drifted away, "The queen had traveled to Japan in search of a servant, someone who would be loyal to her, someone who was strong who could protect her." A scoff sounded from her lips, "She was looking for a pet, a prized possession of novelty." Sakiya's hands formed into fists. "She went from village to village, through towns, searching for a warrior worthy to protect her. Then, she caught news of a young and promising Onna Bugeisha – me."

She took in a breath and her eyes closed. "She searched for me until she found me. When night had fallen across the land and I was sound asleep, she crept into my room and turned me. I remember waking in pain, crying out. I tried to fight her off but of course she was too strong. And, I have been her servant ever since that fateful night."

My chest was tight with pain and sorrow. "How horrible..."

When her eyes opened once more, she began picking at her nails, "She calls me her little samurai as a mockery. A slap to the face because I was never able to truly become an Onna Bugeisha. She had taken that away from me, taken my life away from me."

I met her gaze, there was pity in her own eyes. "I suppose we are similar in that way – the queen stole my life from me and stole one from you."

Catherine appeared then, lingering in the hall. Her ghostly form floating within the air. The frayed ends of her dress swayed as if they were in water, her hair doing the same. "And my life, as well." She added to the conversation.

Sakiya gazed upon the ghostly woman. Her brow creased as she shook her head. "And many others." She sighed. "I understand if you feel a hatred toward me, Natalia. For the murders of your friends. I don't know if I ever told you how deeply sorry I am, I wish I could say I had no other choice – but we all have a choice and I had chosen wrong."

My hands reached for hers and grasped them. My heart did ache for the people that had been lost to this world but there was no hatred within it. "Those deaths are on the queen's hands, not yours. Yes, there was a choice, but the choice was probably death and then they would all have been killed anyways. That's how she works, you know that, I know that. So, I do not blame you nor do I hate you, Sakiya."

Water lined her eyes as she gazed upon our clasped hands. "I never was given the chance to know you in your past life, but I am glad to know you in this one, Natalia."

"I'm glad to know you as well." I offered a smile.

And she returned it.

The door opened. Aron waltzed in, his brown eyes taking in our joined hands. "Did I ruin a moment?"

Sakiya rolled her eyes, "As usual."

Aron bowed low at the waist, "Apologies, my dear vampire lover, and little witch."

Roman stepped beside the werewolf and clasped a hand on the man's shoulder, "Why don't we let the girls have some private time?"

Aron straightened himself and stood beside his friend, draping an arm across roman's shoulders. "I could use a drink, what about you, Roman? I know you vampires are always thirsty."

Roman had told me of his nightly routine, that he did in fact drink blood from humans. But he never killed. But he also told me how hard it was to suppress the beast that lurked deep inside him, how it howled for the kill, for the final drop of that sweet blood it craved so fiercely.

A chuckle sounded from Roman as he brushed Aron's arm off, "Always." Then, his blue gaze found mine as he approached the couch where we sat. Bending low, his lips brushed against my forehead. "We'll return soon."

"Be safe." I whispered to him.

He smiled before the duo closed the door behind them. Sakiya turned her attention toward me, "I know witches have certain powers. And I wonder, if you could see into my memories? I would like to show you the days of when I trained to be an Onna Bugeisha."

I offered my hands to her, palms up. Tasha and Sasha had ventured through my past life memories, I remember the ritual – the candles and the smell of burning sage – but I doubted I would need such to glimpse into her memories, they wouldn't be locked away like mine had been.

My heart tugged at the thought of the twins. But, I knew they were alive – within my heart I knew. They were strong, and they would not die so easily.

Sakiya's hands lay atop my own, with a smile to her, I closed my eyes. Taking in a breath, I tapped into that well of magic deep within me – awakening it. It churned at my command and spilled out into my being. My veins warmed as it flowed like a molten river. There was a gasp of breath from Sakiya – not of pain but of surprise. Perhaps she has never truly allowed a witch to work magic on her.

At first, it proved hard to enter her memories as she fought against my magic. It was as if she had erected a barrier across her mind. My magic wrapped around it, calming and soothing. I could have forced my way through, but I chose not to. I wished for Sakiya to trust me, to open up to me. So, I allowed her to ease the barrier on her own. Then, the barrier began to fall away as I was allowed inside her mind.

THE ONNA BUGEISHA

Sakiya and I had entered into the memory of her choosing, walking along that bright path together. We emerged into bright sunlight, a cool breeze that wrapped around our beings and whispered through our hair. Pink petals drifted lazily along the wind, fluttering within the air, spiraling and dancing.

To my side, Sakiya stood, a reminiscent smile upon her face as her eyes took in the sight before her. Tears seemed to glisten within the corners of her dark eyes. My hand found hers and gently squeezed.

"This field was my sanctuary. I came here often as a girl after my parents had passed in battle." She gazed around her upon the many trees that surrounded us. "Often times I came here in solitude to practice what I had learned in my training."

Then, a figure appeared, cresting over the top of a hill. Sakiya's smile widened as the figure made its way toward the center of the field – of the trees. It was a young woman, midnight hair intricately braided down her back.

"That was my mother's kimono." Sakiya's voice had a gleam to it – the old memories resurfacing and the feelings that came along with them.

The kimono was simple yet beautiful. Black with pink and red flowers sewn across the dark silk, the vibrant colors standing out almost like stars against the night sky.

"My grandmother gifted it to me on the eve of my fourteenth birthday." My eyes then found the weapon that the woman carried with her. The shaft of it was long and dark, with a sharpened blade at one end that seemed to have a lethal curve to it. "And the naginata there, was my father's."

The past Sakiya raised the weapon before her – grasping it with both hands – and the blade sliced silently through the air before her, cutting a single pink petal in two. She spun, her midnight braid whipping behind her, and thrust the naginata forward, spearing another petal on the tip of the lethal blade. Her face remained calm; emotion erased from her delicate face.

"I believe this was a few nights before the vampire queen had come for me. I had yet to finish my training, I was so close, but never attained it. That true title of Onna Bugeisha, never truly fought in my first battle." A sigh escaped her, "When I learned of my parents passing, I wished to become what my mother was. A warrior. I wished to be strong, not just for them, not just for me, but for those who couldn't find the strength."

She gazed upon the woman before her, a solemn look within her eyes, sadness creasing around them. Sakiya watched her past self execute the most delicate of moves, the blade glinting in the sun's light.

"I believe that you earned that title, Sakiya. You were – are – an Onna Bugeisha. A warrior."

Her hand squeezed mine as a single tear rolled down her cheek. "Thank you, Natalia."

THE WITCH

When we had left Sakiya's memories, she excused herself, wishing to have some alone time. Tears had been cascading down her cheeks when I had opened my eyes. I never truly knew – understood – just how much she had lost. Her parents, the chance to become a warrior, and her own life.

But as I had watched the woman leave, I knew she was much more than the queen's servant – she always had been much more than that. She was strong, a woman with a warrior's heart. A woman who has faced loss and took strength from it, turned into something that would help others. She trained to become a warrior for those who couldn't, for the parents she had lost, she had become a warrior for herself.

Chapter Twenty Three

The Wolves

THE FOLLOWING EVENING, we had ventured out into the late hours of the night. Our little group disappearing into the shadows that we traveled through, allowing them to devour us whole. Soon our feet found pavement and golden light from the aged streetlamps. Stores lined along the sidewalk, closed for the night till morning returned.

The further we walked, the quieter it seemed to become. My breath hitched as the bar came into sight. Caution tape marking the entrance to the building. A hand had found mine, fingers entwining. Roman gave my hand a gentle squeeze. Though we walked on the opposite sidewalk, I could have sworn I could still smell the tang of blood coating the air.

Tears prickled within my eyes as I thought of Cindy, the bartender that had become almost like a mother to me. The ring on my finger seemed to burn in memory of her. I forced the tears back. Cindy's death would be avenged, the vampire queen would pay for every death that marked her hands.

We continued along our silent walk, a few blocks later we found ourselves passing Miss Lola's dance studio, the building that had become like a second home to me. It has been awhile since I stepped foot inside there, my body ached at the memories of the ribbons, wishing to tangle amongst them again.

A silent prayer was sent to the Earth for sparing at least Miss Lola's life, a life the vampire queen has not stolen. And I prayed she never would. I made a promise to return there once this was over, once the queen was dead.

"Do you think they'll honestly meet us?" Roman's voice had broken through the silence.

I glanced over my shoulder toward Aron. A wolfish grin crossing his lips, "I know we dogs hate your blood sucking asses, but if it means stopping that bitch, then I'm sure they'll show."

Sakiya raised a brow, "And after the queen is dead, will they come hunting us like dogs?"

Aron wrapped a muscular arm around her waist, pulling her close. "Oh, my dear vampire lover, I'm sure they'll come to love you just as I do." He pressed a kiss to the crown of her head.

The cemetery was in sight, my heart leapt in my chest. Our group approached the iron gate and we entered the land of the sleeping dead. We followed along the stone path passing by headstones marking graves. My skin crawled as it felt as though watchful eyes were upon us. I scanned the darkness – the trees that scattered through the cemetery – for signs of the wolf pack. Nothing moved within the shadows, a sound didn't whisper through the silence.

Aron had promised that the werewolves would show that they would aid us in our fight against the vampire queen. I held tight to that hope – that promise.

We came to a halt on top of a hill in the center of the cemetery. Here we would wait in anticipation for the werewolves to come. The breeze was a cold chill, almost as if Death itself were here trailing its fingertips across our skin – marking us – claiming us.

Aron stood before our group; hands shoved into his pant pockets. His dark, shoulder length hair whispered in the breeze. Anxiousness radiated off his being, his back muscles growing taunt beneath the white, long sleeved shirt he wore.

These were his people, werewolves. Known as the vampires' greatest enemy. People who took on the form of wolves, who had strength that no human could imagine, sight and hearing like no other. Immortal beings that walked this earth, like the vampires.

Soon we saw movement in the shadows. Figures began to prowl forth, some on four legs others on two. A group of four approached us, the other werewolves lingered in the darkness. Their eyes watching us closely.

I watched as Aron's shoulders sagged in relief.

Three men and one woman approached us. The woman had skin that was kissed by the sun, fiery hair falling in bouncy curls past her shoulders. Her emerald eyes scanned our small group, her thick brows lowered as her gaze met with mine. A snarl formed on her thin lips, a warning for all of us.

The man that stood beside her wrapped an arm around her waist. He was a head taller than her, his auburn hair kept in a long ponytail that snaked over his shoulder. I noted the scar that marred his left cheek. Those hazel eyes of his took me in as I stared upon the scar. A grin seemed to tug at the corners of his lips.

The other two men lingered behind the couple, standing close together. One man was slender in build but lacking nothing in height. The other was bulkier, the sleeves of his shirt seemed to almost burst from the muscle in the man's arms.

Aron and the auburn-haired werewolf approached each other, and wide grins broke out across their faces. Skipping the usual handshake that was called for in meetings, they went for death gripping hugs, chuckles sounding from them.

"Ah, it's been some time, brother Aron." The man's voice was deep and husky, pleasurable to the ears.

"Wouldn't be so long if you learned how to keep your ass at home and learned to enjoy yourself."

The man shrugged. "An alpha never has time to rest."

Aron crossed his arms over his chest, "I'm afraid you won't have down time for a while, old friend."

"I've heard you wish for our aid against the vampire queen, Marcus informed me."

The slender built man grunted behind the alpha werewolf. His face was stoic – revealing nothing of his true feelings for the request.

"And what has your decision come to be, Jason?" There was apprehension in Aron's voice.

The man locked gazes with the woman by his side, she inclined her head to him before matching gazes with Aron. "We have decided to aid you, the ones of us who wish it." She spoke.

Jason approached Aron and clasped a hand on his shoulder, "You know you have my aid. But the others make this decision for themselves, I will not force them if they do not wish it."

Aron nodded his head, "Thank you, brother."

Jason turned his back on Aron and faced the pack of werewolves that lurked deep within the shadows. I watched as yellow eyes flashed in the darkness. The alpha extended his arms as he spoke, "A request has been presented to me – to us. We have been asked to aid our brother Aron in his quest to bring an end to the vampire queen." At the mention of her, growls erupted through the air. "As you know, she's sent many of her kind on the hunt for us, wishing to bring extinction upon our kind. She has come too close to that. Now, she threatens others. And they have asked for our help. What say you?"

For a moment, silence had settled itself upon the cemetery. Even the breeze no longer whispered through the air. And I dared to allow my hope to falter, to lose faith.

Until, one wolf stepped out from the shadows. The moonlight bathed the white wolf in its glow. Icy, piercing eyes met my own. And then, it raised its head into the air and a howl escaped it. The sound reverberated within my bones. Others soon joined in like a symphony, stepping forth from the darkness. Goosebumps prickled along my arms at the haunting sound. Relief washed over my body as the howls echoed off into the night.

Jason turned to face Aron once more, a wide grin spread across his face. "Well, brother, I suppose you have an answer."

Aron approached the alpha and they clasped arms, "Thank you, old friend. October twentieth is the date, the vampire masquerade, and you already know what time of the day we'll need you."

Jason nodded his head as he released his hold on Aron's forearm. "Until then, Aron."

"Until then." He nodded.

As we left the cemetery behind us, a thought had flickered across my mind. Meeting Roman's gaze, I asked, "May we check on my friends while we're out?"

"Of course."

My chest was in knots as worry had begun to consume me entirely. My palms had become clammy with a sheen of sweat coating them. I bit my bottom lip till blood was drawn forth.

The twins are strong – I needed to remind myself – *they will be alive.*

But it seemed as though no matter how many times I told myself that, I found the words harder to believe. The queen wished for everyone who has ever known me to be dead and so far, she has succeeded in killing off my family, killing Cindy and even the man who worked at the small store.

And as we approached the home of the twins, I was not prepared for the scene that my eyes gazed upon. My knees had given out beneath me, smashing into the grassy ground. Arms encircled me as choked sobs escaped my lips and echoed through the night. My body shook as I cried.

The home was in ruin. Caving in and left in shambles. It appeared as though a fire had devoured the home. The garden was nothing but ashes.

An empty shell remained of the home, the glass within each window had shattered from the heat of the flames. And I knew what we would find if we were to enter that home. The twins... My hands curled into fists, my nails digging into the palms of my hands until crimson wept from them.

Why? Why did everyone my heart held dear have to suffer or die by her hands?

The tears burned down my cheeks, my vision blurry. Snot had begun to drip from my nose, but I did not care.

How much more could she take from me? How many more lives will she steal until she's satisfied? Until she has destroyed every bit of my soul.

A hand gently brushed through my hair as I buried my face into Roman's chest, unleashing all my tears and burdens. Until my sorrow had drenched him. Gently he rocked my body back and forth, holding me while I wept.

When the last set of tears fell down my cheeks, I wiped them away. The twins wouldn't want me to mourn them like this. They would want me to celebrate their lives. They would want me to fight.

And fight, I would.

The queen would not be prepared for when I faced her.

For when we all faced her.

Chapter Twenty Four

In The Past

IN THE FEW days that had come and went, when the sun had risen and fallen and the moon took its place, it felt as though I were lost within a dream. My body and mind had grown numb. I was lost within my own thoughts, within the fog that had encased me. Nothing felt real anymore.

Roman consoled me every day and every night. Catherine lingered beside me but never speaking, allowing her presence to speak for her. Sakiya spoke to me of understanding, speaking words of comfort. But still I could not drag myself from the fog. It was too thick, too heavy. And it weighed upon my heart – my soul.

I had told myself that I would be strong for the twins, but it proved hard to do so. After seeing with my own eyes what had become of their home, after learning about Cindy and the others. It all became too much to bear. The queen wished to break me, and slowly she was winning.

I felt a presence approach me from behind and joined my side by the window. My eyes drifted toward Aron, but our gazes never met. He was focused toward the outside world, where the sun warmed the Earth in its blessing light. And though my body was warmed by its rays as they filtered through the window, that warmth never reached my soul.

Slowly the sun began to set far below the horizon, taking the light of the day with it and soon darkness would creep upon our world.

There were a few moments of hushed silence before the werewolf spoke. “I know what it’s like to lose loved ones in such horrible ways.” My gaze flickered back to him. “Long before I met Roman, my family and I were part of a pack – Jason’s. We were one of the largest here, until the vampire queen began to send her blood sucking dogs after us.”

Aron’s voice grew dark, grim. A shadow seemed to cast itself over his face, his brown eyes growing vacant. “We were attacked. We fought but there were too many of them. I watched my family get slaughtered.” A vein in his neck throbbed. “I tried to help them, but those damned vampires kept me away.” Slowly, he blinked. Refocusing and returning to this world, leaving his memories. “I lost many friends that day as well.”

His dark gaze meeting mine with a fierceness but also understanding. “You must be strong, for them and for those around you. If you allow yourself to fall into despair, to give up, then the enemy has won.” His hand came to rest upon my shoulder. "Do not let that bitch win. Fight for the lives that were lost. Fight for those that are still living."

A warmth burned behind my eyes as tears began to swell, spilling over and streaming down my cheeks. Aron brought me into a tight embrace, his arms wrapped around me as I sobbed into him.

He was right, I couldn't give up, I needed to fight. I knew I had too. And I needed my mind cleared and focused for when the day came when we all faced the vampire queen and brought her reign to a bloody end.

Bringing myself out of his embrace, I wiped away my tears. The last tears I would cry because of her. "Thank you, Aron."

The werewolf grinned, "Anytime, little witch."

My eyes fell away from his, "I'm sorry about your family." My voice spoke gently. I never knew about his past, what he had suffered through. And I knew it could not be easy sharing something so heart wrenching.

"I have had my time to come to peace with their deaths, I know they are resting now, in a place that is far better than here." I heard the werewolf breathe in deeply, "And one day, I'll see them again."

I met his gaze again, "I just hope that one day won't be too soon."

He winked a brown eye, "It'll take a lot more than some blood suckers to kill me."

Later on, after Roman had left to feed when night came upon the world, the door opened, causing both Aron and I to cast our gazes upon Sakiya. She strutted into the room with envelopes held within her hands. The werewolf approached her with a grin, "Brought the mail, my dear?"

She shook her head with a roll of her eyes, "Where's Roman?"

"He's out feeding." Aron's dark gaze flickered back to the envelopes, "What are those?"

Sakiya tossed them upon the couch, "Invitations from the queen to the masquerade. There is one for *each* of us." Her dark gaze lingered upon the werewolf.

His eyes settled upon the woman before him, "Wicked bitch." Aron wrapped an arm around her waist and brought her body close to his, "But that doesn't matter, my vampire lover, she'll be long gone from this world soon."

Leaving the window, I approached the couch and plucked a cream-colored envelope from it. My own named was inked across it in dark lettering. Breaking the wax seal, I tore the invitation free. My past death date stared back at me in bold, dark lettering. The only thing to be found upon the paper. It was mocking, taunting even. I could almost hear the queen's laughter within my mind.

As anger became me, I allowed my magic to unbottle and fill my being. Heat scorched through my veins and my hands ignited as flames danced upon my skin. My eyes watching as the fire devoured the paper within my hands until it was nothing but ash that crumble to the floor before my feet.

Aron and Sakiya said nothing, only watching the flames crackle upon my hands. "It's coming soon, and I cannot wait to burn that wicked creature from this Earth." I had not recognized my own voice.

There was a darkness hidden within me. Something that had steadily built with each death that weighed upon my heart. The shadows within me feasting upon my sorrow and despair, thriving form it. That very darkness was consuming me. My magic churning and morphing into something that was no longer light but something that was twisted and cruel.

The flames still crackled upon my hands, but they begin to transform as I allowed my sorrow to consume me, to engulf my being. I watched as the fire darkened and turned into midnight. The flames turning into wisps and shadows that danced atop the palms of my hands. Slowly they slithered across my skin, wrapping around my forearms.

"Little witch?" Aron spoke but his voice had grown distant.

"Natalia." Sakiya made to take a step closer, but the werewolf held her back.

A ghostly face appeared within the room then, "My friend, come back to us." Catherine spoke gently.

This is what the humans feared. The dark side of witches, how the shadows became us. How we allowed that darkness to feast upon our souls. Turning into the very creatures that they feared. Why so many witches had been burned those long years ago – why they had burned me. Out of fear.

For witches were crafted from both the light and the darkness.

But now, I had become what they hated most.

I was spiraling and there was no coming back. Drowning within the depths of my being, the shadows grasping ahold of my soul and dragging me ever deeper.

I was gone.

Natalia was no more.

THE VAMPIRE

When I had returned to my home, there was nothing but a chilling silence that greeted me. There were no voices whispering in the apartment within the factory. No Natalia or Sakiya laughing and sharing life stories. No Aron joking and pestering.

Silence.

Then, something echoed within my ears. Not voices but whispers of something that was not mortal. Darkness calling out into the night. The scent of magic filled the air, but it was not the sweet smell of flowers, it smelled as though there were mildew festering. My footsteps echoed throughout the factory as I hurried up the stairs, each step groaning beneath me as the steel grew old and rusted.

When I burst through the door, that was when I saw her.

Sakiya and Aron backed against the wall, eyes wide. Catherine lingering within the shadows of the apartment.

And then there was Natalia. Her body covered in shadows. They coiled around her arms and legs, dark wisps flickering around the witch. There was a creeping cold that entered the room. Natalia did not speak. She did not move. Hardly seeming to be part of this world anymore.

And when I peered into her eyes, I found they were no longer blue as an ocean but dark as midnight. Reminding me too much of my own eyes when I allowed the beast to roam free.

The very beast I had to become every night when I fed.

I took a step toward her, "Natalia." I spoke gently.

"Roman, I would trend carefully. The little witch seems to be having a bad day." Aron warned.

I shook my head and advanced. That was when her gaze flickered. Those dark eyes falling upon me. I saw a shift within her gaze as she seemed to recognize me.

"Natalia." I spoke her name once more.

Slowly, so slowly, she cocked her head to the side as she watched me approach. She did not speak, did not move. Only watched.

I stood before her and the shadows that encased her reached out for me. The cold tendrils wrapping around my ankles and moving upward. They coiled around my arms and tugged me closer to her.

"Natalia, my love, come back."

Her eyes stared coldly into mine, "I do not feel anything while like this. I do not feel the ache of a crying heart. The cracks within a broken soul. Like this, I control the fear and sorrow within me."

Carefully, I reached a hand toward her and caressed her cheek. "I know what it is like to feel your despair devouring you as if that is all that's left of you. But it's not. I spent too many years trapped within my darkness but then I found my light once more." Natalia's eyes softened as she slowly blinked, slowly coming forth from her depths. "That light is you, and I need you to come back to me, Natalia. Please. I do not wish to lose you again."

"Please." My voice trembled.

Then, the darkness surrounding her began to flicker.

THE WITCH

I heard it – that familiar voice. It called out to me, seeking me. It reached my ears within the depths of my being. My body curled within itself as his words wound around me like a warm blanket, beckoning me forth.

Please. He had said, begging for me to return to him.

But there was so much comfort to be found here as the shadows draped around my being, holding me. But I knew I could not linger here any longer. There was something I had to do. People waiting for me. I had to return, to swallow that darkness and lock it within its cage once more.

The shadows reluctantly released their hold on me as I allowed Roman's voice to lead me to the surface, to drag me from the darkness.

And once more, I embraced the light.

A gasp escaped my lips as my head tipped back, my legs going weak beneath me. The shadows that coiled around my body slithered beneath my skin; the darkness being called back.

Warm arms embraced me as I fell, cradling me close. Looking up, my gaze met with a haunting blue. "Roman."

There was a gentle smile upon his lips, "I'm here, Natalia. I'm here."

My heart beat at his words, my chest warming as I returned the smile.

Casting my gaze around the room, I found confused and worried eyes watching me. "Did I hurt anyone?"

Aron grinned, "No but you did give us a fright, little witch. Thought we lost ya there."

Roman helped me back onto my feet. "I'm sorry. I've never allowed the darkness to claim me like that. Many witches don't return once they venture along that path." I glanced toward the man beside me, "Thank you, Roman. For bringing me back."

Gently his hand caressed my cheek, "What had caused that?"

Sakiya approached the couch and plucked one of the envelopes from it and approached Roman, handing it over. "Your mother. She sent one for each of us."

He glanced upon it before taking it from her hand. A growl rumbled within his chest as he tore the invitation in two. *"Damn her."*

"In two days' time, she will be, blood sucker. The masquerade is near, and the werewolves are ready to tear their teeth into her flesh." Aron said.

"Good, her reign will soon come to an end."

Chapter Twenty Five

Days Pass

THE DARKNESS THAT I had awakened within me seemed to claw at its cage, wishing to be set free once more. I remembered how it felt to unleash it, to allow the shadows to embrace me. I had fallen into myself, being encased by the darkness that dwelled within me. It caressed me like a loving mother. Wishing to keep me forever safe, forever within my depths.

And I was going to allow it to keep me prisoner. To allow the darkness to control my being, to act on my despair. I had traveled that dark path that many witches never returned from – never looked back. But I had. With the aid of one person.

Roman.

He had saved me from myself. And I would forever be grateful. But there was that lingering dread of my coming death that loomed above my shoulders. My end would greet me soon and my heart grew heavy for the ones I would be leaving behind. For the friends I would sadden with my death. For the lover I would leave once again. Shattering the heart that had just mended.

Would he turn into that monster again? Allowing his sorrow to claim him as I had? Would he ever return to the Roman that the world knew? Or be forever trapped as the beast?

A sigh escaped my lips as I stepped away from the window within my room. Catherine was lingering above the bed, allowing Pax to swat at the ghostly ends of her dress.

"Are you ever going to tell him, Natalia?"

As I approached the door, my hand rested upon the knob. "I can't."

"You know it'll hurt him."

Turning the knob, I said, "It'll hurt him either way."

Then, I stepped into the silent hallway. The sun was shining upon the world and Sakiya was nowhere to be found. She had ventured out last night with Aron trailing her. But now the werewolf could be found asleep on the couch, heavy snores escaping the man.

With quiet footsteps, I approached the door that led into Roman's room. No sounds could be heard coming from the other side as I knocked upon the door gently.

The knob turned and Roman soon stood before me. Brown hair a disarray, sweatpants once more hanging low upon his waist. His face softened at the sight of me, his shoulders relaxing.

"Hello, Natalia."

I offered a smile, "May I?" I gestured to the room.

He took a step back, "You're always welcome in my room, you don't have to knock."

Once I stepped inside, he closed the door. Before he could speak, I cupped his face within my hands and brought my lips to his. A soft growl rumbled within his chest as his hands found my hips, bringing my body closer to his. His fingers gripping my sides with hunger.

My body pressed against his, feeling every dip and curve of his muscles. If my last day was arriving soon, I wanted to have one more day with Roman. One more day where our bodies became one. Our souls molding together as we made love.

Roman slipped his tongue inside my mouth where it danced with my own. I lured him back to the bed, never breaking the kiss. His hands lowered until they cupped behind my knees and lifted me from the ground, my legs wrapping around his body as he lay me upon the bed.

As he lowered his mouth to my neck, his hands began to work the robe off my body. Sliding the dark silk away from my breasts. His hands fondling them. A soft moan had escaped my lips.

Once more, he brought his mouth to mine as he lowered his sweatpants. There were no whispered words shared between us as our bodies became one. Wrapping around one another, embracing each other. Limbs tangling upon wrinkled bedsheets.

THE MOTHER

The flames crackled and danced within the fireplace, devouring the logs they embraced. My finger tapped upon the wine glass held within my hand. The blood within it almost gone as it slipped down my throat.

As I took the last sip, my gaze ventured to the floor. To the spot I had murdered my own mother. Her body was long since gone, servants scurrying forth and retrieving it, disposing of it. Allowing the sun to cast its rays upon my mother's corpse and it turned into nothing but ash beneath the sunlight.

There was a knock upon the door, "Come in."

A woman entered the room, my most prized guard. She knelt before my chair; head bowed. She held no fear even with knowing that I knew of her lover. If it had been any other guard, I would have struck them down, but not Sakiya.

"My little samurai," my voice purred, "Take these to Roman and his mutts."

I extended the envelopes to her and she lightly plucked them from my grasp. "This shall be a masquerade that no one would soon forget."

THE WITCH

Roman and Aron once more traveled out into the night. One more night of prowling within the shadows before the masquerade arrived. He had pulled me close to him and placed a kiss upon my lips. "I'll return soon." He spoke.

Leaning into his palm, I held his gaze. "Be safe."

Aron approached then and clapped a hand on his shoulder, "Don't worry, I'll keep this blood sucker out of trouble."

A sigh escaped Sakiya across the room, "That's not comforting, Aron. You're just as bad as Roman – if not worse."

The werewolf chuckled and a winked an eye at the vampire before the two left into the shadows. Leaving Sakiya and I alone within the room.

"Sakiya, may I ask a favor?"

She turned those dark eyes upon me, "Of course, Natalia. What is it?"

"I want to unlock the rest of my powers. Tasha and Sasha said they were sealed away and I needed to awaken them." I clasped a hand over my heart at the mention of their names, "I think in order for me to do that, I have to go deep within myself. Can you keep an eye on me? Make sure that I do not fall into the darkness? If you see shadows around me, wake me."

Sakiya nodded her head, "I can do that."

"Thank you."

As I seated myself upon the couch, my legs crossed over one another, Catherine appeared. Her ghostly, grey eyes flooding with worry, "Are you sure you should do this? Is this safe?"

A sigh escaped me, "I have to do this. So that when we face the queen, I'm prepared."

Catherine cast her gaze toward Sakiya, and she did not mention my coming death. Keeping it secret until I reached my end.

Then, taking in a breath, I closed my eyes, and descended into my soul.

Both darkness and light had greeted me during my descent. Both reaching their grasping hands toward me. I felt as the shadows coiled around my ankles, slithering up my legs like serpents. Their cold chill embracing my body.

Then I felt the touch of warmth upon my hands and arms as the light wrapped itself around my being, grasping ahold of my hands. Glitters of gold flickered within the darkness of my being as the magic swirled around.

But I soon found my descent had been halted as I hit a wall within my soul. A slick, glass-like surface was before me. And I found my own reflection staring back. The shadows and light swayed behind me within the reflection. I watched as they reached toward it, reached as if they were grasping for something.

The other part of themselves.

They seemed to whisper into my ears as they embraced my body once more. Cold and warmth wrapping around my body all at once.

For if I wanted to unleash my magic – I needed to embrace both the light and the dark within my soul. To awaken every piece that had been locked away.

Approaching the wall, I reached a hand toward it and watched as my reflection did the same. The surface was slick and cold against my hand like water. The surface rippled as my fingers came in contact with it. My reflection distorting.

Closing my eyes, I took in a steadying breath.

It was time.

My magic swirled around me and slithered down along my arm. The shadows and light spiraling down my arm until they too, touched the surface.

The wall glimmered and whispered voices began to echo all around within the darkness. Echoing within my ears. My magic on the other side was calling out to me. Wishing to reach me.

So, I pushed against the barrier. My hand slowly disappearing into the wall. I felt as it pushed against me, but I urged my body forth. The surface of the wall had turned into a thick substance that wrapped around my body like a cool blanket of water.

And with one, final push, I had broken through the barrier.

I felt as something awakened. Something stirred within my soul. Within my very depths. The magic around me seemed to cry out with joy as it had been reunited with its lost half.

And as I gazed ahead, there I stood.

But my hair had returned to its natural color of midnight.

And I realized that the woman I stared upon – was my former self.

The me from a past life.

"Alexandria." My voice echoed around as if we were within a well.

The woman did not speak, she simply smiled and approached me with an offered hand. Without thinking, I reached for her. And when our hands clasped, golden light erupted within the darkness.

A gasp escaped my lips as I felt the last piece of my soul awaken. And when I had opened my eyes once more, I found both Sakiya and Catherine before me. Their eyes wide and watching.

"What is it?"

Their gazes drifted down and my eyes followed their path until I saw my magic spilling out into the room. Golden and bright like Tasha and Sasha's had been. It swirled around me within the air, glimmering within the room. Warmth enveloped my being.

"You unlocked your magic." Sakiya spoke.

I nodded my head and curled my hands into fists within my lap, "And now I'll be ready to face the queen."

THE VAMPIRE

"Are you sure you should do this, Roman?"

We stood before my mother's home. The structure looming above us within the darkness. Shadows coiling around the building. The guards positioned at the gates watched us closely with narrowed eyes.

"Yes. But I think it best if you remain here."

"What? And miss pissing off your dear mother by dragging my muddy paws through her home?"

A chuckle escaped me as I clapped a hand upon his shoulder, "Be a good boy and stay here."

Aron bowed low at the waist, "As you wish, master."

I shook my head and approached.

The guards said nothing, not even acknowledging me with a nod of their heads as I passed them by. Entering the home, even the servants kept their heads down as they scurried away into the shadows.

My knuckles rasped upon the wooden doors that led to my mother's favorite room.

"Come in, my dear son." Her voice sounded from the other side.

The doors creaked open as I stepped foot within the room. Mother was seated before the fire, the flames crackling and dancing upon the logs. The only light within the room.

"I didn't think you would pay me another visit, Roman." She took a sip from her wine glass, blood staining her lips.

"Why are you doing this? Why can't you leave us alone? Why did you kill all those humans?"

For a moment, I contemplated killing my mother here and now. To end this. But I knew I would never make it past those doors. The guards and servants would tear me limb from limb and begin their hunt for Aron and Natalia.

She sat there in silence, those piercing eyes of her staring into the dancing flames. Her nail tracing atop the glass. "Why must you deny what you truly are, Roman? Prince of the Vampires. A monster. Why hide it? It is what you are. What you always will be." A scoff sounded from her, "As for the humans, it is what they deserved."

I shook my head, "You're wrong, mother. I'll never be what you are. And we won't be attending the masquerade."

A laugh escaped her wicked lips as her head tipped back. "Ah, my dear son, have you forgotten that I swore to hunt your little witch and that mutt you call your friend?" She finally faced me, her eyes piercing, "If you do not come to the masquerade, then you and all your friends shall regret it, Roman."

"I came here to reason with you. But I see that shall never happen." A snarl freed itself from my lips as I stormed toward the door.

As I walked through, her voice called out to me. "Don't forget to wear red."

Then, her laughter followed me.

THE WITCH

Aron and Roman had returned, both of them casting their gazes upon me once they stepped foot into the room. Aron sniffed at the air. Roman tilting his head to the side.

"Little witch smells of magic." The werewolf said.

"I unlocked the last bit of it." I smiled at them.

Roman approached the couch and cupped my face within his palms, "You never cease to amaze me, Natalia."

My hand came to rest upon his own and as I stared into his eyes, I found a deep trouble within him. "What troubles you?"

A sigh escaped him, and he brushed his lips against my brow. "My mother, as usual. I went to her. I do not wish for you to attend the masquerade. But I know she'll hunt us until the end of time."

Aron approached Roman, clapping a hand upon his shoulder. "Don't worry, we'll take care of that blood sucker."

Roman's hands fell from my face and he turned his back upon us, walking down the hall to his room, and disappearing within. My heart ached for him – crying out for him.

"He worries of losing you, Natalia." Sakiya seated herself beside me. "He needs some time alone. To think, clear his head." She placed her hand atop my own.

The werewolf leaned against the wall, "He worries too much. We'll be just fine. Right, little witch?" He winked a dark eye at me.

Forcing a smile, I said, "Of course."

Then I met Catherine's gaze. Her eyes so full of sorrow that I could not bear to look into them anymore.

For the words I spoke were coated with lies.

Chapter Twenty Six

A Masquerade of Nightmares

THE NIGHT HAD ARRIVED. Sakiya had knocked upon my door, awakening me. Sleep evaded me through most of the day as I tried to sleep for the coming battle. But whenever my lids drifted close and I found myself falling into the land of sleep; the nightmare had plagued me. Mocking and tormenting me. Reminding me that my death would soon come.

When I opened the door, I found that Sakiya was already dressed for the masquerade, a beautiful midnight and crimson dress fitted upon her slim body. The sleeves hung low upon her shoulders and reached into points atop her hands. A crimson band of fabric wrapped around her narrow waist. A pool of midnight rippled past her ankles upon the floor.

Within her hands, she held a ruby dress. Black lace ruffled atop the skirt. "The queen gifted me many dresses. She loved dressing me as though I were a doll." She shrugged her shoulders, "Perhaps I was to her, a play thing. A trophy." She offered a smile, "But I thought it would suit you."

Approaching her, I placed my hand atop her own, "Soon she'll pay for all she's done." Then, I smiled to her, "But thank you, Sakiya."

Once I had slipped into the dress, I seated myself upon the bed and Sakiya began to comb through my purple hair. Brushing it to one side and braiding the strands together. As we sat there, a meow echoed within the silence of the room and Pax leapt onto the bed, crawling into my lap. Purrs escaped him as my fingers combed through his fur. He nudged his head into the palm of hand, licking my fingers.

It was then that my heart began to ache. For I would be leaving my furry companion behind within the world. But I hoped that Roman or Sakiya would take care of Pax when I no longer could. Or perhaps Sakiya would – she had said that she loved cats. And Pax had taken a liking to the vampire.

"All done." She said as she stood from the bed.

I smiled, "Thank you again, Sakiya."

Catherine appeared then, a smile upon her lips. "You look beautiful, my friend." And though she smiled, I could see the sorrow within her grey eyes.

"Thank you, Catherine."

Our gazes held for a heartbeat. Both of us knowing this would be the last time she would see me within this body. For when next we met, I would be a spirit wandering the world.

Catherine gave a slight nod of her head. She would be here waiting for my return. She would be the one to guide me within the afterlife.

Sakiya then offered her hand to me, I slid my own into her palm and allowed her to help me from the bed. Pax leapt from my lap and curled into a furry ball upon the bed, drifting off to sleep.

"It is no trouble, Natalia. Now come, I'm sure Roman is itching to know how beautiful you look."

A giggled laugh escaped my lips as we stepped forth from my room and into the hall. Immediately I was greeted by a gaze of haunting blue. Whatever conversation Roman and Aron had been having, was dropped.

Sakiya led me down the hall until I stood before Roman. A smile appeared upon his lips, eyes brightening as they gazed upon me. "You look breathtaking, my love."

My gaze slid down his body. His brown hair had been combed back to the side, away from his face. He wore a fitted black vest with a crimson long-sleeved shirt beneath it tucked into black trousers.

"And you look quite handsome."

His hand found itself upon my waist, drawing me close to him, his other resting upon my cheek. His thumb gently stroking it. "I wish that I could take you to a true masquerade not run by my mother. But I swear to you, that once this is over, I'll take you. I'll take you to see the world, Natalia."

There was so much promise within his eyes. So much happiness at the thought of the future – *our future.* My heart broke staring into those eyes of his. Looking upon his beaming face.

I would be causing him so much heartache and I hoped that he would not fall into that darkness again. Hoped that he would not venture through the world plagued by my death. That he would find happiness.

Then, Aron approached Sakiya. A wolfish grin upon his lips. "Ah, my dear vampire lover, you stole my breath away. You look appetizing."

Sakiya rolled her eyes, "You're such an animal." But she smiled back to the werewolf.

"Ready to tear some teeth into some blood suckers?"

Roman's hand slid beneath my chin and he tilted my head, lowering his until our lips met. It was brief but I could feel his love within the kiss. His warmth embracing me.

"Let's go." Taking my hand, he led me through the door into the night.

THE MOTHER

A silken, crimson dress poured over my body like a cascade of water. The straps light upon my shoulders, the neck line dipping low between my breasts. The dress fitted against the slight curves of my body and flooded to the ground like a pool of blood. A long slit running up one of my legs.

A servant had come into the room and fashioned my long, golden hair atop my head. Pinning it in place. My bangs sweeping down across one eye. The simple, poor thing was too much a coward to look into my eyes. Causing a smile to play upon my lips. Her hands having a slight tremble to them as they worked through my hair.

Once she had finished, she quickly scurried from the room.

Rising from my chair, I stood before the fire, sipping upon my glass of blood. Allowing it to stain my lips. Coating them in crimson.

There was a knock upon the door. "My queen, the masquerade shall begin soon."

A smirk curled upon my lips. Soon that little witch would be here. And soon, her blood shall be mine.

A laugh escaped my lips, "Too bad you couldn't be here to see this mother." Raising my glass into the air, I said, "A toast to you and your burning soul."

THE WITCH

The night air whipped through my hair as we traveled through the darkened sky. Roman holding me within his arms though I argued that I could fly on my own, but he insisted. Telling me to save my magic for the fight. Below us, a wolf of midnight fur ran upon the earth. Sakiya flying just above him, watching for any of the queen's servants.

The night was still and silent. Not a soul could be found lingering about the world. As if the earth itself had fallen into a deep slumber. Its creatures curling in on themselves and allowing the world of dreams to claim their beings.

It did not take long for us to arrive at the masquerade – the world seeming to urge my life to meet its end and soon it would. For my nightmare had predicted my death since the beginning and now, I would walk into the queen's trap.

A grand building bloomed from the darkness of the trees. Lantern light flickering with dancing flames around the large estate. The ground had been fenced in, seeming as though there was no end to the blacked metal. Roman lowered from the sky and gently placed me upon the earth, my heels clicking against the cobblestones that led toward the gate. And standing there, were two vampires. Their eyes already darkened as they gazed upon us with widening smiles, their fangs glinting in the moonlight.

Swallowing down my fear, I reached for Roman's hand and entwined my fingers through his. He answered with a reassuring squeeze before leading me toward the gates. Sakiya and Aron walking just behind us.

Roman cast his haunted gaze over his shoulder and met the gazes of his two longest friends. No words were shared between them, and there needn't be. Enough was spoken through their eyes and Roman nodded his head to them, thanking them for everything. And in turn, they nodded their heads to him.

When we approached the vampires, Roman moved me behind him. And before he could speak, one of the guards did for him. "Ah, the little prince has returned home." Mockery sounded within his voice. Those dark eyes drifting toward me and his tongue flicked from his mouth and traced across his fangs.

"Allow us in so we may get this night over and done with." There was a growl in Roman's voice as he addressed the man.

Stepping aside, he nodded his head to the other vampire, and he began to unlock the gate. As it swung open, the vampire called out, "It shall be a night of blood, *little prince.*"

I tensed as my nightmare began to manifest before my eyes. Of the vampires drinking the blood from my veins. As the pain in my stomach became real. Closing my eyes, I took in a steadying breath. I needed to be strong. And the queen must fall.

As we approached the doors, Roman led me up the three stairs. Each step closer I took, my feet felt as though they were being weighed down. And I was dragging myself because I knew once I stepped through those doors, I would be greeted by death.

Before we entered, Roman turned toward me and took my face within his hands. And there within his eyes, I saw the fear that he had been hiding. It raged like a storm within his gaze. Threatening to drown him.

"Natalia," His voice rasped my name, "You are the light in my life. My peace. I am nothing without you. I have loved you for decades and I shall love you for many more."

Tears prickled behind my eyes. My chest aching. Cracks forming within my heart for I knew my coming death would shatter him. But this needed to be done. I played a role in bringing down the queen. And I would play it till the very end.

"I love you, Roman. From now till my heart stops beating."

He leaned down and brushed his lips against mine. I fell into him, giving into the kiss and embracing the warmth of him. For this would be the last I would ever feel it. The last I would feel his lips against my own.

It was then that all of our shared memories together – both from this life and the last – began to dance through my mind. From the first times that we met. Till our last moments together.

When the kiss had reached its end, Roman drew me into his embrace, those strong arms wrapping around me protectively. Fearing that if he let me go, that I would vanish from his hands. I rested my head against his chest, taking in the scent of him. My hands curling into the fabric of his shirt.

From behind us, I could hear Aron and Sakiya. They too, were saying their goodbyes in case one or both of them did not make it out of this alive. I peeked my gaze toward them and found Aron drawing Sakiya forth with one arm and tilting her chin with his free hand. There was love within his eyes and a playful grin upon his lips.

"You know I love you, my dear vampire lover."

Sakiya scoffed with a roll of her eyes, "You're an animal."

Aron leaned down, their lips a breath away from one another, "You wouldn't have me any other way."

She smiled as she slipped her fingers into his dark hair, "Never." Before sealing her lips over his, she whispered, "I love you."

Aron held her close, his hands gripping her sides. But I could see the worry that creased his face. Fear could be found lurking in each of us on this night as we stepped through those doors that would decide each of our fates. Though mine had already been set in stone once I took my first breath in this world.

As the werewolf and vampire untangled themselves from each other, Aron wrapped an arm around Sakiya's waist, and they approached the doors.

Roman cast his haunting gaze past the two, searching the shadows. "When will they arrive?"

Aron clapped a hand on his shoulder, "Soon enough. I'm sure we can handle your mother's blood sucking dogs on our own until then."

Roman nodded his head and cast that gaze upon me once more. His hand reaching out and stroking my cheek for a moment before he turned toward the doors. Without another word spoken, he placed his hands upon the knobs and turned them.

We had arrived at the masquerade.

Chapter Twenty Seven

Death Awaits

WHEN WE ENTERED the masquerade, any music that had filtered through the air had been silenced. The melody strangled until its notes died away. And every vampire within the room, turned their attention upon us. Their gazes weighing heavily upon me as their eyes never drifted away. Many of them grinned wickedly as they flicked their tongues across their fangs. But I would not be intimidated by them.

Clapping echoed through the room and the vampires departed, and the queen herself stepped into view. A crimson, silk dress poured down her being, and as she walked, it trailed behind her like a river of blood. A long slit ran up the side of the dress, exposing her pale leg.

I hated to admit that the queen was breathtaking – as all vampires were. Their curse came with beauty. Her golden tresses had been fashioned atop her head, her bangs sweeping over one, ghostly eye. In one hand, she held a wine glass, but I knew it was not wine that swirled within that glass.

Roman tensed at the sight of his mother, a snarl forming upon his lips. Moving me behind him, he placed himself between his mother and I. She arched a finely plucked brow at her son, a smirk upon her lips.

"Roman, are you not going to introduce me to your woman? Or are you ashamed of her?"

A growl sounded from him, *"You won't go near her."*

A dark laugh escaped the queen, "Oh, my son, I mean your witch no harm. I simply wish to meet her properly. Our little fight didn't leave much room for introductions."

When Roman did not move, her smile faltered, her lips falling into a flat line. "Fine. Have it your way then." Casting her ghostly gaze over her shoulder, she nodded her head and a group of vampires stepped forth. "We can do this far easier if you simply allow me to meet her or I could tear you away from her, the choice is yours, son."

"No." Darkness coated his voice, echoing through the room.

The queen simply shrugged her shoulders, "Fine. Remove him."

As the vampires moved toward him, I placed my hand on his arm and stepped around Roman. The queen smiled and raised a hand into the air, the vampires stopping in their tracks. Her grin had returned.

"Come to me, my dear witch." The queen offered a pale hand.

As I made to step forth, Roman grasped my arm and tugged me back. "Natalia, don't trust her."

I couldn't bring myself to stare too long into those eyes. The eyes that had glimpsed into my soul and knew me entire. Placing my hand onto his chest, I stepped away from him. "It's alright." My voice was gentle as I spoke, calming his rage. My hand reaching up to caress his cheek within my palm, "It's alright." I said again.

The tension in him seemed to ease at my touch. Subtly, he nodded his head. Dropping my hand from his face, I turned to face the vampire queen and slipped my hand into her offered palm. Her skin was cold against my own – deathly cold.

Her thumb traced over my fingers, closing her eyes she took in a deep breath. "Ah, I can practically taste your magic. You are a strong witch. Just as you were in your past life."

A prickle of rage stung beneath my flesh. She mocked my death, taunted me. Straightening my spine, I locked my gaze with hers. "I do not fear you."

A chuckle sounded from her as she dropped my hand. "Foolish as you are strong. A clever person would know to fear someone such as I. Would bow before my feet and beg for their life. But you, Natalia, do not. And I must say, I admire that about you – in both lives." A long sigh blew forth from her lips, "But now, this life has reached its end."

"YOU WILL NOT LAY A DAMNED HAND ON HER!" Roman roared, darkness coating his eyes as he bared his fangs at his mother.

And when he made to lunge at her, the queen simply snapped her fingers and the group of vampires hurdled toward him. Roman swung his arm back and cracked one against the head, the vampire sent tumbling to the ground. But the others quickly piled atop him, forcing him to his knees and holding his arms back. Another grabbing a fistful of his hair and jerking his head back. Roman snarled and thrashed against the vampires that held him. A wildness within his now dark eyes.

Aron bellowed and shifted into his wolf form, a hulking beast dropping to all fours. With a growl, the werewolf lunged at the vampires holding his friend, Sakiya falling into step beside him. But another group of vampires tackled the two to the ground. And though they fought, there were too many of them. They were trapped.

The werewolf snapped his teeth at the vampires holding him, barely grazing one of their arms. The bite would slowly poison them, but it wasn't large enough to kill them. The vampire hissed and swatted Aron on the head.

"Alright now, that's quite enough. The fun is about to begin." The queen announced, turning that ghostly gaze upon me. "Natalia, would you care for a drink?"

At that, a servant scurried forth balancing a silver platter upon the palm of her hand. One, lone wine glass could be found upon it. The servant bowed and offered the drink to me. Raising a brow, I eyed the queen.

"Go on, take it." She urged.

My gaze drifted back to the glass, staring at the liquid within wearily. And it was then that I realized, my death had greeted me. All those nights spent trapped within the same nightmare that played over and over again. Here it was laid out before my eyes. The poison that would take my life away. That would eat its way through my stomach and kill me slowly. A painful, drawn out death.

Holding the queen's gaze, I reached for the glass and plucked it from the tray. The servant hurriedly scurried away. I stared down into the dark liquid and I could have sworn I heard it wicked laughter as it swirled within the glass. My hand trembling as I held it.

"Well, should we make a toast, Natalia?" The queen extended her glass.

I raised my brow to her, "And what shall we be toasting too?"

"My reign and your death, my dear."

"NO!" Roman's voice reverberated throughout the room. Shattering my heart and tears began to prickle within my eyes. *"YOU WILL NOT TAKE HER AWAY FROM ME AGAIN! I'LL KILL YOU! I'LL TEAR YOU APART!"*

He thrashed against the vampires that held him. Sakiya and Aron fighting to break free. But there was no escaping for them. They were all trapped here. The vampire queen had won – for now.

Casting my gaze over my shoulder, I was met with Roman's. Pure and utter rage distorted his features. He had become the embodiment of a true vampire. "I swear that you won't die here, Natalia. I lost you once, I won't lose you again."

It was then that the tears had fallen, cascading down my cheeks in warm streams. I shook my head. "No, Roman. I will."

His brow creased, a look of confusion within his dark eyes. "What do you mean?"

"There is something I haven't told you. Because I knew if I told you, you would refuse to let me come and your mother would have hunted us down."

A pur sounded from the queen, "Oh, keeping secrets? Do you wish share it with us, dear Natalia?"

I cut a narrowed glance at the queen but her smile only widened like a feral feline about to pounce on its prey. Facing Roman once more, I spilled the truth to the world. The dark secret I kept hidden. "I've had the same nightmare for months now, almost every night I dreamt of my death. Each night I found myself collapsing onto a floor and vampires surrounded me, and then they lunged for me while I lay dying. I realized that I had foreseen my death and now it has arrived."

Roman's eyes drifted toward the glass in my hand. Shaking his head, his voice rasped, "No. Natalia don't drink it. We can survive this – *together.*"

The fear had settled into him, the darkness of his eyes fading away revealing that sapphire blue once more. The eyes that shattered whatever remained of my heart.

Heels clicked against the floor and an icy hand rested upon my shoulder as the queen stood beside me. "I'm afraid if she doesn't drink it, then you all shall die. And then, Natalia will still die no matter what she chooses." Grasping ahold of my chin, she jerked my head and forced me to look at her. "Now, the choice is yours, Natalia. Drink the poison or watch them die one by one. Their lives are in your hands."

"You would kill your own son? Your own flesh and blood?"

The queen narrowed her eyes, "That is what it means to be a true vampire. A true monster. You must sacrifice *everything.*"

I shook my head free of her grasp. "I once hated you, but now I only feel pity for you."

A snarl curled upon her lips, "I don't want your damned pity. Now, *drink.*" A hiss escaped her lips.

I couldn't bring myself to look at Roman for I knew it would destroy me completely. "Promise me something, Roman."

"Natalia... please..." His voice pleaded to my ears.

Shaking my head, "Promise me that you'll live. That you won't grieve my death for the rest of your years. Promise me that you won't fall into darkness, Roman. Promise me."

"I love you, Natalia. I am sorry I failed you again. I'm sorry I couldn't protect you. I'm sorry..." His voice shattered as he choked back his tears, but they still forced their way through.

"Sakiya, Aron, thank you for being my friends. Watch over Roman for me."

A whimper sounded from the werewolf. And it was Sakiya who spoke, "It was an honor to call you my friend, Natalia. And I am sorry as well that I couldn't save you. Perhaps in the next life we'll find each other."

A saddened smile tugged at my lips at that thought. Yes, they would find each other again. In another life. Another time.

But now, this life had reached its end.

"Come, Natalia, let us drink together."

Meeting the queen's gaze, she clinked her glass against mine. And with a heavy heart, I lifted the glass to my lips. Blocking out the sounds of Roman's screams as he watched me drink the poison.

When it flowed across my tongue, I felt its bite as it began to devour me. It burned on its way down, scorching my throat. The glass fell from my hand as my body trembled. The glass shattered across the floor. My stomach churned and knotted. A pained gasp escaping my lips as I fell to the unforgiving ground. Curling into myself as the poison ate its way through my body.

Wicked laughter echoed through the air as the queen stood over my dying body. Her ghostly eyes watching with joy as the poison laced through my veins. Burning whatever was in its path.

The queen knelt beside me, but my vision had begun to blur. A cold hand brushed my purple tresses from my face. "Ah I must say it is very satisfying to see you in pain, little witch. And soon, we shall feast upon your sweet blood. Thank you, for playing this game with me. But I have won, and you have lost." Behind the queen, a group of vampires lurked forth, looming over my body. Watching and waiting to feast upon my blood.

A coughing fit had seized me then. My throat parched and burning, my tongue dry. My soul was on fire. And when I tried to summon my magic, it did not answer my calls. The poison slowly eating away at it.

"I shall take my time feeding from you-" But the queen's words had been silenced when the symphony of howls echoed through the air.

The sound of glass shattering and fighting broke out within the masquerade. Hisses and snarls filling the room as vampires lunged at the attacking werewolves. They had arrived but a moment too late.

"KILL THEM ALL!" The queen demanded, calling for her loyal followers.

And it was then that golden light flooded through the room. My vision cleared enough for me to see Sasha and Tasha entering the room. Their beings engulfed in a golden halo as they unleashed their magic upon the world. They were alive. And they were here.

They were alive.

And they were beautiful. Their magic pouring from their beings and leaking into the world. Vampires shrieked as their golden light enveloped their beings, engulfing them entire, burning the flesh from their bones.

Amidst the chaos, I felt warm arms embracing my body, plucking me from the floor, cradling me close. Through my blurry vision, I found Roman's blue gaze. The sounds of howls filled my ears as the werewolves tore through the vampires.

"Stay with me, Natalia." Roman's voice spoke, "Don't leave me again."

But the poison had eaten its way through my body. Slowly, it was making its way into my heart. Its beat beginning to slow. "Roman..."

Something wet landed upon my cheek. A tear, I realized. "You're safe now." His voice sounded choked. "Stay with me." There was a light brush of fingertips against the skin of my throat as he combed aside my hair. "I won't let you die again."

My vision had left me. His voice growing muffled. My mind encased by a thick fog as my heart slowed its beat.

"NO!" A voice shrieked within my room.

Then there was a pain within my neck. Something sharp piercing my flesh. A silent gasp escaped my lips as my skin set afire. I tried to lift a hand to summon upon my magic but there was nothing left. No strength. No energy.

There was nothing.

Then, that fire made its way through my being. It coursed through my veins like molten lava. My fingers and toes curled as a scream formed upon my lips. I wanted to claw at my flesh and set those fires free. I was being burned from the inside out.

Arms still wrapped around my being, "I've got you." Roman whispered into my hair. "I've got you."

It felt as though my soul had been set aflame, the fire eating away at it. My magic shrieked within my being, recoiling within my depths, hiding itself from the fire.

It was then that I had realized what I was becoming; a vampire.

No longer would I be a witch. But the magic still lingered within me, still sang within my veins. I could still hear its whispers.

I had become something new entirely.

When I opened my eyes once more, I saw with clarity. Roman was staring down upon me, tears glistened upon his cheeks. "Natalia." He whispered softly.

My hand reached up to cup his cheek within my palm. Everything felt odd to me, my own body feeling foreign. "Roman." I said.

A wide smile spread across his lips as his hand covered over mine, leaning into my palm.

"HOW COULD YOU!" A voice shrieked through the chaos of the room.

As Roman helped me to stand, I faced the vampire queen. There were fallen bodies laid before her feet – vampires and werewolves alike. Crimson dripped from her sharpened nails, leaking from the corners of her lips. There was a deranged look within her dark eyes.

"It is over mother." Roman stood before me, shielding me from his mother's view.

"Oh no, my son, it is far from over. The witch and I haven't had a turn to play."

A snarl rippled from him, "And you won't."

Gently, I placed my hand upon his shoulders and stepped from behind him. "It's time for this to end."

Roman reached a hand toward me, grasping my own. "Natalia, she's my mother, let me deal with her."

Casting my gaze back, it shifted from blue to darkness. As my fangs lengthened, I felt the magic stirring within my being as well as I called it forth from the depths it hid within.

"She is my murderer. My family's murderer. Everyone has protected me, fought for me, now it is my turn to protect you."

Roman's brow creased as worry flooded his features, but he slowly released his hold upon my hand and nodded his head.

Then, I faced the vampire queen.

All around us, the fighting waged on. Vampires hissing and snarling as werewolves lunged. Tasha and Sasha summoning upon their golden magic, igniting the room with its light. Sakiya maneuvered through the room as if she were a shadow, striking any down who stood for the queen. Aron kept close to her, tearing his teeth into any vampire who dared lunge at her.

Laughter sounded from the queen, "Not a little witch, anymore are you? You're nothing without your magic."

A grin tugged upon my lips, "Who said I was without magic?"

Her brow creased, "You are a vampire now, you are no longer a witch."

Before, there had never been any accounts of witches keeping their magic once an immortal turned them. But I had. Summoning upon my magic, I called it forth the darkness that lurked within myself. The shadows slithered forth from beneath my flesh and coiled around my arms and legs. A golden halo ignited around my being.

The queen gazed upon the darkness and light that embraced me and took a step back, "No. How is it possible? *What are you?*"

A smile caressed my lips, "A creature."

Her haunting gaze narrowed and slowly darkened. "Whatever you may be, I'll still kill you. I'll continue to do so in whatever life you are born in. I'll never stop hunting you."

"Then I suppose I must bring an end to you."

"You are nothing!" She shrieked, "You are food and nothing more!"

The vampire queen lunged, golden hair whipping behind her. Midnight eyes trained upon me. She reached out a clawed hand, ready to tear into my throat. But she would never get that chance.

Extending my arm, the shadows leapt forth, spiraling within the air toward the vampire. A shriek escaped her and as the darkness coiled around her being and lifted her body into the air. She thrashed against the shadows hold but to no avail.

"Release me you damned creature!" The queen snarled.

"I can't do that. You are a threat to the world and to those I care for. Your reign has reached its end – and your life. You will pay for my family that your murdered. For killing me and attempting too once more. For everything you've done, you shall pay." Casting my gaze around the room, I found that many of the queen's vampires were scattered across the floor, others had fled into the shadows of the night. "But, I believe there are others who want to punish you before you leave this world."

It was then that Sakiya and Aron took a step forth. Sasha and Tasha falling in behind them. Roman wrapping his arm around my waist and drawing me close to him as he pulled me back a few steps, allowing the others to approach the queen that dangled within the air.

And it was Sakiya who took that first step and stood before the queen. Those ghostly eyes narrowed upon the woman before her. "Ah, my sweet samurai. Have you come to free your queen and seen the error of your ways?"

Sakiya offered a feline grin as she flashed her sharp nails, "I have come for the debut you owe me. For the life you have stolen from me. And for the years you spent mocking my pain."

A scoff sounded from the queen, "You shall never be the warrior you desperately dreamed of being."

Sakiya narrowed those dark eyes, "I am more than you shall ever be."

With a snarl, she lashed out at the woman. Her nails raking across the queen's face, peeling back her skin. Crimson weeping forth from the wounds. Four scratches stretched from the queen's temple down to her chin. Stealing away her beauty – her vanity.

An ear-piercing shriek sounded through the room.

"I'LL KILL YOU! I'LL KILL ALL OF YOU!"

With a smile, Sakiya took a step back from the queen. Her dark eyes as bright as the queen's blood that dripped from her fingers.

Sasha and Tasha stepped forth then. Their golden magic radiating from their beings. A wicked smile found itself on Tasha's lips as a sphere of golden light manifested above the palm of her hand. "I have to admit I love seeing you suffer. This is for tormenting our friend. For burning our home. This is for all witches you have killed."

Sasha fell into step beside her sister both of them extending their hands toward the vampire queen. The golden light within their palms ignited and shot toward the queen. Screeches sounded from her as she thrashed against the shadows that held her. Their light melted away the flesh from her arms, revealing bone to the world. Crimson poured forth and pooled on the floor beneath her.

"YOU ARE NOTHING BUT FOOD!"

"It is you that is nothing." Sasha said as the two sisters stepped back from the queen.

The werewolf stepped forth then, a cocky grin on his lips as he waltzed up to the vampire queen. "You wanting me dead was the least of my problems; your vampires weren't quick enough to catch me." She snarled at him, "But what you have done to Roman, to Sakiya, and to Natalia. Now, that is my problem." His auburn gaze drifted across the room, lingering upon the dead wolves. "The lives you have stolen tonight, is my problem."

Aron took a step closer to her and placed his booted foot on her knee. They held gazes and he smiled. The queen shrieked once more as he kicked her kneecap back, her leg bending at an awkward angle. The bone shattering and crumbling into dust. Then, he did the same with the other knee. Her legs dangling and bent at awkward angles. Rage and pain distorted her features. Her mouth gaping open as shrieks escaped her lips.

"I'll leave the rest to the witch." With a cocky grin, Aron took a low bow and retreated to stand beside Sakiya, bringing her body close to his.

Then, it was their turn with the queen. Roman walked by my side as we stood before her. A feral look was within the queen's eyes as they narrowed upon us. Her lips curled back into a snarl as she bared her fangs at us, snapping them at us as she bit at the air. The queen was spiraling into madness.

"All I have to say to you, mother, is that this world shall be a far better place without your monstrous presence. Be sure to say hello to grandmother for me in whatever damned afterlife you find yourself in."

The queen tilted her head back as cackling laughter sounded from her, echoing through the room. "I shall be seeing you there, *son.*"

With a shake of his head, he turned that gaze upon me. His hand fell upon my lower back and nodded his head. It was time for his mother to leave this world. It was time for the reign of the vampire queen to end.

Taking a step forth, the queen's eyes lingered upon me. "You are nothing, Natalia. And you will never be anything."

Raising my hand, a golden halo enveloped around it. "I feel sorry for you. For someone to hate as you do, means you never knew love. And your sadness turned into hatred. You lash out on those who have what you never had. And for that, I pity you."

Something flickered within her gaze, her features softening. With a shake of her head, she lowered it. "Get it over with. I welcome death."

I nodded my head, "Then this is where our paths part."

The queen said nothing more. Waiting for death to claim her and take her to the afterlife that waited. Sadness nipped at my heart, though this woman killed my family and even me, though she tormented others, there was pain hidden away within her heart. Sorrow that had eaten away at her soul, festering until it turned into darkness. A darkness that she allowed to swallow her entire. Where she took comfort in the shadows.

The golden light brightened, and a beam shot forth toward the vampire queen. It was then that she looked up and a small smile softened on her lips and she closed those ghostly eyes, welcoming death.

When the light engulfed her being, it blinded the room. Vampires shielding their eyes as hisses escaped them. And when the light flickered away nothing remained of the once vampire queen. Even the ash that became of her body had been burned by the light.

Her reign was over.

Chapter Twenty Eight

A Final Goodbye

THE remaining vampires within the room, turned their gazes from the spot where their queen once was, to Roman and I. He moved himself in front of me, Sakiya and Aron stepping to either side of him. They we were ready – *we* – were ready to face them if they turned on us. If seeing their fallen queen ignited something within them. But what came next, neither of us expected.

The vampires fell onto their knees and bowed low to the ground before us. The werewolves casting their gazes from them, to us. One of the queen's former servants lifted her head and a smile found itself upon her lips. Silver beginning to line those green eyes.

"You've freed us." Her voice rasped. "We're free from her."

A vampire male lifted his head next, "You are the king of vampires, Roman. And we bow before you. We serve you."

But Roman shook his head, "No, I'm not. You are free."

The servant girl spoke again, "But this is our home. We have nowhere else to go. Do you wish us to leave?"

My heart ached for her. Placing my hand on Roman's arm, I said, "Roman, these people need you. You'll be a better ruler than your mother. You are not her."

Turning his blue gaze upon the vampires once more, he took in each of their hopeful faces. How they all beamed at him, eager and willing to serve. How each of them smiled upon him. "Wouldn't my grandmother take my mother's place?"

Sakiya approached then, her dark eyes upon him, "Your mother killed her."

A scoff sounded from Roman, "Good riddance to them both." With a long sigh, Roman nodded his head, "Alright, I'll do it." Facing me, his hand found itself upon my cheek, "But there is one thing I must ask you."

"What is it?"

Kneeling on his knee, he took my hand in his. A warm smile finding itself upon his lips, "Natalia, will you rule by my side as queen, as my equal?"

Tears swelled within my eyes as my heart leapt with joy. I nodded my head, "Yes. Yes!"

Roman stood from the floor and wrapped his arms around me, sweeping me off my feet and twirling me. Laughter escaped us as tears streamed down my cheeks. When my feet touched the floor once more, Roman's lips met with mine and I melted into him. Embracing him, my heart reaching out for his. The vampires within the room cheered and clapped their hands. Even the werewolves raised their heads and howled, the sound echoing through the room.

When Roman and I broke free of one another, we found Aron approaching the leader of the wolves; Jason. The two clasped hands and brought one another into a hug, clapping their hands on each other's backs.

"Thank you, brother." Aron said.

Jason pulled back and nodded his head, "If you ever need us, you know where to find us."

Aron offered a wolfish grin, "I'll be sure to howl."

With a chuckle, Jason then turned his gaze upon Roman and approached him. Offering his hand, Roman took it. "I congratulate you, king. May you rule better than the one before you."

Roman nodded his head, "Thank you. And I swear that the vampires under my ruling shall not hunt your kind."

Jason offered a smile, "Thank you. Now, it is time for us to depart."

One of the werewolves shifted and a woman approached Jason, he drew her into him and placed a tender kiss upon her lips. Placing a hand upon his cheek, she said, "Come, let us go home."

His hand rested against hers that lingered upon his cheek. "Yes, let us go."

With that, the leader of the werewolves and his woman turned into wolves once more and led the pack from the estate. Many of them carrying the bodies of their fallen, taking them home to mourn them and give them a proper burial.

Then, the twin witches stepped forth. Stepping away from Roman, I offered my hands to them. Sasha taking one and Tasha, the other. "I thought you were dead." Tears swelled within my eyes. "I saw your home and I thought the queen had killed you. I thought..."

Tasha shook her head and offered a smile, "Darling, I told you we would not die. Witches are hard creatures to kill. After Sasha and I killed the queen's dogs, she fled. We went into hiding but when we left, the barrier fell from our house and when the queen returned, she burned it."

Not being able to contain myself, I dropped their hands and tossed my arms around the women. Bringing them into my embrace. A soft laugh escaped Sasha as they wrapped their arms around me. Sobs sounded from my lips as tears wept from my eyes. My friends were alive. They were here. The queen hadn't taken them from me. And she would never get the chance too.

The twins stepped back and Sasha's gaze lingered upon me. *I congratulate you, Natalia. You shall make a wonderful queen.*

Tears burned down my cheeks as I signed, *Thank you, you are always welcomed here.*

Sasha placed a hand on her sister's shoulder. "I think it is time for us to leave. We still have much work left to do on our home. We shall be seeing you soon, dear."

I nodded my head, "Thank you both, for everything."

"Always." She smiled.

And then, the twins left. Golden light radiating from their beings as they took flight into the night, dancing amongst the stars.

As the vampires within the room began to depart, a ghostly figure presented herself before us. Sakiya and Aron standing beside Roman and I as we stared upon my ghostly companion. There was a smile to be found upon her face. Her grey eyes sparkling as she stared at me, as if she could hardly believe I were alive.

"My dear friend..." Her voice was a haunting echo within the room. "I came here expecting to find your spirit but instead I find you alive and well. The dream did not come true."

Casting my gaze to Roman, I said, "Actually, it did."

Catherine cocked her head to the side, her hair rippling. "What do you mean?"

Smiles found themselves upon our faces. "It wasn't a dream about my death," my hand rested upon his chest just above his heart, "But of my rebirth."

Her gaze slid between Roman and I and then realization had stuck her. "You're a vampire. But your magic..."

I clutched my hand over my chest, "Still with me."

Catherine clapped her hands together and drifted toward me. "My friend, you are truly amazing, and I love you dearly."

"And I love you too, Catherine. I guess you can't teach me about being a ghost or ghostly things now." A laugh sounded from my lips.

Roman cleared his throat, drawing our attention. "So, Catherine knew about your dream?"

I nodded my head, "She's known about it since the beginning before I met you again. I couldn't bring myself to tell you because I had a part to play in the queen's end."

Roman caressed my cheek within his hand, "No more secrets that involve your life."

Leaning into his palm, I said, "I promise."

"Since there are no more secrets, I have one I must share now." Catherine drew each of our attentions.

Arching my brow, I asked, "What do you mean?"

"When you told me that you dreamed of how I died and who killed me, I saw the light."

"The light?" I blinked at her, my mouth gaping open.

She nodded her head. "Yes."

"That's great!" But then, it struck me. "You can move on."

Catherine reached out her ghostly hands. Turning my hands palms up, hers lingered just above mine. "My time has come and though my soul is heavy leaving you behind, I know you'll be fine." Her grey gaze flickered to the people gathered around me. "I know they'll watch over you as I have all these years. And these years have been the best years of my life – or after my life – and I do not regret a single second."

My heart ached but I knew this is what Catherine needed. She needed to be free, to move on, no longer trapped to this world. Tears cascaded down my cheeks as I nodded my head. "Thank you, Catherine, for everything. You have been a great friend to me in both of my lives and you'll be missed. But I know you'll be happy. You'll be *free.*"

Catherine cast her gaze over her shoulder, a smile appearing on her lips. "They're waiting for me." Her voice whispered.

And I knew who she meant. Her family was beckoning her. It was time for her to reunite with them. "Go." My voice rasped; the word heavy upon my lips.

Turning that grey gaze back to me, I found ghostly tears upon her face. And I also found that a hint of auburn was returning to her irises. Her grey hair transforming to gold. "Goodbye, dear friend."

"Goodbye, Catherine."

Her hands fell away from mine and she turned her back to us. Roman wrapped me in his embrace and I rested my head against his chest as I watched my friend leave this world behind. Her body lowered from the air, her feet meeting with the ground and she reached a hand out. Her fingers seeming to wrap around a doorknob and when she pulled back, a white light spilled out into their world.

And before Catherine stepped through, she cast a last glance over her shoulder, and I found the color had returned to her skin. Her tresses golden once more and falling from the air to sway at her hips. Those auburn eyes bright as she took each of us in.

With a smile and a parting nod, she faced the light once more, and stepped through. And Catherine was gone from this world, moving on to join her family once more.

We stood there for a long moment, my eyes never venturing away from that spot. As if I were expecting her to return to the world, to us, to me. But, she wouldn't. And now she could truly be happy.

Now, it was our turn to be happy.

Epilogue

THE MONTHS HAD come and went. Roman and I settling into our newfound roles. The vampires eager and happy to serve us – sometimes too eager. The werewolves would often visit, any tension that had built between our species had dispersed. The werewolves no longer being hunted – no longer facing extinction. We now shared this world together in peace. Though many vampires did not agree with this and fled, never to be seen again.

As for my shop, I still worked in it. Sasha and Tasha helping me, they worked during the day time and I took to working the night hours. My shop was open twenty-fours a day and many witches took joy in the new hours. But I no longer lived in it. Roman, Aron, Sakiya, and many others helped to move my personal belongings from there and from Roman's old home. The once darkly decorated estate came to life with colored tapestries and different assortments of décor.

Pax took a quick liking to his new home, having many different rooms to explore and claim as his own. The vampires grew a fond attachment to my furry companion quickly. One of the servants came up to me crying one day while holding the purring the cat. And when I had asked her what was wrong, she told me it would shatter her heart when it came to the day of Pax's final breath. But I had reassured her, telling her that once when I was younger, I placed a spell on Pax so that he would never die. Though I had never used it on myself, not that I needed it anymore.

Her tears had quickly dried and a bright smile appeared on her face.

Sakiya and Aron decided to share a room together, the two were never found apart, finally able to share their love with the world. No longer having to hide after decades of keeping it secret. A few months after the queen's death, Sakiya and Aron had traveled to Japan. It had been decades since she had stepped foot in her birthplace. The two stayed there for a couple weeks before returning. Sakiya seeming happier, her soul lighter. The two becoming much closer. Aron seeming to have a new appreciation for the strong woman by his side.

My mind always drifted to Catherine, wishing her well. There was an emptiness in my life as she moved on. But I knew that she was happier, that she was with her family where she truly belonged. And perhaps one day, we will meet again.

As for Roman and I, we were finally gifted our happy ending. Finding each other once in a past life but being torn apart all too soon. After decades of searching, our souls found each other once more. Traveling through time and space to complete the halves of our hearts.

Our souls were home.

And we welcomed two children into this world.

A set of twins. The girl was named Catherine. The boy was named Ronan. One after my dearest friend, and one after Roman's long-lost father.

We had found our happy ending.

MY OTHER BOOKS:

SHADOWS AND NIGHT

(CHILDREN OF DARK)

BLOOD AND NIGHT

(CHILDREN OF DARK)

DEATH AND NIGHT

(CHILDREN OF DARK)

THE NIGHTWALKERS DUOLOGY

THE ENCHANTRESS AND THE WEREWOLF

A TALE OF TWO PACKS

THREE YEAR WINTER

SPAWN OF FOX

HUNTED

CONTINUE READING FOR CHAPTER ONE OF, SHADOWS AND NIGHT!

CHAPTER ONE

A BLOOD CONDENTAI

"The beginning of every story is a mystery until the final chapters."

THE NIGHT SEEMED TO BREATHE, and as it exhaled, more shadows cast themselves across the land. Veils of darkness draped over the world – or just this portion of the land. The part of it ruled by the Goddess of Dark; Severina.

A land that only knew eternal darkness. A land where the sun nor the moon never blessed it with their light. A land whose people became the monsters that lurked within the shadows. People who craved blood just as much as they craved the darkness that their Goddess blessed them and this land of Ventaria with.

Eternal night for the children of the Goddess so that they may prowl and hunt until the eternity of darkness claimed their souls and they returned to their Goddess's side and remain there until time itself turned to dust.

Many lives faded with time, bodies growling feeble and aged. Hearts that grew weak and struggled to beat. Lungs that grew shriveled and could hardly hold a breath. Other lives had to be taken by force and if they weren't, then their lives never ended. Seeing the darkness through the ages of eyes that appeared youthful but held wisdom from the centuries.

And Valina, was one of those that had a life of never-ending night. Her crimson eyes seeming youthful but lurking just behind those strange irises was vast pools of knowledge and wisdom. Collected and stored in the vault that she called her mind.

She was one of few, for her kind were not exactly the rarest in the world – but close enough to it. For there were some, not many, who had the power of all the *Condentai.* The Goddess seemed to favor some of her children over others and Valina was one of the favored.

For Valina was a *Blood Condentai.*

A special person with the power to control one's life force; blood. A person who could stop the flow of it in your veins, cause it to erupt your heart, make your eyes weep with crimson. A *Blood Condentai* could even call it forth from your body, rising from it like a veil of mist, and use it as they will it. For blood was at their command and it bowed before them.

And it even kept their seemingly dead heart beating. For all they needed was blood, nothing more and nothing less.

Valina now was on the prowl for that very substance. Her body craving that thick crimson. She was crouched on the edge of a cliff that overlooked the town before her. Her crimson eyes watching the people scurry along the cobblestone street. Picking her prey was easy; if she wasn't in the mood for a fight she would find another *Condentai* or human that wouldn't prove as challenging.

Valina pondered for a moment, testing her mood. And it seemed as though the daggers sheathed at her sides called out to her. And so, she answered their pleas. Her slender, gloved fingers wrapped around the black leather hilts and they hissed as she drew forth the long, obsidian blades. Her gaze traced along the sharp curve and tip of the daggers, tracing along the only sliver of color to be found on her weapons; crimson, which was no surprise.

Valina bowed her head and her grey lids sealed over her eyes. *"Goddess of Dark, hear my prayer, bless me on this night of hunt and many more forward."*

And when her crimson eyes viewed the world before her once more, the beast that had been slumbering within her, had awaken. And it was thirsty for *blood.*

Rising from her crouch, her body took a leap into the air. Down she plummeted, her black cloak swept up by the wind, her hood flying back allowing the length of her silky midnight hair to feel the rush of the air's fingers through her locks. Her leather boots hit the ground, the earth trembling beneath her feet, a thin cloud of dust wafted into the air when she landed.

Her gaze flickered over to her left, her eyes tracing along the cobblestone road that led into the town not too far ahead. But tonight, she would not venture there, no. She turned her attention toward the right, where the vast darkness of forest waited. And there, she would hunt for her prey. With a feral grin, she marched toward those awaiting, crooked hands of the trees, stepping between the aged bodies of them, and set off into the darkness.

The shadows seemed to watch Valina as she ventured through the darkness, her eyes allowing her to see perfectly, even in total dark. On light feet she treaded the forest, her pointed ears listening closely to the sounds that disturbed the quiet, to the creatures prowling and waiting in the gathering shadows.

Valina caught sight of one of the forest dwelling creatures. A tarantula. All eight of its crimson eyes stared back at her. The creature was no average sized arachnid. Its body was the size of a small cottage, its eight legs stretching longer than the tallest trees in the forest, its fangs were sharp and coated in poison. The creature made no move toward Valina, the tarantulas of the forest thought of *Blood Condentai* as one of their own. Both of them hunters of blood. Slowly the creature backed into the shadows, allowing them to swallow its body.

Valina smirked at the tarantula. For it was one of the Earth Goddess's children but the ones that crossed over into the land of the Goddess of Dark, well, Severina turned them into something of her own making. As more of a mockery to Sybil, to take something of hers as Sybil had once done to Severina.

Deeper and further she traveled, the blades spinning and dancing within the palms of her hands as she walked.

Then, her feet stilled. The twirling blades had ceased their dance. A smirk quirked at the corners of her lips. Her prey had arrived. Already her mouth seemed to water with eagerness for it knew that soon it would be drowning in blood.

Without looking behind her, she twirled around, her cloak spanning out, and threw one of her obsidian daggers. It flipped head over end through the air. The blade sliced through the wind, aimed at Valina's prey. To any mortal eye, they would not have seen Valina move.

But her prey was no mortal.

A tall, grey skinned man like Valina caught the hilt of the dagger a breath before it met with his exposed chest. His crimson eyes gleamed as a smile curled on his thin lips.

"Ah, my dear Valina, am I your prey for the evening?" His voice was sultry, speaking slow but not too much so. Just enough to radiate with confidence, enough to drive a woman mad.

But Valina was not driven mad. Though his voice was pleasing to the ear, she never fell victim to it. "My prey lately has been too easy; my daggers are crying for a challenge."

The man bowed deeply. His long, silky black hair swept over his shoulder just on one side for the other side of his head was completely shaved – allowing his pointed ear to show. "Always a pleasure challenging you, dear Valina. But I must say, my skills have improved greatly since our blades last met. I hope you can keep up."

Valina knelt into a crouch, the smirk still playing upon her lips. "You always underestimate me, Ventar. Whenever shall you learn?"

"Perhaps when that pretty blade of yours pierces my heart."

"Be careful of what you wish for, Ventar."

And in a blur of movement, Valina was nothing more than a breath of air. She was there and then within a blink, she was not. Her body moving too fast for eyes to track. But, Ventar's could track her. For he was of her kind, a *Blood Condentai.*

He simply side stepped, and she retrieved her dagger from his hand. Her palm heavy with its reassuring weight. Her ears caught the sound of blades hissing from their sheaths. Ventar had reached behind him to withdraw two long, obsidian swords.

"Do you think your daggers can hold up against these, my dear?" He twirled the swords in his hands, his voice and posture radiating with confidence.

Valina's grip tightened on the hilts of her long daggers. "Oh, Ventar, my daggers have never failed me."

She lunged forward. His sword slicing through the air toward her and she dodged to the left. Extending her hand, she swiped the dagger at his exposed side. The sharpened blade kissed his grey skin, a thin line of crimson appearing, tear drops weeping from the wound.

Valina could have ended the fight then, but she preferred to play with her prey.

Raising the blade to her mouth, her tongue flickered out and stole a taste of his blood. At once her mouth was in a frenzy as the sweet liquid met with her taste buds.

Ventar watched with a cocky smile upon his face. "My blood pleases you, does it not? I must say I would not allow anyone else the pleasure of it, my dear Valina."

"Do not take it as a compliment, Ventar. *All* blood pleases me – pleases *us*."

Ventar said nothing, only approaching her with a predator's movement. His crimson eyes locked with her own. He bent his knees and then lunged. Quickly, Valina tossed up her daggers to meet with his blades. The sounds of them meeting rang out through the dark forest. She felt as he pressed his weight into his swords, but she pushed back with equal strength.

Ventar grinned and when he did, she caught sight of his fangs. "How long do you think you can do this?"

She grinned back, flashing her own sharp teeth. "Forever but I do not feel like wasting my time." She swept out a leg and knocked Ventar's feet from beneath him.

She did not, however, get a chance to leap upon her prey – that would have proven too easy. Ventar thrust his swords toward her as she advanced on him, causing her to leap back. The man was on his feet once more. He did not speak as he dashed forward, brandishing his swords. Her daggers met them once more. Knocking them aside as they tried to strike her. She would not allow her blood to be spilled on this night – or any night.

And when Ventar advanced on her again, she cast a quick glance behind her. Taking a few steps back, she raised her daggers once more to meet with his swords. And when he pushed, she allowed him to push her back. He grinned because he thought he would win, that he would claim her blood. But he was only playing into her trap.

No smile crossed her lips, she did not wish for him to see the deception being played upon him. When her back was pushed against the tree, she allowed the blades of his swords to get dangerously close to her face. Ventar leaned close to her, a victorious smile playing upon his lips, his fangs ready for their claim of blood.

"My dear Valina, you are a strong opponent, but you cannot best me. Now, allow me my drink of blood." He leaned close to her, his mouth lingering above her exposed neck.

It was then that she allowed her smile to show, "Never."

She reared her head back and smashed it against his long, thin nose. A howl escaped him as he staggered back, and she twirled then, sheathing one dagger within the blink of an eye – and ran two steps up the trunk of the aged tree and leapt into the air. Her back arching as she flew and when she landed upon her feet, she was already facing his back.

Ventar had no time to react, to understand that he had been tricked like a child. Her other unsheathed obsidian blade pressed against his exposed neck.

Valina's lips were close to his ear, as she whispered, "You have been bested, Ventar. Now, drop your weapons and allow me my drink."

His swords clattered to the ground as he hung his arms by sides and lowered his knees to the earth. There was no frown to be found upon his face, only a grin. "Never have I been able to best you, my dear. If only we were allowed to control one another's blood, perhaps then I would have a chance."

Blood Condentai could not control one of their own kinds' blood.

"Perhaps not even then." Grabbing a fist full of his silky, midnight hair, she moved his head to the side – exposing his slender neck. Lowering her mouth to his pulsating veins, her fangs grazed his skin. A slight moan escaped Ventar and she knocked him on the head with her free hand, "Do not make this a sexual pleasure for yourself, Ventar."

A chuckle escaped him, but he said nothing more as her fangs pierced his skin, sinking deep, and warm blood flowed into her mouth – sweeping across her tongue as she drank. Her eyes rolled into the back of her head as she became lost within the bloodlust, the hunger. The sweetness enveloped her mind like a silky blanket, the warmness of it coating her soul. She believed that nothing else in the world could taste as sweet as blood, the very thing that kept every living soul alive, herself included.

But, her feeding had to come to an end. Slowly, she removed her fangs from his neck and backed away, releasing her hold on his hair. As he stood, he sheathed his swords and bowed to her.

"Always a pleasure, my dear Valina." And before she could speak, he stood before her and leaned close to her ear, "Perhaps one day I shall win a taste of your blood." And when he moved his head, she felt the wetness of his tongue lick at the corner of her mouth. He dodged the swipe of her dagger. "You had some of my blood on your mouth." He winked.

"Bastard." She hissed.

"The best kind." And then, he vanished into the shadows.

Valina tracked through the forest, wandering through the shadows, and made her way back to where she had started. The cobblestone street soon came into sight. Her black, leather boots padded softly along the stones. The walk was mostly spent in silence for many souls within the town and within the forest were asleep – others waiting patiently in the shadows to strike at their prey.

Many of the shops, homes, and cathedrals she passed were swallowed in darkness, it did not bother her or anyone for the land itself was nothing but darkness, but sometimes lanterns were lit to allow those without the vision of night to see – meaning the humans that lived amongst them.

The grey and black stoned buildings were eerie with silence and Valina liked the silence, it allowed her mind to wander. Some of the black metal street lamps had been left lit, flames crackling and dancing within their glass prisons, swaying to the left and right as the wind brushed against them. The silver metal chains the lanterns hung from creaking in the wind as it rocked on the curled black hook all the lanterns hung from.

Further ahead, past the town and the forest, was a castle that rested at the very top of the highest hill in the land. The castle itself gave anyone who gazed upon it shivers tingling along their spine. Valina was no exception to this. It felt as though an icy, skeletal hand traced its boney fingers along her spine. Her body trembled.

The grey stone loomed above the land, a black metal fence rising high from the ground and wrapping around the grounds of the castle. Crooked, sharp ends pointed into the sky, keeping anyone from daring to scale the fence. But, many tried, and many were left skewered to the pointed ends as a lesson, a warning. As of now, skeletons hung from some and a few fresh bodies hung from others. Sometimes the king would display his enemies' bodies, spies and rebels, for all eyes to see.

Valina dragged her gaze away from the castle. Not many things troubled her, but the sight of the castle was one of the few that did. And she hated more than anything to admit to that. But she was not the only one who lived in fear here, for everyone did.

Soon enough, she found herself facing a four-way split in the cobblestone road. Taking the left road, she wandered down along past the homes that lined the road. A few still having lanterns lit and igniting the path before her – not that she needed it.

Her feet came to a stop before the last home on the street, just close to the edge of the forest. The building was large enough, the grey stone sparkling as if the building were still new though it was as old as she – three hundred. She had built this home with her own hands and it took her many years. Pride always swelled in her chest at the very sight of it.

Opening the silver gate, she walked up the three steps, her eyes glancing at the black lanterns, hanging before her black painted door, and saw flames alive within them. Reaching her gloved hand into her pocket, she retrieved a silver key with a skull crafted at the top and plunged it into the lock. It clicked, and the door opened. Immediately, her nostrils were assaulted with the smell of incense.

Locking the door behind her, Valina set to work removing her cloak and hanging it upon one of the silver hooks on the grey stone wall. Removing her boots, she set them beside the door. Unbuckling the belt that her sheaths filled with daggers hung from, she hooked them on another hook beside her cloak. Finally, she removed her gloves and set them in a silver dish that rested upon a dark wood table on the opposite wall of the hooks.

Before her stretched a dark wooden stair case with black metal railing. On either side of the staircase were doorless doorways to other parts of the house, black painted wood decorated the outer parts of them, dark carvings of decaying flowers and skulls crafted into it. The first floor held the kitchen and living room. Another door just under the staircase led into a bathroom.

As Valina stepped through the doorway that led into the living room, her fingers traced along the carved wood, it took her many months to carve each and every intricate detail. As she leaned her head back, at the top center of the doorway was a carving of her Goddess; Severina. Her long black hair flowing down into the wood, her hands outstretched with shadows twirling from her fingertips.

"And the hunter has returned to its home." She heard a whispered and distant voice speak to her.

Stepping into the living room, she found a short woman standing before an open curtained window. The black silk pushed aside to allow the full view of the darkness to be seen. The woman's back was faced toward Valina as she leaned against the wall, her arms crossed over her plump chest.

"Yes, I have, Ashari." She said to her best friend and occasional lover.

Ashari's white hair fell down her back softly and swept at the floor behind her bare feet. Her dainty, pale hand clutching the dark fabric of the curtain – such a sharp contrast. "It was getting late, the shadows growing deeper, I began to wonder if I should send a spirit to search for you."

Ashari was a *Ghost Condentai* allowing her to speak to the dead and bend their ghostly bodies to her will, sometimes even allowing the dead to speak through her if their own spirits could not speak. Like if something truly tragic happened to them before they died; if their tongue had been cut out, their lips sewed together, acid poured down their throat. Then they could speak through Ashari.

Sometimes, Ashari would go on her own hunts for the ghostly victims, avenging them so that their souls were no longer tied to this world and they can join their Goddess. Other times, if the person deserved death, she allowed them to remain as their own form of torture – to be stuck here with only the *Ghost Condentai* and other spirits to speak too.

"As you can see, I am alright. No need to send a ghostly dog sniffing for me."

Finally, Ashari faced her. Those silver eyes meeting her crimson gaze and a small smile pulled at the woman's plump lips. "I am glad to see you home safely."

"I hope I didn't have you standing there too long."

Ashari moved the curtains back to conceal the windows and made her way to the fireplace. "Not long at all. But, I can see from the way your eyes glow that the feeding was well tonight."

Her mouth watered at the thought of Ventar's blood. "Very well, if I might say."

"And it is safe to assume that your prey was no easy target. I can see the way your hair is mussed and how your heart is still beating faster than normal."

Ashari was an observant woman, sometimes too much so. "I wanted a little bit of challenge tonight."

Valina made her way to the red velveted couch. It was also crafted from dark wood, like the rest of her furniture, the legs curling into rounded points that rested upon the floor. The velvet framed by the wood.

"The hunter seeking its prey." She spoke in her whispered voice. "And the hunter's prey, I am assuming was, Ventar. Am I safe in assuming so?"

Too observant. "Yes."

The fireplace roared to life, flames licking the logs within it. Crackling could be heard as the fire devoured the wood. A warm glow cast itself over the room.

"Two souls attracted to one another, their thirst undeniable, one shall drink and the other shall thirst." Sometimes, Valina wished Ashari wouldn't speak in those haunting riddles. But she had grown used to it over the last hundred years, it was a trait of the *Ghost Condentai.* And sometimes, Valina enjoyed the riddles, just not when they involved Ventar.

Ashari plucked something from the fireplace mantle and moved across the room with fluid grace. "This arrived for you."

Valina took the envelope and tore it open, retrieving the letter within;

My Dearest Valina,

I write to you in hopes that you'll attend my yearly ball. My heart was greatly saddened when your lovely face could not be found within the crowd of dancing bodies. If you chose to arrive this year or not, there shall be a dress sent to you either way. It shall arrive two days after this letter makes it to your gracious hands, just in time for the ball.

Sincerely, Your King Valnar

Though his words were sweet, they were anything but. The king was a mad man that was given too much power. He was another of her kind and she was thankful for that at least. He could not control her mind, body, or organs like the other *Condentai* could.

For many years Valina has tried to keep low, away from his sight, but one can only hide for so long until they are found. And when his eyes found her, he wished for nothing more than to make her his. And she was owned by no man. Her body and mind her own. But the Goddess only knew how long the king could keep hearing no before he took matters into his own hands.

"What are you going to do?" Ashari asked, still standing before her, her silver eyes glancing down at the letter.

Valina stood, Ashari moving aside, and approached the fireplace. With a flick of her wrist, she tossed the letter into the fire and watched as the flames devoured it. "I cannot miss another ball. Last year he was furious that I did not attend." Valina had heard that he had killed three servants in a fit of rage, one of them was a *Blood Condentai* – and her kind were scarce enough and with one of their deaths being on her shoulders. If only she would have attended, they would still be alive. "I do not wish to know what would happen if I did not make an appearance two years in a row."

Ashari said nothing, for there was nothing to say. The woman approached her and placed a tender hand upon Valina's shoulder. For a long while, the women stood there watching the flames.